"There is s...
say to you, Ri...
accustomed...
close proximity to a gentleman."

Ridiculous pleasure coursed through Richard at her words. He did not seem able to help himself. But the nervousness in her eyes puzzled him. He wanted to draw her into his arms and comfort her. He wanted to kiss her. Richard tried to concentrate.

"Deborah," he said. "If you are wanting to change your mind because you still do not trust me, then I must remind you that I promised to do nothing that you did not desire, and I will keep to that." His voice came out more roughly than he had intended and her eyes flew to his.

Her gaze touched his face and skittered away. "You do not understand," she said. "I have been trying to pluck up the courage to tell you. When I said that I wished to change the terms of our betrothal you misunderstood me—I want you to make love to me. For the duration of our betrothal, I want you to be my lover."

* * *

***One Night of Scandal***
**Harlequin Historical #763—August 2005**

**Dear Reader,**

*It is 1803, and along the coast of Suffolk the threat of French invasion is at its highest. Smugglers, pirates, treasure seekers and spies are all drawn to the quiet Midwinter villages, where the comfortable surface of village life conceals treason and danger as well as romance and excitement....*

This is the world that I have inhabited for the past year whilst I wrote the BLUESTOCKING BRIDES trilogy. It has been a wonderful experience. I have always loved the county of Suffolk for its remoteness, the peace of the woods, the wind in the reeds at the water's edge and the sunset over the sea. It is one of the most atmospheric and inspiring places for a storyteller.

About a year ago I was reading a book about "The Great Terror," the years between 1801 and 1805, when Britain was permanently on the alert against the threat of Napoleonic invasion. It made me wonder what life would have been like in the coastal villages of Britain, where there was always the chance that the business of everyday living would conceal something more dangerous. I thought about a group of gentlemen dedicated to hunting down a spy—gentlemen for whom romance was no part of the plan, but who found that the ladies of Midwinter were more than a match for them! And so the idea of the BLUESTOCKING BRIDES trilogy was born....

I hope that you enjoy these stories of love and romance in the Midwinter villages! It has been a real pleasure to write this trilogy.

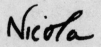

# Nicola Cornick

## One Night of Scandal

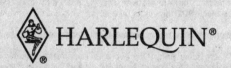

# HARLEQUIN®

TORONTO • NEW YORK • LONDON
AMSTERDAM • PARIS • SYDNEY • HAMBURG
STOCKHOLM • ATHENS • TOKYO • MILAN • MADRID
PRAGUE • WARSAW • BUDAPEST • AUCKLAND

ISBN 0-373-29363-1

ONE NIGHT OF SCANDAL

Copyright © 2004 by Nicola Cornick

*Available from Harlequin Historical and*
**NICOLA CORNICK**

*The Virtuous Cyprian* #566
*Lady Polly* #574
*The Love Match* #599
"The Rake's Bride"
*Miss Verey's Proposal* #604
*The Blanchland Secret* #630
*Lady Allerton's Wager* #651
*The Notorious Marriage* #659
*The Earl's Prize* #684
*The Chaperon Bride* #692
*Wayward Widow* #700
*The Penniless Bride* #725
*The Notorious Lord* #759
*One Night of Scandal* #763

*Bluestocking Brides

**Look for**

*The Rake's Mistress*

**Coming September 2005**

Please address questions and book requests to:
Harlequin Reader Service
U.S.: 3010 Walden Ave., P.O. Box 1325, Buffalo, NY 14269
Canadian: P.O. Box 609, Fort Erie, Ont. L2A 5X3

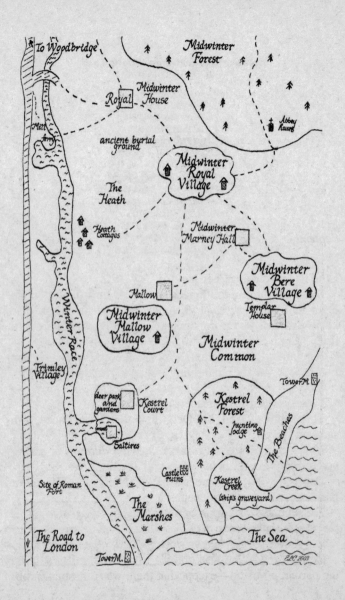

# Chapter One

*September 1803*

She had overplayed her hand.

Deborah Stratton drummed her fingers impatiently on the letter that was resting on the top of the walnut desk. She knew exactly what it contained, but she read it for a third time, just so that it could annoy her all over again.

Her father, Lord Walton, wrote in a deceptively pleasant manner. It was the underlying message that troubled Deborah.

*I am gratified to hear of your betrothal…*

That sounded kind, but Deb knew that it was laced with sarcasm.

*However, your suitor seems somewhat dilatory in asking my permission to pay his addresses to you…*

Deborah winced. There was no denying that. Her suitor had been very remiss indeed.

*The imminent occasion of your brother's marriage seems the ideal opportunity to introduce the gentleman to your family so that he can secure my approval, albeit belatedly…*

Deb frowned. She was obliged to agree that it would be the perfect occasion—except that there was one small problem. There could be no introduction, for her suitor did not exist. He was a figment of her imagination. He had been invented with the express intention of persuading her father to cease interfering in her business.

Lord Walton had been pressing his younger daughter to return home to Bath for some time. His letters had become ever more urgent. He wrote that it was inappropriate for a young widow in Deborah's situation to live alone but for a female companion. Far better to return to the family seat where she could resume her place in Bath society and he would be spared the expense of financing a separate household for her.

It was, in fact, a request that Lord Walton could enforce easily whenever he chose by the simple expedient of withdrawing her allowance. Deb knew this and she had written back in desperation, explaining that she had recently contracted a betrothal to a Suffolk gentleman and wished to remain in Midwinter Mallow. This, her father's reply, had arrived by return of post.

*We shall look forward to seeing both of you in two months' time for Guy's wedding…*

Deb pushed the letter aside and sat back in the walnut chair. Her ruse had backfired spectacularly, just as her companion, Mrs Aintree, had warned her that it would. She knew that it was all her own fault. She had got herself into a tangle, as she was wont to do, and now she would have to get herself out again.

Deb got to her feet and marched into the breakfast room where Clarissa Aintree was still at the table, reading the local newspaper. Mrs Aintree, a practical lady of indeterminate age who had once been Deborah's governess, was accustomed to her former charge's impulsive nature. Sometimes her warnings were heeded and sometimes they were not. This had been one of the latter occasions.

Mrs Aintree put the paper aside and took a sip of tea, her blue eyes regarding Deborah's stormy face with mild amusement.

'I assume that your father did not respond to your letter quite as you intended?' she enquired.

'No!' Deborah slumped into her seat disconsolately and poured herself another cup of chocolate. Then she paused with a sigh, resting her chin on her hand.

'I thought that Papa might be so pleased to think me safely betrothed that he would agree to my remaining in Midwinter, but instead he says that he wishes to meet my fiancé and that I must bring him to Guy's wedding!'

Mrs Aintree murmured something that sounded like 'I told you so'.

Deborah got up again and strode restlessly across to the window. 'I know you told me so, Clarrie, but I thought—' She broke off. 'Oh, I am so cross!'

'With yourself?' Mrs Aintree asked shrewdly.

Deb gave her a sharp look. 'Yes! And with Olivia! She was the one who told Papa in her letters that this is a dangerous neighbourhood in which to live.'

'It is,' Mrs Aintree pointed out blandly.

'I know! But if Olivia had not written thus to him, then he would never have summoned me home to Bath.'

Mrs Aintree ate a piece of toast. She ate it thoughtfully and slowly. Then she said, 'Your papa is not a stupid man, Deborah. I am sure that he is quite well aware of the dangers of French invasion here in Suffolk.'

Deb sighed. She knew that was true and that it was unfair to blame her sister, Olivia Marney, for telling tales. Even so, she felt aggrieved.

'Yes, but Liv mentioned the increase in smuggling and the rumour that there are spies at work in the neighbourhood and…oh, a hundred and one other things to alarm Papa!

She knew that he had been seeking an excuse to summon me home and so she presented him with one…' Deborah paused. 'Indeed, if I did not know her better, I might think that she had done it on purpose!'

'That is unworthy of you,' Mrs Aintree said calmly. 'Your sister would never deal you Spanish coin, Deborah, as well you know. She has been a tower of strength to you. Not that she cannot have been tempted to get rid of you over the years, given the way that people say you flirt with her husband.'

A hint of colour came into Deborah's cheeks. 'I do not flirt with Ross,' she said, a little defensively. 'You know that is untrue, Clarrie. It is just that we are very alike and we enjoy each other's company. Indeed, I wish that Liv and Ross could settle their differences. It is devilishly uncomfortable to spend time with them when they bicker like magpies.'

Mrs Aintree gave her a severe look that put Deborah forcibly in mind of the days when she had been a recalcitrant schoolgirl.

'No doubt Olivia suffers from it rather more than you do,' she said.

Deborah gave a gusty sigh. 'Oh, I know that I am a selfish creature,' she said, 'but what am I to do?' She threw herself down in her chair again, half-heartedly buttered a piece of toast and then pushed it aside. 'I cannot produce my fiancé for my father's approval, for he does not exist.'

Mrs Aintree shook her head sadly. 'I have told you before, Deborah dear, that one deception leads inevitably to another. I suggest that you tell your father the truth.'

Deborah wrinkled up her nose. She could see both the logic and sense of Mrs Aintree's advice, but matters were not that simple.

'You know I cannot do that, Clarrie. If I confess that there is no betrothal, Papa will see me removed to Bath before you can say purse strings!'

Mrs Aintree frowned. 'Would that be so bad? You are often saying that you miss the diversions of a town. I know that at the beginning you thought it best to live quietly, but it is not right for a young lady such as yourself to be immured in the country with nothing to entertain you. And the company in Bath can be very elegant—' Mrs Aintree stopped, glancing at Deborah's strained, white face. 'No, how foolish of me. It would not serve at all.'

Deborah shook her head. 'If that were all that there was to it, then you know that I would heed your words, Clarrie. But it is not!' She rubbed her forehead in a gesture of despair. 'You know that I love my family, but I would run mad within a day if I had to live with them again. Too much has happened for us to try and pretend otherwise, yet my parents behave as though nothing has changed. Mama wants to throw me in the path of any man who has fortune and address, just as she did before I was wed. As for Papa...' She hesitated. 'He has an unshakeable belief that he knows what is right for all of us, and he has not given up hope of promoting a match for me with cousin Harry. He wrote to me on the subject not two months since and put me in a dreadful turmoil. That was the reason that I invented my fictitious suitor in the first place!'

Mrs Aintree nodded, her face sympathetic. 'You know that Lord Walton only wishes to secure your future, Deborah,' she said, striving to give the balanced view. 'Most people would consider it a dreadful shame that you would not countenance remarriage when you are young and attractive and have your entire life before you—'

Deb made a sharp movement that sent the remaining chocolate slopping into her saucer in a miniature tidal wave.

'No! I cannot marry now. Not after Neil...'

Mrs Aintree touched her hand. 'I know. I understand.'

Deb turned away, her face tense. She seldom spoke of her short marriage to Neil Stratton, if marriage it could be called. The memory was still acutely painful after the passage of three years and she had learned a swift and bitter lesson, one she would never forget. She had been a silly, flighty girl of nineteen when she had eloped, and she had been looking for a means of escape from the stifling restrictions of life at Walton Hall. She had thought that she loved Neil, but it had not been long before she realised that she had been deeply mistaken in him and that his feelings for her were no more than a charade. Her marriage had been a sham and it had left her with an abiding fear of making the same mistakes again.

Deb's elopement had been yet another impulsive act in a long line that led back to her days in the schoolroom. In her childhood, her scrapes had generally been of a relatively harmless nature, such as releasing mice down the staircase at Olivia's come-out ball or putting spiders in Guy's socks to make him wail. The elopement had had rather more severe consequences for her life. After that, Deb had recognised that she was prone to act on impulse and had tried hard to temper her more rash actions by stopping to think first. It did not come naturally to her. Sometimes she was able to repress her impulses and sometimes she could not.

Deb nibbled the corner of the piece of toast. So the mention of her imminent betrothal had failed to throw her father off the scent. Nevertheless, she could not afford to give in now. She would *not* admit that she had made it up, return meekly to Bath and to the impossible prospect of being married off to her cousin Harry. She needed a plan.

She watched Mrs Aintree out of the corner of her eye. Clarrie had always had an uncanny knack for spotting when Deb was hatching a plot, but now her companion looked quite serene, as though she thought the matter settled. Deb knew that it was not. Somehow, a temporary fiancé must be found.

If only she could produce a gentleman for her father's approval, then the whole matter might be dealt with and forgotten quickly. It would not do simply to turn up at Walton Hall and *pretend* to be an engaged woman. Her father was shrewd and would smell an enormous rat if she arrived without the necessary gentleman in tow. No, she needed a *real* gentleman to endorse her story. The counterfeit betrothal would buy her time, and once she had returned to Midwinter she could write vaguely to her parents about her wedding plans, finally letting it be known that the engagement had ended with mutual goodwill some twelve months later. No doubt by then the threat of invasion would have receded, cousin Harry would have found another bride, and her father could be persuaded to let her stay in Midwinter Mallow.

The plan seemed sound, but even Deborah could see the huge flaw in the strategy. She did not have a fiancé and, further, she had no idea how to find a suitable gentleman to fill the role.

Deb made a quick inventory of her male acquaintance. It did not take long, for the list was small, society in the Midwinter villages having few eligible gentlemen. It was one of the reasons why she had chosen to live there; she did not wish to be troubled by masculine attention. Most of the men she knew were already married, like her brother-in-law, Ross Marney, or Lord Northcote of Burgh. There was Sir John Norton, of course. He was a bachelor. The drawback there was that she did not like him. And then there was the Duke of Kestrel, who was far too eminent to involve in such a plan, and his brother, Lord Richard Kestrel, who was far too... Deb paused. The first idea that had come into her head when she thought of Richard Kestrel was that he was far too *attractive* for her to ask him to be her counterfeit fiancé. The thought made her acutely uncomfortable and she shifted on the dining-chair's embroidered cushion. Richard Kestrel was too attractive, too dangerous, too forceful and too…*everything*…to be in the least bit suitable. If she were looking to find a lover rather than a husband, then he would be ideal. Deb gave herself a little shake, uncertain where that idea had come from. She wanted neither lover nor husband and the inevitable trouble that would follow with both.

Her inventory over, Deb sat back with a sigh. The lack of appropriate candidates at least spared her the embarrassment of having to approach a gentleman of her acquaintance and ask him to pose as her temporary suitor. Perhaps it would be easier to make a business arrangement with a stranger instead. She could pay someone to act the part.

Various objections rose in her mind and Deb dealt with them one by one. She had no money other than her allowance, which her father could remove at any moment. That was a practical consideration, but she was sure she could find a way around it. Perhaps she could persuade Ross to fund her. It was not an insuperable problem.

Far more daunting was the thought of pretending to be engaged to a stranger. Yet if she were to hire an actor, for example, it might be quite easy. He would know how to carry off the part. And they would only be visiting Walton Hall for a week at the most.

A feeling of nervousness gnawed at Deb's stomach. Every instinct that she possessed told her that it was a foolish, ridiculous and even downright dangerous idea to hire herself a husband. She should not even be countenancing it. Ladies simply did not behave in such a manner.

And yet, what alternative did she have? She did not wish to return to Bath and a life she had left behind three years ago. She did not want to marry cousin Harry. She did not want to marry *anyone*. That was impossible.

The newspaper rustled as Mrs Aintree turned the pages. She was reading the *Suffolk Chronicle*, which Deborah knew carried advertisements for everything from the efficacious effects of bear's grease on the hair to Mr Elliston's patented beaver hats. As she watched her companion skimming each page, an idea slowly began to form in Deborah's head. Perhaps she could place an advertisement for a fiancé in the newspaper. After all, people were always advertising for servants and this was not so very different. She needed a gentleman to perform a specific task. She was prepared to pay him. The newspaper was a way in which she might find him. She would have to be careful, of course—she would need to make sure that she involved someone else in the interview process and that she took up proper references for the gentleman concerned, but the fundamental idea might just work.

Deborah considered the plan whilst buttering another piece of toast with renewed enthusiasm. It was not an orthodox manner in which to find a fiancé, but there was no doubt that such a businesslike approach had its merits. The more she thought about it, the more she could see that it was akin to interviewing a butler or some other employee. There was also another big advantage. If she made a business arrangement, there would be no unfortunate misunderstandings about love.

During the three years that she had lived in Midwinter, Deb had been subjected to the attentions of various suitors, several of whom had professed an ardent regard for her. She had found the experience uncomfortable, given that she had a distaste for marriage and no wish to mislead a gentleman into thinking she would make another match. When she had gently tried to dissuade her admirers they had all, without exception, taken offence, as though it was impossible to accept that any one of their suits could not be irresistible to her. The whole experience had left Deb even more set against a love match and with the reputation for being as cold as ice. Under the circumstances, a business transaction had to be the best option.

Her appetite restored and her decision made, Deborah wolfed down the rest of the piece of toast and another one besides, which she larded with strawberry jam, before excusing herself and returning to the small study where she had left her father's letter. It was a sunny day in late summer and she was itching to get outside. A ride would be most pleasant before the heat of the day grew too extreme. And that afternoon she had planned to walk over to Midwinter Marney Hall to see Olivia. But first she had a task to accomplish.

Drawing pen and paper towards her, Deb started to draft out her advertisement: *Lady seeks temporary fiancé…*

She paused. That sounded a little abrupt. People might think that she was mad. She needed to be rather more subtle in her first communication. Still, she felt it should not prove too difficult to sketch out a suitable notice, for Mrs Aintree had told her that, of all the Walton family, she was the one most accomplished at her letters. She bent to the task again.

A half-hour later, she had come up with something with which she was almost satisfied.

*A lady requires the assistance of a gentleman. If any gentleman of honour, discretion and chivalry will venture to answer this notice and despatch a reply to Lady Incognita at the Bell and Steelyard Inn, Woodbridge, Suffolk, then he shall have no reason to repent his generosity.*

Deb bit the end of her pen as she considered the wording, then she blotted the page and sealed the note decisively.

There was no time for hesitation. They were to depart for the wedding in Somerset in less than two months' time, and, if she was to advertise and interview a suitable candidate, she needed to start at once.

She crept back in to the breakfast room, the letter tucked under her arm. Mrs Aintree had gone, but the newspaper fortunately remained and it was the work of only a moment to discover the address for advertisements and the price for a modest three lines of text. Deb rang the bell for the maid and placed the letter in her hand, with instructions for the gardener's boy to take the gig into Woodbridge and deliver the letter at once. Then, feeling slightly breathless at her own audacity, she made her way upstairs to change into riding dress. She squashed an unworthy desire to run after the maid and snatch the letter back. Nothing ventured, nothing gained. And, after all, if she disliked the tone of any of the replies, she need not answer them. No one would ever know.

Within another half-hour she was out in the stable yard and was waiting for Beauty to be saddled. The fresh morning air restored her spirits. She decided to ride without a groom and whilst she was out, to consider the attributes that she required in a transient fiancé.

She trotted down the drive and out on to the lane. Her fiancé would have to be a gentleman, of course, or at least someone who could consistently act the part. She could not foist some upstart upon her family and expect them to accept him. On the other hand, he had to be biddable. *She* was the one in charge of this situation and required her betrothed to recognise that fact. He could not challenge her authority. He would do as she told him. Smiling slightly, she set Beauty at the fence and galloped off into the fields.

Lord Richard Kestrel had been cantering full tilt along the lane that passed Mallow House when he saw Mrs Stratton's gig approaching, driven at a cracking pace by the gardener's boy. The gig passed within two inches of him and one of its rickety wheels almost came clear of the road. The boy righted it without the least appearance of concern and continued on his way whistling. But a letter that had been on the seat beside him slid from the cart and came to rest on top of a tall spike of thistles at the side of the road. Richard bent down, plucked it from its perch and looked at it with interest. It was written in Deborah Stratton's strong hand, which he had previously read on one memorable occasion, and it was addressed to the editor of the *Suffolk Chronicle*. Richard dusted the missive down, caught up with the gig and passed it over to the gardener's boy, who stowed it away gratefully.

As Richard turned his horse, he wondered idly why the Honourable Mrs Stratton would be writing to the newspapers. Perhaps she was inviting more ladies to join the Midwinter reading group. Or more likely she was writing to the editor to complain about the preponderance of rakes in the Midwinter villages that summer. Richard knew that Mrs Stratton had no very good opinion of rakes in general and of himself in particular.

Richard took the green lane that passed to the east of Deb Stratton's property and slowed his highly bred black hunter to a decorous trot. The horse flickered its ears with disappointment, but Richard had no wish to meet his maker on that particular morning and it seemed that almost everyone abroad had let the fresh summer air go to their heads. Tempting as it was to kick the horse to a gallop, Richard had an instinctive feeling that caution should be the order of the day.

The thought had scarcely left his mind when there was the tremor of hooves on the dry earth, and Deborah Stratton herself rode out on to the lane on a big brown mare that was almost a match for Richard's hunter. The horse saw them before Deb did and it took fright, rearing up and pirouetting around. Deb brought the mare ruthlessly under control in a flurry of flying hooves and sat panting slightly, her hat askew, her cheeks stung pink with cool morning air and indignation.

'Good morning, Mrs Stratton,' Richard said. 'Are you practising to join the Spanish Riding School in Vienna?'

He saw Deb Stratton's pansy-blue eyes narrow on him with intense dislike. She always looked rather comical when she was angry, like a child having a tantrum. Her face was too pretty and too amiable to express annoyance convincingly, and for all that she was two and twenty, she looked much younger. From the thick, fair curling hair that rioted beneath her hat, to the pert nose, full mouth and resolute chin, she looked like a schoolroom chit who had been thwarted and was in a sulk.

'Good morning, Lord Richard,' she said. She was having difficulty keeping her tone even slightly polite. 'I would rather join a school renowned for its discipline than be a circus rider like you.'

Richard grinned. One of the many things that he liked about Mrs Stratton was that her nature was so open that she found it well nigh impossible to adopt the prevarications required by polite society. With him, she did not even try.

They had met two years previously and almost from the start Deborah had made it perfectly clear that she found him to be nothing but a rake and a scoundrel, and she would be the happiest woman on earth if she were never to see him again. Richard's reputation, which had drawn so many women to him like moths to a dangerous flame, had done him no favours at all in her eyes. He had quickly realised that Deb was that most fascinating combination of qualities, a passionate woman who appeared to have the morals of a puritan. Her antagonism had only piqued his interest. And, being a rake, he had known at once that he had to have her.

Their acquaintance had developed in the most fascinating way. Richard had begun to suspect that, for all her protestations, Deb was not indifferent to him. He was too experienced with women not to recognise that her dislike was turning to reluctant attraction. The very fact that she deliberately avoided his company spoke of her struggle with her own feelings. The knowledge had prompted him to make a serious miscalculation. He had asked her to be his mistress.

It was unlike him to be so inept in matters of the heart, but he had assumed that he could overcome any scruples Deb might possess and persuade her into an *affaire*. A slapped cheek had demonstrated just how passionate her nature was—and how far he had misjudged the situation. Then, lest he had not quite understood her message, she had sent him a very sharp letter, telling him to keep out of her way in future. Ordering him, in fact.

Richard had had no intention of doing so and he was assisted in the matter by the fact that society in the Midwinter villages was small and they were forever being thrown into each other's company. Deb had tried to ignore him and Richard had delighted in teasing her by straying close to the line that she had drawn. She had reacted disdainfully, yet underneath he had sensed that her reluctant attraction to him was still there and that it troubled her deeply. It also stirred in him a desire greater than he had ever known.

But then two things had happened to change the balance of the situation. Firstly, Richard had renewed his friendship with Ross Marney, under whom he had served at sea. Ross was his senior by several years and there had always been a mutual respect between the two of them. Now that they were living in the same neighbourhood, this quickly grew into a warmer friendship. Which made Deb, as Ross's sister-in-law, firmly out of bounds to Richard. She became that most tempting but untouchable of creatures, the woman that he wanted but simply could not have.

As if this were not bad enough, Richard had crowned his folly with a final piece of madness. He had fallen in love with Deb and his ambitions had changed. Now he wanted to marry her.

He was not entirely sure how or why it had happened. True, they were forever in company together and shared an interest in riding and the pleasures of the outdoors. Even so, it seemed inexplicable to him. He was not a man who had ever looked to marry, for his elder brother had the responsibility of providing an heir to the dukedom of Kestrel. More to the point, he had never met a woman that he wanted to wed. Until now. And now, of course, his choice had fixed upon someone who would barely give him the time of day, let alone her hand in marriage.

Richard had told himself many times that his ardour was the natural result of being denied something that he wanted. He told himself that he would soon overcome this temporary difficulty and be cured.

He knew that he deceived himself.

It was also clear that he had not a hope in hell of achieving his ambition of marriage to Deborah, for whilst he had been languishing like a lovestruck boy rather than a man of experience, Deb's feelings for him had undergone no such radical change. She still despised his reputation and, as a result, would not let him close. It was barely surprising, given that he had marked his card when he had asked her to be his mistress.

Richard knew that he could not undo the past. For years he had revelled in his status as one of the most dangerous

rakes in London. He had exploited it, enjoyed it to the full.
Now it could deny him the one thing that he wanted above
all else. It was an irony that he could appreciate.

And in addition there was another obstacle. Richard had
heard from Ross Marney amongst others that Deb's first
marriage had been very unhappy and that she did not look
to wed again. Taken all in all, the barriers seemed formi-
dable. And yet Richard knew that he was going to try. His
courtship would not be in the least conventional, but it was
his most ardent intention to oblige Deb to admit her feelings
and to persuade her that, despite her misgivings, they were
meant to be together.

He brought his horse alongside hers and was amused
when she twitched her reins to draw a little way away from
him.

'I beg your pardon,' he said smoothly. 'I was attempting
to compliment your riding skills. You controlled your horse
magnificently back there. But perhaps you do not care for
compliments from a circus rider?'

Deb turned her face away so that all he could see was
her charming profile beneath the brim of her saucy hat.

'I certainly do not seek compliments from you, Lord
Richard,' she said. 'They are as worthless as withered
weeds.'

'How poetic,' Richard said. 'Do you study the romantic
poets at the Midwinter ladies' reading group this summer,
Mrs Stratton?'

Deborah's voluptuous mouth pursed tightly, as though
someone had pulled a drawstring. It made Richard want to
kiss her. He repressed the jolt of desire that ran through him
and soothed Merlin to a stately walk. The hunter tossed its
head in disgust.

'We are studying the works of Andrew Marvell,' Deborah
said, 'though I do not expect that you will have heard of

him, Lord Richard. I have yet to learn that intellectual pursuits are your strong point.'

Richard, who had taken a double First at Oxford, merely smiled. 'You have yet to learn anything about my strong points, as I recall, Mrs Stratton. When I offered to demonstrate them to you, you declined.'

Deborah blushed slightly, but did not look at him. 'Of course I did! I am no lightskirt prepared to help you enliven your time in the country. By the by, when *do* you return to London, Lord Richard? Surely it must be soon? Time seems to pass so slowly these days.'

Richard laughed. 'I am desolate to disappoint you, ma'am, but I fear that the time for my departure has not yet come. However, you need not repine. You have done an excellent job of avoiding me this summer thus far. Look at the way you cut me dead at Lady Sally Saltire's most recent ball! It was masterly. It is merely our bad luck that we bumped into each other today. I am sure that it will not happen again.'

Deb looked down her nose at him. 'I hope not. Midwinter used to be such a peaceful place, but these days it is bursting with all manner of undesirable characters.'

Richard laughed. 'You may classify me with the riff-raff, Mrs Stratton, but I am not convinced that you see me as undesirable…'

He watched in amusement as Deborah bit her lip, clearly torn between giving him another huge set down and a natural courtesy that told her she was behaving very rudely towards him. She was quite the most transparent person that he had ever met but, in a society that dealt so much in the counterfeit, it was refreshing.

She pulled her horse a little ahead of his on the grassy track and glanced back over her shoulder.

'One of the pleasures of riding for me is that I may do it

alone,' she said pointedly. 'I bid you good day, Lord Richard.'

Richard put his gloved hand on her reins to slow her down. She looked sharply at his hand and her face froze with disapproval.

'My lord?' Her tone was arctic.

'A moment, Mrs Stratton,' Richard said, as their horses drew level. 'Since it is so rare that I have the pleasure of riding with a companion who is my equal in skill, how do you feel about a wager? If you can outrun me, then you have won the right to your solitude.'

Deborah's eyes snapped. Before Richard could even draw breathe, she had whipped the reins out of his hand, turned the horse and dug her heels into its flank. She passed so close to him that he was forced to pull the hunter to one side for fear of being ridden down.

Richard paused for only a second before swinging Merlin around and following. He had intended to be chivalrous and to offer Deb a head start, but now he saw that no quarter was expected. She had set her mare at a gate that led into a wide field running downhill towards the river and was already at least a furlong ahead of him.

Smiling grimly, Richard gave chase. Deb was crouched low in the saddle and cut a flying figure in her red riding dress as she lay almost flat against the horse's neck. She had the advantage of knowing the ground better than he; she did not hesitate as the mare thundered over the grassy turf towards the water. The wind snatched her riding hat from her head so that her hair tumbled about her shoulders and streamed behind her like a Valkyrie's.

Richard was gaining on her now and, no matter how she wheeled and turned, closed the gap between them, forcing her towards a small copse of trees at the edge of the river. Finally, when she could see that there was no way to escape him, she drew rein and led the horse at a docile walk under the canopy of leaves.

Richard watched her closely. He would not put it past her to try and trick him now and slip past him out of the woods. She looked frustrated and defiant, her breast heaving with exertion under the constraint of the tight red jacket.

'What a streak of wildness you have in you, Mrs Stratton,' Richard said slowly. 'I have always surmised that you possess the desire to kick aside the rules of society and be free.' He turned his horse so that they were facing one another, bringing the hunter alongside until his knee brushed hers. She did not move away, but rather sat frozen in the saddle, her blue eyes wide and fixed on him.

'You did not ask what the penalty would be if you lost the wager,' Richard added gently.

He took one gloved hand from the reins and slid it behind her head, into the tangle of her windswept hair, drawing her closer to him. The horses pressed together, crushing his leg between their heated bodies. It was a damnably uncomfortable way to kiss a lady, but it was worth every moment to him, for he had been wanting to kiss Deb Stratton for a very long time indeed. Her lips were soft and cool, and she tasted of fresh air and faintly of honey, and there was some other less definable taste that was Deborah herself, and it went straight to his head—and to other parts of him that responded instantaneously. He first closed his teeth about her voluptuous bottom lip, then released it and slid his tongue into her mouth, courting a response until she kissed him back, hesitantly at first and then with growing passion. The touch and the taste of her fused in his mind with the bright sunlight and the chill of the breeze, and desire flooded through him until he was within an inch of pulling her from the horse and making love to her there on the bed of leaves beneath the trees.

He gathered her more closely against him, sliding his hands gently down her back, alive to every curve and line of her body beneath the enticingly trim riding habit. He had never ached so much for a woman before, nor lost touch with all reality other than that which he held in his arms. But Deb was soft and vibrant, and when she leaned closer to him and with a little sigh matched the stroke of his tongue with her own, he was powerless to resist.

The horses shifted and pulled them apart, and Richard reluctantly let Deborah go. He moved back, his eyes on her face. She looked completely bemused for a second, dazed and dazzled, and he felt a violent satisfaction to have so thoroughly undermined her defences. Then her expression warmed into anger.

'I *knew* you were a rake!' she said furiously.

'I am so pleased to have been able to prove you correct,' Richard replied.

Deborah made a noise of disgust. 'I could have outrun you had I been riding astride.'

'Now that,' Richard said with appreciation, 'I should have liked to see.'

Deborah made another squawk like an infuriated hen and set the horse to walk along the path out of the wood. It was a narrow track and Richard let her go first. Last autumn's bracken mingled with the pine needles underfoot and the horses' hooves made a crunching sound on the undergrowth. Deborah was holding herself upright, ramrod straight. There was indignation in every line of her figure. It made Richard want to laugh. He was willing to bet that half her annoyance stemmed from the fact that she had not been able to help responding to him. And what a response. It scorched him to remember it.

'You did kiss me back,' he pointed out mildly.

That gained him a stormy look from those deep blue eyes. 'I have no recollection of it.'

'You have a short memory, then. Come here and allow me to remind you.'

Deb quickened her horse's pace to a trot and burst out of the shade and into the open field again. 'Is my penalty for losing the wager also to find that I cannot lose your company, Lord Richard?' she demanded.

Richard smiled. 'I feel that I should escort you home, Mrs Stratton. One may come across all kinds of rogues if one has the folly to ride out without a groom in attendance.'

Deborah raised her whip and tapped it thoughtfully against the palm of her hand. 'Perhaps I could deal with them.'

'I thought that I had already demonstrated that you could not?'

Richard watched in amusement as Deborah's fist clenched more tightly about the handle of the whip. The leather of her gloves strained across her knuckles. Her intentions were all too clear.

'I find my need for solitude to be quite overwhelming now, Lord Richard,' she said coldly. 'Sufficient to defend it with violence, even.'

Richard laughed. 'You have no need to go so far, Mrs Stratton. I can take a hint as well as the next man.'

He thought that she almost smiled then, despite herself. 'All evidence to the contrary, Lord Richard,' she said. 'I have always thought you remarkably slow to understand.'

Richard quietened Merlin, who had picked up the tension in the air and was sidestepping nervously.

'Perhaps you are underestimating me?' he said softly.

'I doubt it,' Deb snapped. 'My estimation of you has always been that you are a thorough-going rake, and I have seen nothing to contradict that.'

'I cannot fault your assessment of me,' Richard said. 'All that I question is your own response. You are not as indifferent to me as you pretend.'

He saw the colour come into Deborah's cheeks then and thought it a mixture of indignation and guilt. She did not wish to admit her attraction to him, but because she was of so honest a disposition she was having difficulty with lies and half-truths.

'You are mistaken,' she said.

'I do not think so.'

'You are conceited.'

'Possibly. That still does not prove that you dislike me.'

'I dislike you intensely.'

'And that does not prove that you are not attracted to me.' Richard threw up a hand. 'Come, Mrs Stratton—Deborah—admit the truth.'

'I did not give you the right to address me by name, my lord,' Deborah snapped.

'No, you just gave me a passionate kiss in the woods. I concede that one does not need to be on first-name terms to do such a thing. Indeed, you could make love to me and never need to call me by my name—'

He saw the flash of fury in her eyes, but he did not flinch as the whip came down. It hit the mare's flank rather than his face, and the creature took off across the fields as though it had the fires of hell snapping at its heels.

This time Richard let Deborah go, watching with admiration as she leaned from the saddle to retrieve her hat from the grass without even slowing the horse's stride. With a whimsical smile on his face, he turned Merlin in the opposite direction and cantered back towards Kestrel Court along the track that ran beside the edge of the river, the Winter Race. The path was soft and sandy beneath Merlin's hooves and the horse settled to a tidy pace leaving Richard at liberty to think about Deborah Stratton. He had forced himself to self-control when dealing with her, but she had brought out every primitive and masculine instinct within him. It was damnably difficult to behave like a gentleman when all he wanted to do was carry her off.

Richard sighed, deliberately allowing the tension to drain from his body. It had been an interesting morning. First there had been the mysterious letter addressed to the editor of the *Suffolk Chronicle*. He wanted to know what that had been about. Then there had been his encounter with Deborah herself, as madcap and passionate and yet as determinedly strait-laced as ever. Their meeting had only strengthened Richard's determination to pursue his unconventional wooing. And since he could never pretend to be a sober man, and since she thought him a rake, a rake's courtship was what she would get.

# Chapter Two

'Is there something the matter, Deborah?' Olivia Marney enquired of her sister when, later that day, they were sitting on the veranda at Midwinter Marney Hall partaking of tea. 'You have barely sat still for five minutes at a time this afternoon and you seem most agitated. What can have happened to upset you?'

Deborah plumped herself down on the cushioned seat of the wicker chair and toyed with the spray of lilac that she had wrenched from a nearby bush. Its bruised petals gave off a sweet perfume. Deb laid the spray aside with a sigh. No doubt Olivia, who had put years of effort into the gardens at Marney, would be watching her with concern in case she destroyed her life's work in one fell swoop. The way Deb was feeling, it was a distinct possibility.

'I am sorry I am such poor company,' she said. 'I feel quite liverish today. Maybe it is the sun.'

'Hmm.' Olivia poured her sister another cup of tea and pushed the plate with the homemade fruitcake in Deb's direction. 'It has never bothered you before. I thought that you went out riding this morning?'

'I did.' Deb moodily swallowed a mouthful of tea. It tasted too strong and she wished that she had asked for lemonade instead. She put her cup down and studied the prospect across the lawns to the ornamental shrubbery. It was cool and leafy, and should have been soothing to the spirits. Deb found that it was not.

'Did you not enjoy yourself?' Olivia was enquiring. 'Usually riding puts you in such a pleasant frame of mind.'

Deb frowned. 'No, I did not enjoy myself. I was plagued by that rogue, Richard Kestrel. He insisted on accompanying me for some of the way. He quite spoiled my outing.'

Olivia's brow cleared. 'Oh, I see. It is Lord Richard who has put you in this vile mood! I should have guessed. No one else has his talent for upsetting you.'

'He kissed me,' Deb said. 'Can you believe the audacity of the man?'

There was a clatter as Olivia dropped her silver spoon on the tiled floor. She bent to retrieve it, sitting up with a slight flush on her face. 'Good gracious, Deb, you should warn me before you make an announcement like that! Nothing half as exciting ever happens at Midwinter Marney Hall.'

Deb was momentarily distracted from her own thoughts. 'Do you mean that Ross never kisses you, Liv?'

'Never,' her sister said. 'We have been married six years, you know, so it is hardly to be expected. Besides, we quarrel so much that there is never time for anything else. But we were not speaking of my situation, were we, Deborah? Tell me what happened.'

Deb shrugged slightly. She found that she did not wish to confide the whole tale of her encounter with Richard Kestrel, for it might involve some awkward explanations and she was not at all sure of the precise nature of her feelings. Olivia was famously perceptive, and would hit at once on the idea that Deb was in some strange way attracted to the rakish Lord Richard. Indeed, when Richard had tried to seduce Deb the previous year and Deb in a flurry of outrage and shock had unburdened herself to her sister, Olivia had merely smiled in a maddening way and said that she had been expecting it for several months. She had seemed a great deal less surprised than Deb was herself, and not particularly shocked.

'It was no great matter,' Deb said now, glossing over the ill-advised race and the fact that she had lost it. 'We were riding through Winter Wood and Lord Richard took the opportunity of the secluded surroundings to steal a kiss.'

She sighed sharply. 'I suppose that it was my fault for lowering my guard. After all, I know what type of man he is.'

A tiny frown touched Olivia's face. Looking at her, Deb wished that she could achieve Olivia's effortlessly cool façade. Such an outward show of composure would be of great use when dealing with the advances of a rake like Lord Richard Kestrel. Alas for her, Deb felt that she wore her heart on her sleeve, and, no matter how she tried, she was incapable of hiding her feelings. When a scoundrel like Lord Richard provoked her she reacted impulsively. It always got her into trouble.

Deb sighed and stirred her tea, forgetting that she had already done it once and that she did not take sugar anyway. She wished that she could achieve Olivia's levels of serenity. Her sister seldom lost her temper and always appeared tranquil. Occasionally Deb would wonder if Olivia had no warmer feelings at all, for she never saw evidence of them. She had even wondered if this was responsible for the estrangement between Olivia and her husband Ross. Ross was by temperament quite similar to Deb herself for he had a quick temper. Deb had always thought this was one of the reasons why they dealt together so well. Olivia, in contrast, was tranquil and self-possessed. She reminded Deb of violets and cool water, whereas if she had to characterise her own temperament she would have thought of hot coals and scarlet roses.

Olivia's frown had deepened slightly. 'Is it possible to kiss on horseback?' she enquired now. 'I had always imagined it would be a little difficult. I take it that you *were* on horseback at this point?'

'Of course we were!' Deb tried not to sound too sharp. 'You do not think that I dismounted so that he could kiss me properly, do you?'

Olivia raised her brows at her sister's tone. 'There is no need to be snappish. You might have been tempted.'

'Well, I was not,' Deb said untruthfully. 'Lord Richard takes the most shocking liberties and I do all I can to discourage him.'

'So you *were* on horseback and it *is* possible to kiss properly in that situation,' Olivia mused. 'How interesting!'

Deb sighed crossly. For once she did not feel that her sister, normally so sympathetic, was giving her appropriate support.

'It was not *interesting*, Liv,' she said. 'It was quite outrageous.'

'Oh, pooh,' Olivia said. 'Outrageous, indeed! I wish I had your difficulties, Deb. You would not hear me complaining.'

'Liv!' Deb was genuinely scandalised. Despite the unsatisfactory state of her marriage, Olivia had never indicated for a second that she would look elsewhere for consolation.

Olivia shrugged, but her blue eyes were twinkling. 'No need to sound so huffy, Deb. I did but wish to point out that most ladies would give their best gown to be in your shoes as far as Lord Richard Kestrel was concerned—yes, and throw in their jewels as well, into the bargain!'

Deb snorted. 'What nonsense—'

'You protest too much,' Olivia said, plucking a grape from the silver bowl of fruit at her elbow. She looked back at her sister and her gaze was shrewd. 'Cut line, Deb. You know that you like him. There is no point in trying to gammon me—or yourself either.'

There was silence that fizzed with indignation and then Deb subsided with a little sigh.

'Oh dear, I confess that you might be right. How is it that you know me so well, Liv?'

'Years of observation,' her sister said calmly. 'You are easy to read, Deb. You like Lord Richard Kestrel, you enjoyed his kisses and, though you are shocked at yourself for even considering it, you are wondering just how far you could let him go before you got into difficulties.'

'Liv!' Deb said again. The colour flooded her face. Her sister's assessment was uncannily accurate.

'Well?'

Deb rubbed a hand across her forehead. 'I admit that I enjoy Lord Richard's company,' she said, feeling a certain relief that she could discuss her feelings honestly with Olivia. 'He has a very engaging manner, in an impudent sort of a way...'

'And his compliments are very pretty.'

'True, but very practised.'

'And are his kisses practised too?'

Deb traced patterns on the top of the wicker table. For all her belief that Lord Richard was nothing more than a rake, there had been something sweet about his kisses, something that had evoked a shockingly strong response from her.

'I do not know,' she said reluctantly. 'I have very little means of comparison. I imagine that a man of his reputation must be very good at kissing, which is why I felt so...' She waved her hands about descriptively.

'So...' Olivia prompted.

'So dizzy and shivery and excited...' Deb shivered again

now, thinking about it. She was obliged to admit that there
had been something between the two of them from the moment that they had met on the bridleway. It had been like
flint striking steel; a spark, a flare and then the flame caught.
It mattered not whether she liked Richard or not. Something
had ignited as soon as their eyes had met.

Olivia laughed. 'Yet you wish to run away from him?
Oh, Deb!'

Deb drank some of her cooling tea. 'I find it disturbing
to be so attracted to a man whose way of life I utterly reject,'
she said.

'I imagine,' Olivia said shrewdly, 'that you find it disturbing to be attracted to a man at all when you swore you
would never trust one ever again.'

Deb shrugged awkwardly. 'At the time—after Neil's betrayal—I could not imagine ever finding a man I could like.'
She looked out across the cool green acres of the garden.
'Now I am not so naïve as to believe I could not have
feelings for someone, but…' she frowned '…I could never
act on them.'

'Never?' Olivia looked quizzical.

Deb fidgeted. 'I could never contemplate marriage…' She
fidgeted with her teacup again then looked up to meet her
sister's level gaze. 'I cannot quite believe it, Liv, but lately
I *have* had thoughts…' she hesitated, then continued more
firmly '…thoughts of what it might be like to take Richard
Kestrel as a lover. What could be more shocking than that?'

A quiver of breeze ran along the veranda, sending ripples
across the little ornamental pond where the fat goldfish
basked and stirring the branches of the lilac so that its scent
suffused the air.

Even now, Olivia's calm was not impaired. 'There are
plenty of things more shocking,' she said. 'I can see that

you would not be much taken with marriage but you might find that to take a lover would be far more pleasurable…'

Deb stared at her. 'How would you know?'

'I do not,' Olivia said calmly. 'I am only speculating.'

Deb shook her head. 'It is a scandalous plan. I do not support such behaviour and neither do you.' She sighed. 'Goodness knows, after the huge outrage over my elopement, I simply should not be thinking of compounding my folly with this. It is the sort of fantasy that is all very well in theory, but must never be made a reality. It is far too dangerous.' She wriggled in her chair. 'Anyway, Lord Richard is not the sole cause of my ill temper. I had a letter from Papa today.'

'Ah, I see.' To Deb's relief, Olivia let the subject of Richard Kestrel drop. 'Is Papa pressing you to return to the fold?'

'More than that, he is commanding me.' Deb licked her finger and picked up the cake crumbs from the plate in most unladylike fashion. 'He threatens to cut off my allowance if I do not return to live at Walton Hall.'

Olivia made a little sound of distress. 'That is harsh, although I know he only wants what is best for you, Deb. I do not suppose you can countenance it?'

'No.' Deb put the plate down. 'It is not simply the difficulty of returning home after three years away, Liv. That would be restrictive and unpleasant, but nowhere near as difficult as refusing the match with cousin Harry—again.'

Her sister shuddered. 'Is that what Papa is proposing?'

'I fear so,' Deb said. 'I spoilt his plans when I eloped with Neil and now he sees an opportunity to make the match that I rejected the first time around.'

Olivia's gaze was troubled. 'Surely Papa would not force a match? I know that he can be very autocratic but, if you were unwilling, surely he would not persist?'

Deb looked at her, but did not say anything. The silence

was eloquent. They were both remembering their father's determination to marry all his children off advantageously, a determination that brooked no opposition.

'If not cousin Harry, then someone else,' Deb said bluntly. 'You know that he will not be happy until he sees me safely—and legitimately—married.'

Olivia grimaced sympathetically. She tilted the brim of her straw hat against the sun, which was creeping round the edge of the roof.

'So what will you do? You cannot avoid returning to Bath for Guy's wedding, unless you invent some fictitious illness.'

It was on the tip of Deb's tongue to tell her sister that it was not an illness she planned to invent but a fictitious betrothal. She just managed to hold her peace in time. Despite Olivia's surprisingly broadminded stance on the subject of taking a lover, Deb knew that she would be shocked to know that her sister had advertised for a fiancé. It simply was not done. It would be time enough to tell Olivia what she planned when she had found a suitable gentleman, even then, she was certain that her sister would cut up rough.

'I do not know what I shall do,' she said, 'though I am certain that I will think of something. Oh, if only there was not this annoying threat of invasion to add weight to Papa's argument! It is most inconvenient.'

Olivia laughed. 'What is inconvenient? Bonaparte's plans? Do you think that he should have consulted your convenience before he assembled his fleet off Boulogne?'

Deb gave a little giggle. 'No, of course not. How absurd you are! I merely mean that Papa does not consider it safe for me to be living alone with only Clarrie and the servants, for all that you and Ross are but a few miles away.'

'You may come and live here with my blessing,' Olivia

said drily. 'You would not be getting in anybody's way and it would be nice to have someone to talk to.'

Deb gave her a troubled look. 'Truly, Liv, is it so bad? I know that there was a time when you hoped to give Ross an heir…'

'Not much chance of that now,' Olivia said, even more drily. 'I have yet to learn that it is possible to conceive an heir when the husband spends all his time improving his estate and the wife spends all her energies on her garden. We may be designing a most elegant home, but we are not propagating a future generation to appreciate it—'

She broke off, looking flustered for the first time in Deborah's memory. Ross Marney had come through the folding French windows and out on to the veranda just as his wife was speaking. It was impossible to tell how much of the conversation he had heard.

'Good afternoon, Ross,' Deb said, seeing that Olivia was rendered temporarily speechless. She got to her feet. 'May I pour you some tea?'

Ross bent to kiss her cheek. He was of sturdy build, with black hair and intense blue eyes. When Olivia had first married him, Deb, then an impressionable sixteen-year-old, had had quite a crush on him. These days she could laugh at her girlish infatuations, but she still considered him a handsome man.

'I think that you should allow your sister to dispense the refreshments,' Ross said, with an unfathomable look at Olivia, 'since she is complaining that that is all the propagation that she is permitted to do.'

An awkward silence fell. There were two spots of colour high on Olivia's cheekbones as she poured the tea. The spout of the pot rattled against the china as her hand shook slightly, and Deb felt a rush of sympathy. It was too bad of

Ross to make his wife feel so uncomfortable. He should have pretended that he had not heard.

'We were speaking of our trip to Somerset,' she said, trying once again to break the silence. 'It is only two months until Guy's wedding.'

'Plenty of time for him to reconsider, then, before he makes a decision he may live to regret,' Ross said. He took his cup with a curt word of thanks and strolled away down the grassy slope on to the lawn.

Deb was halfway out of her chair when Olivia put her hand on her sister's arm.

'Deb, do not!' she implored in a whisper. 'I know that you only mean to help, but it does not do any good...'

Deb subsided back in her chair. She picked up her own cup and drank the cooling liquid. Sometimes in the past she had interfered in Ross and Olivia's disagreements when her sister's refusal to stand up to her husband had so infuriated her that she could not let a subject pass. Olivia had never reproached her, but sometimes Deb had had the impression that her intervention had made things worse rather than better. She felt exasperated. Olivia was a pattern card of goodness and Ross Marney was a nice man, handsome, generous and kind. So why, oh, why was it not possible for the two of them to co-exist in harmony? She wanted to bang their heads together.

'I suppose that I should go,' she said slowly.

'Do not hurry away on Ross's account,' Olivia said, and Deb heard the note of bitterness in her voice ring clear as a bell. 'He won't speak to me of this. We never do talk.'

Deb wrinkled up her face. Her knowledge of married life was small, consisting of five weeks before Neil Stratton had departed to the wars. That month had hardly been the bliss that she had been expecting. Even so, she knew that if a husband and wife never spoke to each other then they could hardly expect other aspects of their relationship to improve. She opened her mouth to offer some advice, saw the expression on Olivia's face and closed it again.

'You do not understand,' Olivia said rapidly. 'Please let it go, Deborah.'

Deb got up and hugged her sister hard, spilling Olivia's tea in the process. Her sister bore the embrace stoically, even going so far as to give Deb a brief, convulsive hug in return. She dabbed at the tea stains on her dress, head bent. All the animation that Deb had seen in her earlier in the afternoon had vanished.

'Would you care to take the carriage back to Mallow?' Olivia enquired. 'It is hot to be walking.'

'No, thank you,' Deb said. 'I shall go through the woods. It will give me time to think.'

A faint spark of amusement lit Olivia's face again. 'About Richard Kestrel? You do not fear to find him lurking behind a tree waiting to pounce again?'

Deb laughed. 'If he does, he will get all the odium that should rightly be reserved for Ross. It would be poetic justice.'

Olivia put out her hand quickly. 'You will be here for my musicale tonight?' she asked, and Deb could hear and understand the pleading tone in her voice. It was the first time she had seen a crack in Olivia's perfect façade and it made her fearful. The marriage must be in dire straits indeed.

'I was not planning to be here,' she said doubtfully. 'Is it that Estelle creature from the theatre in Woodbridge who is coming to perform?'

'Miss Estella La Salle,' Olivia said reprovingly. 'It is quite a coup for me that she has agreed to sing for us, Deb. She is much sought after and very fashionable in the Prince of Wales's circle.'

'Only because the Hertfords have made such a fuss over

her,' Deb said. 'They must be tone deaf! I love you dearly, Liv, but I am not sure that even for you I can sit through Miss La Salle's caterwauling.'

'You are the one who is tone deaf,' Olivia responded. Her tone changed. 'Oh please, Deb…'

Deb caught sight of Ross disappearing into the shrubbery. He was swiping at the tops of some of the rose bushes and looked to be in a very bad mood indeed.

'Oh, very well,' she said hastily. 'I shall be here for as long as I can stand it!'

Olivia gave her another brief hug and Deb went down the shallow bank and on to the lawn in the same direction that Ross had gone. She was not intending to speak to him for she was not certain that she could be civil, but as she made her way down from the veranda, Ross came across the lawn and fell into step beside her. After giving him one angry, speaking look, Deb tolerated his company in silence. In this manner they walked across the lawn and reached the wooden gate that led out of the garden, across the ha-ha and into the surrounding park.

'You may leave me here, Ross,' Deb said tightly. 'Thank you for your escort.'

Ross put his hand on the gate to prevent her exit. 'Deb, I am sorry.'

'I am not the one to whom you should be apologising,' Deb said, raising a hand to shade her eyes from the sun so that she could glare at him all the better. 'I do not know how Liv has endured your behaviour for so long, Ross. If I were in her shoes, I would have taken my gardening shears to you before now.'

'I know,' Ross said. There was a look of deep unhappiness in his blue eyes.

'And you would deserve it!' Deb added.

'I know that too.' A rueful grin touched Ross's mouth,

lightening the tired lines of his face for a moment. 'Dear Deborah, it is so refreshing to have these sisterly chats with you! You go straight to the heart of the matter instead of pretending that there is no difficulty.'

'Well, do not expect me to give you absolution,' Deb said sharply. She drew him into the shade of a spreading oak that bordered the garden. 'That is better. I cannot judge how repentant you are if I am squinting into the sun.' She scanned his face. 'Hmm. You do look a little bit cast down, I suppose. Well, you have only yourself to blame, Ross. I could shake both you and Olivia, you know. I am so fond of you both and I cannot comprehend why you cannot like each other.'

'Oh, I *like* Olivia,' Ross said wryly. 'I like her a lot. That is half the trouble!'

'I do not mean in *that* way,' Deb said, frowning at him. 'Men are all the same! You bring everything down to whether a woman is attractive to you or not and matters are never that simple.'

'That is because men are simple creatures at heart,' Ross said, looking out across Midwinter Marney land towards the sea. 'All I desire is a home, a wife who cares for me and an heir…'

'Try not to sound too maudlin,' Deb said tartly. 'You do not deserve those things unless you settle your differences with Olivia.' Her face softened and she took his hand. She could never be angry with Ross for long, for she owed him a huge debt of gratitude and she knew what a very kind person he was at heart.

'Dearest Ross,' she said, 'it grieves me to see you both so unhappy. You and Olivia have been so generous to me in the past. I do not know what I would have done without you after Neil died—'

'Don't,' Ross said gruffly. His face set in hard lines. 'You know that we would have done anything to help you, Deb.' Anger darkened his eyes. 'The only thing that I regret is that the fever got to Neil Stratton before I could call him to account.'

Deb sighed and freed herself. 'Don't, Ross. It is all over and done with now. But I do know that you are a kind and honourable man, and that very fact makes your estrangement from Olivia all the worse! If you were a boorish oaf then I could understand it, but you are not! At least, not most of the time.'

'Thank you, Deb,' Ross said ironically. 'That vote of confidence encourages me.'

'You deserve my censure,' Deb said. 'You were positively churlish to Olivia just now. Can you not be nice to her for a change? Talk to her! Take her flowers…'

'She has all the flowers she needs in the garden,' Ross said glumly. 'I tried giving her a bouquet once and she made some remark about preferring to see flowers growing rather than dead in a vase.'

Deb sighed with exasperation. 'That is unfortunate, but why give up as a result?'

'Because I have no notion what it is that Olivia wants,' Ross said, frowning heavily.

Deb sighed again. 'Then why do you not *ask* her, Ross? Must I tell you how to do everything? Sit down and talk to her one day. Take her to the seaside. Buy her a present! I don't know…' Deb shook her head at him. 'Olivia needs you, Ross. She may appear cool and composed on the surface, but underneath she is as vulnerable as anyone else.' She gave him a little push. 'Now go and talk to her!'

But when she reached the place where the path to Midwinter Mallow entered the beech wood, she looked back to see Ross striding away across the fields and could just make

out the forlorn figure of Olivia still sitting on the veranda a
quarter-mile distant in the opposite direction.

With an exasperated sigh, Deb called down a curse upon
the heads of all men and vented her irritation by kicking up
all the old, dry beech leaves from the ground beneath her
feet. It made her feel better, but she knew that something
had to be done to help Olivia. Unless radical steps were
taken to reunite the Marneys, and soon, she could foresee
years of misery for her beloved sister and brother-in-law as
they lived their separate lives under the one roof.

In one way, however, she was obliged to acknowledge
that Ross's arrival on the veranda had been timely, for if he
had not appeared, there was a chance that she might have
blurted out to Olivia all about her decision to appoint a
temporary fiancé and, even worse, about the newspaper advertisement. Deb frowned. For some reason, thinking of her
fleeting fiancé made her think of Richard Kestrel again. She
took a swing at an innocent spray of cow parsley beside the
path. Lord Richard was exactly the sort of man who was
the epitome of what she did *not* want in a counterfeit suitor.
She needed someone who was moderate, agreeable and open
to her guidance. Most certainly she did not need a man who
was dangerous, forceful and devilishly attractive.

Deborah shook her head impatiently. Dwelling on Richard Kestrel's attractions seemed a particularly pointless ex-
ercise at the moment and yet she seemed powerless to dismiss him from her mind. Nor was it helpful that the idle
thought she had had of taking Richard as a lover had somehow taken root and would not be shifted. She knew it was
a scandalous thought and one that she could not act on. It
had better remain no more than a fantasy. And yet it still
gave her no peace at all.

# Chapter Three

'Deb! Deb, wake up!'

The sound of her sister's voice penetrated Deb's pleasant doze. She stirred reluctantly and opened her eyes. The press of visitors in Olivia's music room that evening had dissipated a little, for they had moved into the conservatory to take refreshments. Olivia had taken the rout chair next to hers and was leaning close, shaking her arm with a little impatient gesture. Deb yawned.

'Has Miss La Salle finished?'

'Ten minutes ago!' her sister scolded. She shifted slightly and Deb saw over her shoulder that the infamous singer was now at the far end of the salon, partaking of a glass of wine and surrounded by admiring gentlemen. She smiled faintly.

'Was it good?'

'I cannot believe that you did not hear,' Olivia said. 'How is it possible to sleep through singing like that?'

Deb laughed. 'I found it difficult, certainly, but by no means impossible.'

Olivia shook her head impatiently. 'Well, never mind that now. I need you to find Ross for me, Deborah. He has not made an appearance for the whole evening. It is most embarrassing.'

'Is he sulking,' Deb enquired, 'or is it merely that, like me, he does not care for music?'

A hint of colour came into Olivia's cheeks. 'I do not believe that he has forgiven me this morning's comments and thinks to punish me. And, yes—he does hate singing. He says that Miss La Salle's voice reminds him of wailing cats!'

Deb smothered a laugh. 'Yet you wish to inflict this suffering on him?'

'He must come,' Olivia said, grabbing Deb's sleeve between desperate fingers. 'Everyone has remarked upon his absence. If I am obliged to listen to any more of Lady Benedict's false condolences on having a philistine for a husband, I believe I shall run screaming from the room.'

Deb frowned. 'Why do you not simply request Ross to come and join you?'

Olivia's face puckered. 'He will not pay any notice. *You* ask him, Deb!'

'And if he does refuse, I shall give him a piece of my mind,' Deb agreed. She stood up. 'Where is he?'

'I think he is in his study,' Olivia said. Her face relaxed. 'Thank you, Deb.'

Deb walked slowly out through the double doors and into the hall. She felt exasperated and more than a little upset. Olivia was putting a brave face on matters, but it seemed that her relationship with Ross had degenerated even in the short time since that morning's disagreement. If matters continued like this, they would be completely estranged in a matter of days. Deb, whose hot temper could never bear to let a quarrel fester, fizzed with irritation.

She gave the door of the study a quick, perfunctory knock and burst in.

'Ross, you must go and join Liv in the music room at once!' she declared. 'I do not know what has got into you today. You are acting in the most churlish manner—' She broke off as the man sitting behind the desk rose from his wing chair and she saw him properly for the first time. It was not Ross Marney. It was Richard Kestrel.

'Good evening, Mrs Stratton,' he said.

'What are you doing here?' Deb demanded, shaken out of good manners by both the unexpected sight of Lord Richard looking so elegant in his evening dress and mortification at what she had just inadvertently revealed to him. 'I did not know that you were attending the soirée.'

Richard bowed ironically. 'Very likely you did not see me,' he said. 'I arrived late and you were already asleep by then.'

Deb's red face blushed an even more fiery colour. 'You! Oh! I was not asleep!'

'Yes, you were. I saw you with my own eyes. And what better way to tolerate Miss La Salle's peculiar style of vocal gymnastics than to block them out with pleasant dreams?'

'What? I...' Deb frowned, distracted. 'Does no one like her singing?'

'Very few people, I believe, but as she is a protégée of the Hertfords, everyone pretends that she is marvellous.'

'Well, I think that is ridiculous. But that is nothing to the purpose.' Deb shook her head impatiently. 'I was looking for Ross.'

'I rather gathered that,' Richard said. 'I would not wish to be in his shoes when you find him.'

Deb had not realised that it was possible to blush any harder. She subsided into one of the armchairs by the fire and looked at him with embarrassment. 'I apologise that you should have been the unwitting victim of my ill temper, my lord.'

'Please,' Richard said. 'Do not apologise.' He took the chair across from her. There was a keen look in his dark eyes. 'I understand that you are concerned for your sister's happiness.'

Deb grimaced. 'Is her *un*happiness so apparent to everyone?'

'Only to those of us who know Lord and Lady Marney well, I suspect,' Richard said. 'I hope that they may resolve their difficulties.'

Deb sighed gustily. 'I hope so too. I suppose that I had better go and hunt Ross down.'

'There is no need,' Richard said calmly. 'He left a moment before you arrived. He specifically told me that he was on his way to join his wife and martyr himself for the second half of the evening's concert.'

Deb stared. 'Oh! How very provoking!'

Richard raised his brows. 'What is?'

'Why, that I should come in here and insult you in Ross's place when all the time he was intent on joining Olivia anyway. What a waste of time!'

Richard was laughing. 'My dear Mrs Stratton, you have never had any compunction about insulting me before. I beg you not to worry now.'

'That was different,' Deb said crossly. 'Previously you deserved it.'

'I can see that you have a clearly defined sense of fair play,' Richard commented. He gestured to his glass. 'I beg your pardon—I have been most remiss. Would you care to join me in a glass of wine?'

'No, thank you,' Deb said. She smiled slightly. 'They have a most unpleasant Madeira which is too sweet for me, and I do not care for brandy.'

'A pity,' Richard said. 'I am persuaded that it would be far more enjoyable sitting here and talking to you than returning to the musicale.'

Deb secretly thought so too. The charms of Miss La

Salle's singing could scarcely compete with the stimulating conversation of Lord Richard Kestrel. And yet she was aware of a certain trepidation. The room was warm and softly lit, and it conjured up an intimacy that was surely dangerous when one was conversing alone with a gentleman who was a certified rake. It gave Deb the same feeling that Richard's presence always aroused in her. Her undeniable attraction to him drew her on, but at the same time the cold, hard sense she had learned from experience warned her to run away, and quickly. Still, she did not move.

'Have you made up your mind yet?' Lord Richard enquired affably.

Deb jumped. 'I beg your pardon?'

'Have you made up your mind on whether it is safe to stay?' There was a mocking light in Richard's eyes. 'Common sense might suggest that it is not…'

'Past experience might suggest that it is not!' Deb snapped.

'Very true.' Richard put his head on one side and considered her thoughtfully. His gaze moved over her face feature by feature and Deb felt her skin warm beneath his regard. It felt almost as though he was touching her.

'As it turns out, you are quite safe,' Richard continued. 'I would not have the ill manners to seduce a lady in her brother-in-law's house.'

Deb raised her brows disbelievingly. 'Is that so? And when did this surprising change in your behaviour come about, my lord?'

Richard smiled and Deb's wayward heart skipped a tiny beat. 'When I met you, of course, Mrs Stratton,' he said smoothly. 'However, my good resolutions have not been put to the test before. I am not sure how they would stand up to provocation.'

'So *that* would be your justification!' Deb said scornfully.

'The age-old excuse of a man who is not strong enough to resist temptation!'

Once again, Richard's gaze lingered on the honey-coloured hair curling about her face—and on the indignant set of her mouth. He smiled slightly.

'Yes, the age-old excuse since Adam... Poor Adam, he really wanted to eat that apple, didn't he, and yet he did not have the courage to admit it, but had to blame Eve instead.'

'Typical!'

Richard's gaze narrowed with interest. 'It seems that you do not have a very high opinion of our sex, Mrs Stratton? Why is that?'

Deb shifted a little, suddenly nervous. She had never really thought about it before, but it was true that all her observations of the male sex had led her to form a somewhat critical assessment. There was Ross, of course, who had shown her great kindness and yet exasperated her in equal measure for his inability to settle his differences with Olivia. There was her father, who always thought that he knew what was right and that he had the inalienable right to enforce it. And then there had been Neil Stratton, another good-looking, feckless adventurer who had turned her feelings inside out and shown her the true meaning of dishonourable behaviour. She set her lips in a tight line.

'I do not wish to pursue this subject, my lord.'

Richard nodded slightly, and the tense feeling inside Deborah eased. Thank God he did not press her. She never wanted to tell him the truth, never wanted to tell anyone...

She glanced across at the desk, where Richard had laid aside his book when she had erupted into the room.

'Were you reading when I came in?' she enquired, failing to keep a slight note of disbelief from her voice.

Richard laughed. 'I was. I find it a useful accomplishment. My tutor taught me when I was a boy, you know.'

Deb's eyes narrowed at his teasing. She craned her neck to see the title of the book.

'It is *The Meditations of Marcus Aurelius*,' Richard said obligingly.

Deb nodded sagely. *The Meditations*, indeed! She was certain that he had plucked it at random from the shelves.

'I see,' she said. 'And what do you think of his writings?'

'Bleakly stoical,' Richard said. 'He has a dark view of human life and an obsession with the approach of death. What is your opinion, Mrs Stratton?'

There was a tiny pause. 'I have not read his writings,' Deb admitted.

Richard burst out laughing. 'I see. You were seeking to test me!'

Deb had the grace to look a little shame-faced. 'I thought… That is, I did not think—' She broke off in confusion.

'You did not think that I was given much to reading?' Lord Richard finished for her, a hint of irony in his tone. 'My dear Mrs Stratton, is it possible for you to have a lower opinion of me than the one you already possess?'

'Infinitely,' Deb said sweetly.

Richard's smile deepened. 'And now that you know I read the stoic philosophers, have I gone up at all in your estimation?'

'Oh,' Deb said, 'naturally I am most impressed. However, I do not think that I shall be reading *The Meditations* now that you have told me their style. There is enough to be miserable about in real life.'

Richard conceded the point. 'Perhaps poetry is more to your taste?' he enquired.

'I enjoy that, certainly,' Deb agreed. 'And you, my lord?'

Richard shifted slightly in his chair. 'Yes, I enjoy poetry too.' His gaze met hers very directly. 'I know that you think me an intellectual lightweight, ma'am, and a man with no propensity towards hard work, but I must correct your perception by saying that the only reason I had the chance to study poetry in the first place was because I was at sea. I read scraps of it in between naval actions.'

Deb smiled. She found that she rather liked the idea of Lord Richard Kestrel standing on the bridge of his ship with a book of poetry tucked in his pocket. She fancied that he would have looked rather good in the austere Navy uniform and found herself wishing that she had had the chance to see it.

'I had forgotten that you were in the Navy,' she said, feeling a little ashamed of herself for dismissing him as an idle gentleman of leisure. 'Why did you give it up?'

There was a hair's breadth of a pause in which she had the feeling that she had asked a question of great import.

'I took an injury at the Battle of the Nile and they did not want me on active service any more,' Richard said, after a moment.

'I am sorry,' Deb said. She repressed an impulse to touch his hand. Just for a second she had seen a bleakness, beyond anything she had expected, reflected in his dark eyes. She felt as though the bottom had dropped out of her heart. He had looked so lonely and remote in that moment, a far cry from the society rake of her imaginings.

Then he smiled at her and the image was gone. 'Thank you for your sympathy, Mrs Stratton,' he said. 'It was difficult at the time to abandon something that had given purpose to my life, but…' he shrugged '…there are always other things to do.'

Deb wondered. It could not be easy for a man accustomed to so active and adventurous a life to accept the restrictions of a circumscribed existence. She was unsure how much of what he said was true—and how much a defence.

Richard looked at her and the lines about his eyes crinkled. 'Do not look so stricken, ma'am. I am very well these days and am happy to show you my collection of naval memorabilia any time you wish!'

Deb recovered herself. 'No, thank you, my lord,' she said. 'I suspect that that is an invitation on a par with inspecting your art collection—or your set of etchings!' She glanced at the clock. 'I must go back to the musicale. With good fortune there may only be a few minutes of the concert left.'

'I will escort you back,' Richard said easily. He swallowed the remains of his brandy and got to his feet, holding the door open for her.

The hall was deserted and in shadow. A line of light showed beneath the music-room door and from behind its panels rose the squeaky arpeggios of Miss La Salle torturing a Bach cantata. Both Deb and Richard winced.

Richard put his hand on her arm. 'A moment,' he said. 'I do not think that we wish to go back in there.'

'Well, we cannot continue our conversation out here,' Deb pointed out.

'It was not conversation that I intended to pursue,' Richard said. He turned her gently, inexorably to face him. Deb's breath caught in her throat.

'You said—' Her voice failed her.

'That you were safe from seduction? So you are—for the time being.' Richard's hand came up to brush the line of her jaw with a gentle touch. His face was dark and severe in the shadowed dimness of the hall and she could not read his expression. Her nerves skittered in anticipation, but she did not draw away.

She did not know why she could not resist him. Perhaps it was because of that moment when he had been speaking of his lost naval career and she had looked into his eyes and seen a depth of feeling far more intense than she would ever have expected—and a loneliness that had undermined her defences. It was not that she felt sorry for him, but more that she had been taken off guard. She had glimpsed the private demons of isolation and lack of purpose that tormented Richard Kestrel, and it had given her an entirely new perspective. Oddly, it made her feel vulnerable to him.

She felt his arms go about her, felt his lips on hers. The kiss was brief and fierce and spellbinding. The candlelight seemed to swoop dizzily about her. She felt dazed and star struck, as though she had taken too much wine. A cool shiver ran along her nerves as his tongue touched hers, a featherlight touch. The kiss deepened then and became hungry and demanding, stripping her of her ability to think. This was not like the embrace in the beech wood. That had been sweet and had made her quite light-headed, but it had felt strangely unfinished. This time he held her close and his lips claimed hers with a mastery and a need that she felt powerless to resist. It shook her to the core. It threatened to steal her soul.

With a gasp she pulled herself out of his embrace and put several hasty steps between them. Richard made no move to pull her back into his arms and his face was expressionless, though she saw a muscle move in his cheek. He did not apologise and merely gave her back look for very straight look. In the faint light she saw the blaze in his eyes, hot and hard, and drew her breath in with a short, nervous gasp.

Deb fought for self-control. Her heart was beating wildly but it was not a fear of Richard Kestrel that terrified her, but the need to confront her own feelings. She had never, ever felt the depth of emotion that Richard's touch had stirred in her. She was not sure she liked it. She certainly could not answer the questions that the kiss had posed.

The door of the music room opened and a pool of light

spilled out into the hall. Olivia, Ross and a number of their visitors came streaming through the doors.

'I must find some brandy for our guests,' Deb heard Ross murmur to his wife. 'After such torment they require sustenance as quickly as possible.'

Olivia caught sight of her sister and hurried across the floor.

'There you are!' she said, coming over to Deb's side. 'Whatever happened to you? I thought that you had gone to find Ross and then you disappear for a full half-hour.'

Deb dragged her gaze away from Richard's face and swallowed quickly. 'I beg your pardon, Olivia. Lord Richard and I were discussing literature. I had no notion that so much time had passed.'

Olivia's brows shot up into her hair. She looked from one to the other. 'Literature? How very erudite! Do you care for some refreshment after such intellectual discussion?'

The servants were lighting more candles now and in the sudden, bright glow, Deb felt a little more secure. It was as though the light had banished her danger, at least for the time being. She risked another glance at Richard. He was watching her face and had been doing so for the entire conversation. She repressed a shiver.

'Thank you, ma'am,' Richard said now, wrenching his gaze from Deb and smiling at Olivia. 'I should be glad to take a glass of brandy with Lord Marney.'

'Splendid,' Olivia said. 'Deborah?'

'I shall go home,' Deb said. 'I have the headache. Goodnight, my lord.'

'Mrs Stratton.' Richard bowed. Deb saw a flicker of a smile touch his lips at her formality when only minutes before she had been locked in his arms in a scandalous embrace. She felt a surge of temper. Damn him! He was far too sure of himself—and of her.

'Thank you for the…discussion, ma'am,' Richard continued. 'I found it most stimulating.'

'Thank *you*, my lord,' Deb said. 'I feel so privileged to have been the object of your interest not merely once but twice in the same day.'

Richard bowed again, with immaculate politeness, though Deb could see from his expression that he was not going to ignore her challenge.

'It was a pleasure,' he murmured. 'Any time you wish to continue our debate…'

Deb smiled brilliantly. 'I do not think that would be at all wise, my lord,' she said. 'I have a great desire to discuss Moore next time.' She looked at him and quoted sweetly, '"He was a rake amongst scholars and a scholar amongst rakes…"'

Richard laughed, took her hand and pressed a kiss on it. 'And when his father suggested that he should give up his rakish pursuits and take a wife, he said—'

'"Certainly father, and whose wife shall I take?"' Deb finished the quotation. 'Precisely, my lord. Some rakes never reform.'

Richard released her hand slowly. 'So you think you have my measure, Mrs Stratton? We shall see. Goodnight. I shall look forward to our next meeting.'

Deb gave him an arctic look. 'I doubt that shall be soon, Lord Richard.'

Richard raised his brows expressively. 'Do you? Then perhaps you do not have my measure after all.' He nodded pleasantly to Olivia and strolled away.

Olivia, neglecting her other guests out of sheer curiosity, saw her sister to the door.

'What on earth was that all about, Deb?' she demanded.

'That,' Deb said, pulling on her gloves, and noting that her hands were shaking slightly, 'was about Lord Richard

Kestrel and his *disgraceful* behaviour, Liv. Can you not ban the man from your house?'

'Not really,' Olivia said, taking her literally. 'He is a friend of Ross's after all. But, Deb…surely he cannot have behaved disgracefully twice in a single day?'

'I fear so,' Deb said.

'You *fear* so? What can there be about his behaviour to make you fearful, Deb?'

Deb paused, looking at the tiny pinpoints of stars that pricked the autumn sky. 'It is myself I fear, not Lord Richard,' she said slowly. 'He makes me feel so—'

She stopped, shrugged abruptly and continued in her normal voice, 'I can scarce be the first lady to be in danger of letting her heart rule her head in the matter of Lord Richard Kestrel.'

As the carriage trundled down the lane to Mallow House, Deb thought about Richard Kestrel. He had said that she was safe from seduction, and yet there was more than one way to seduce a lady. It could be done so subtly that the lady in question might not notice until it was almost too late. Her defences were undermined, her emotions engaged. It seemed to Deb that she had known Richard Kestrel for an age and yet suddenly all her preconceived notions of him were being challenged and her prejudices tumbling. She had started to let him close to her. And now that he was close, there was no way on earth that he would let her escape him. It was the most perilous thing that she could have done.

# *Chapter Four*

Lord Richard Kestrel had been reading the *Suffolk Chronicle* with extreme attention for the past three days. It was a newspaper that previously he had dismissed as tiresomely provincial in its outlook. Generally speaking, he preferred to have his newspapers delivered directly from London. Now, however, he pored over every page of the *Chronicle*. His curiosity—and much else—was aroused. What was the communication that Mrs Stratton had sent to the editor of the *Chronicle*? He had scanned the letters page to no avail, had waded his way through endless advertisements for Doctor Solomon's Cordial Balm of Gilead and was losing the will to live over the countless reports of agricultural sales at Woodbridge market.

Then, on the third morning after Olivia Marney's musicale, he found it. His eye was caught by a small notice at the bottom of page six, wedged in between an advert for the erection of a patented thrashing machine and a notice about a zoological collection that boasted a one horned rhinoceros.

*A lady requires the assistance of a gentleman. If any gentleman of honour, discretion and chivalry will venture to answer this notice and despatch a reply to Lady Incognita at the Bell and Steelyard Inn, Woodbridge, Suffolk, then he shall have no reason to repent his generosity.*

A small smile curled Lord Richard's mouth as he considered the identity of Lady Incognita. Could she be none other than the utterly infuriating, utterly entrancing Deborah Stratton? And if so, what assistance did she require from her discreet gentleman? Richard's mind was positively boggling.

There was only one way to find out, of course. Richard went across to the inlaid cherry-wood desk in the window and extracted a pen and an inkhorn from the top left-hand drawer. Sitting down, he pulled the paper towards him and started to write.

'Mrs Lester tells me that the cellars have flooded again,' Mrs Aintree said, over breakfast that morning. 'One of the hams your brother-in-law sent over is quite ruined and the case of wine you laid down is under water.'

'The duck decoy must be blocked again,' Deb said. She was eating a buttered egg with one hand and turning the pages of the *Suffolk Chronicle* with the other whilst she scanned the advertisements. 'I will go and take a look after breakfast.'

'Could you not send to Marney for the gamekeeper to come?' Mrs Aintree suggested, the very slightest edge to her tone. 'It is scarce appropriate for you to be grubbing about in the undergrowth; indeed, it could be positively dangerous.'

Deb laughed. 'Dangerous? The duck decoy? I doubt there is more than a foot of water in it and the ducks are scarcely threatening creatures.'

'That was not what I meant,' Mrs Aintree said severely. 'When are you going to stop behaving like a hoyden, Deborah? Although your father is quite wrong to try and coerce you into marriage, I do believe that the fundamental idea might be of value. With a proper home and family of your own—'

Something like a shaft of pain wedged itself in Deborah's breast and she pushed the remains of the egg aside. 'I have a home here, Clarrie,' she said. She folded the newspaper and stood up. 'Pray excuse me. I shall take a quick look at the pond to see if the sluices are jammed and then I shall send to Ross for assistance.'

As a concession to propriety, Deb went to fetch her bonnet and spencer before venturing out. Neither was strictly necessary in the functional sense, since no one was going to see her and the weather was still mild. She eschewed wearing gloves, but made sure that she tucked her hands out of sight as she passed the breakfast room window. She did not want Mrs Aintree ringing a peal over her for inappropriate dress.

It felt pleasant to be out in the fresh air. Deb had not slept particularly well for the last few nights, the ones that had followed the musicale, and she did not wish to dwell on the reasons why. When Mrs Aintree had mentioned marriage and a home of her own, Deb's thoughts had—ludicrously— swung to Lord Richard Kestrel for a brief moment before she had depressed her own hopes and dreams stillborn. That way lay madness. She had no wish to remarry and, even if she had, her choice would scarcely fall on a man whose reckless charm reminded her all too forcibly of her first, perfidious husband. It was yet another reason why she required a temperate, biddable man to be her pretend fiancé. She was done with rakes.

The duck decoy was tucked away at the bottom of Mallow's overgrown garden near the bridge across the track to Midwinter Bere. Deb knew that Olivia shuddered each time she saw the runaway shrubbery and neglected flowerbeds, but Deb had no money to spare for luxuries such as gardening and too much pride to ask Ross to fund anything other than the most basic of maintenance. The previous owner of Mallow had been a keen sportsman who had even imported a specially trained dog from Holland to hunt ducks with him. He had kept the decoy in good condition, but these days the traps were broken and the bushes that had been planted to shield the pond from the wind had all but gone wild. The ducks splashed happily in the decoy, knowing that they were safer there than on the river. When Deb arrived on the bank they set up a loud squawking and scattered into the undergrowth.

Deb pushed her way through the tangle of shrubs and reached the end of pond, where a sluice gate was supposed to regulate the flow of water out under the bridge and into the Winter Race. Two years before, the sluices had blocked during heavy rains and it was then that the problem with the cellars had first become apparent. In this instance it seemed more a case of neglect than anything else. Deb could see that, during the past summer, grasses had seeded themselves around the sluice gate and the overhanging twigs and branches had grown through the gaps, completely jamming the gate. She pulled half-heartedly at some of the deep-rooted grasses. A little of the soil tumbled from the bank, but the weeds refused to shift. Gardening was not Deb's occupation of choice, so she dusted her hands down on her skirts and straightened up, almost banging her head on an overhanging branch. She would have to ask Ross to send the Marney gardeners over to clear the decoy before the whole area became choked with weeds and the first proper rains of the winter caused more damage. Sometimes she hated to be dependent on Ross's charity, but it could not be helped. She could not do the work herself.

It was as Deb was struggling back towards the path, her

skirts snagging on brambles and the low branches snatching at her hair, that she trod in something soft and squelchy that the ducks had evidently left behind.

'Ugh!' Her foot slipped from beneath her and then she was tumbling over in the soft grass of the bank, her skirts ripping on one of the broken duck traps as she fell through the undergrowth and into the shallow pond below.

It was only about a foot deep, as Deb herself had told Mrs Aintree earlier. Unfortunately, that foot was comprised of slimy green water choked with duck weed and dead plants. Worse, when Deb tried to wrench her skirts free of the broken trap, she found the material stuck fast. She wallowed in the water, tugging on the fabric until something ripped.

'Hell and damnation!'

'You do indeed look like something conjured from the deepest halls of Hades,' an amused male voice confirmed from the bank.

Deb was so taken aback that she lost her footing in the muddy depths of the pond and sat down with a splash.

Lord Richard Kestrel—unforgivably—laughed. 'Is this the latest fashion?' he continued. 'A gown with duck-weed trimmings?'

Deb gave an infuriated snort. Of all the undignified situations in which to be found! It would have to be Lord Richard Kestrel, of all people, who was the last man on earth she wanted to see her at a disadvantage.

'You are trespassing,' she said haughtily.

'I am.' Richard eyed her with deep amusement. 'Would you like me to assist you, Mrs Stratton?'

'No, thank you,' Deb said, struggling to find her feet on the slippery mud of the pool. 'I would like you to go away.'

Lord Richard ignored the request and came forward and offered a hand to her anyway. Deb ignored it.

'Do accept my help,' he encouraged. 'It will save you much trouble in the long run.'

Deb gritted her teeth. 'I would not dream of inconveniencing you.'

'Please have no scruples about that. As I am here already, you may as well take advantage of me.' He grasped her flailing hand and pulled hard, dragging her from the grip of the mud. Deb's ankles came free with a squelching sound and she cannoned into him. They both ended up amongst the bushes, Richard's body breaking Deb's fall. She lay still for a moment, completely winded.

'There was no need to take me quite so literally.'

Deb opened her eyes to look down into Richard's laughing face. With horror she realised that she was lying on top of him, her breasts squashed against his chest and one of his hands curved around her buttocks. Just as she realised this, she felt Richard's hand slide with leisurely intimacy over her body and she gave a horrified gasp and rolled off him. Richard sat up.

'Please do not worry,' he said, scrupulously polite. 'Whilst you have a figure that looks most alluring in a dampened gown, the sight—and the smell—of that mud is enough to kill any ardour stone dead.'

'I am glad that there is something that puts a rein on your rakish habits,' Deb snapped. She pushed a piece of weed out of her eyes and examined her torn skirts. There was a jagged rip down the left-hand side that was quite irreparable and showed far too much petticoat.

'What were you doing in there?' Richard enquired. He seemed genuinely interested. Deb glared. 'I was trying to free the sluice gate,' she said. 'If it comes to that, what are *you* doing here? As I have pointed out already, you are trespassing.'

Richard lay back in the grass, his hands behind his head.

'I was riding past when I heard a splash and a shout. I was afraid that someone might have had an accident.'

He turned his head and looked at her. 'You are not very grateful, Mrs Stratton. I begin to wish that I had left you to your watery fate.'

Deb looked at him and, most unexpectedly, felt an urge to laugh. 'I am sorry about your clothes,' she said, her lips twitching as she took in the mud that was beginning to dry on his pristine hunting jacket. 'I dare say you looked quite nice when you started out. And I am sorry that I interrupted your ride.'

Richard stood up and helped her to her feet.

'Would you care to make up for it by riding out with me later?' he asked abruptly. 'When you have had the opportunity to change into dry clothing, of course.'

Deb hesitated, surprised by a strong urge to accept. She knew that it was madness to consider it, but when had common sense had anything to do with inclination? Yet today she had promised herself would be the beginning of a new, more sensible approach to life in general and Richard Kestrel in particular. She had to extricate herself from this growing attraction before it was too late. She fought a short, sharp battle with herself and shook her head.

'Thank you, but I do not think so, my lord.'

Richard's hand was still on her arm. 'But you would like to,' he said acutely.

Deb flushed, feeling her skin heat from the inside outward. She could lie, at which she was unconscionably bad, or she could tell the truth, or she could yield...

'The last time that I went riding with you proved to be a far from comfortable experience,' she said truthfully. 'I do not think it would be sensible to repeat it.'

Richard smiled, and her heart jolted.

'I see,' he said softly. 'You are afraid of me.'

'No, I am not!' Deb retorted. 'At least, not in the way you imply.'

'Then you are afraid of yourself,' Richard countered perceptively, 'and the way in which your impulses might lead.'

Deb swallowed hard. She knew, and evidently so did Richard Kestrel, that her unruly impulses might lead her into all manner of disastrous situations as far as he was concerned. She tilted her chin to look at him.

'I am merely concerned to be prudent.'

'Do not be,' Richard advised. 'It is far more interesting to indulge your inclinations.'

Deb smiled reluctantly. 'My inclination, Lord Richard, is to return directly to the house and take a hot bath. Good day to you.'

And she grasped her muddy skirts in one hand and escaped with what dignity she could muster, before she changed her mind.

Richard Kestrel put aside the letter that had just reached him from his brother Justin in London and stared unseeing out of the window of Kestrel Court. On his return from his ride he had partaken of a second breakfast and was on his third cup of coffee. It was a glorious September morning with the early sunlight still pink and hazy as it lingered on the mist rising from the river, the Winter Race. It was a shame that he had not been able to persuade Deborah Stratton to accompany him on a ride. It was the most perfect morning for a brisk gallop across country and there was no one he would have enjoyed sharing it with more. Richard briefly considered taking a sail on the Deben, or even swimming in the sea. It looked calm enough today, albeit the water would hold the first icy chill of coming winter. Then his eye fell on the letter once more. Duty called. He could not abandon business for pleasure today.

He settled down to read. In the case of the apprehension of the Midwinter spy, matters did not seem to proceed at all. Justin wrote that there was concern at the Admiralty that the Midwinter spy was still active in the Woodbridge area, passing on information to the French over such matters as the garrison numbers stationed in the town, the defences along that stretch of coast, the tidal waters of the Deben and other rivers, the state of the Volunteers and the preparations against invasion. Enquiries in London had yielded no information on the possible identity of the spy and her network, and Justin was talking of returning to Midwinter soon.

Richard sighed, sitting back and resting his booted feet on the desk. For three months they had been stalking the Midwinter spy, watching and waiting, hoping for a mistake that would give the game away. He and Justin and their younger brother Lucas had whiled away the long hot days of high summer in paying court to the local ladies, chatting to the gentlemen, observing, sifting information, waiting patiently for some clue. None had been forthcoming. The Midwinter spy did not make mistakes.

And now they were at the start of autumn, with the political situation at a critical point and invasion fever spreading panic, and still the spy was working right under their noses.

Richard ran his hand through his hair. It was generally agreed that the spy was one of the ladies of the Midwinter villages, who hid behind a respectable façade whilst organising her treasonable activities. When Justin had first put forward this hypothesis, back in June, Richard had found it as difficult to believe as any gentleman would. Yet the meagre evidence they had suggested that the theory, unlikely as it seemed, had to be true. A female spy had been working on the south coast the previous year and had been traced from Dorset to London to Suffolk, where she had merged effortlessly into local society. The only clue that they had was that many of the Midwinter ladies belonged to a reading group run by Lady Sally Saltire and Richard and his elder brother had long been suspicious that the group was a convenient means of passing information. Yet if this were the case, it meant that the Midwinter spy could only be one of four or five people, all of whom seemed most unlikely suspects.

There was Lady Sally Saltire herself, of course. This was a difficult call, for Lady Sally had been an old flame of Justin Kestrel's before her marriage and Richard knew that Justin, secretly but passionately, still carried a torch for her. Then there was Lily Benedict, who publicly gave the impression of being a devoted wife to her bedridden husband. Richard knew that this, at least, was a pretence. Lady Benedict had given him to understand discreetly but quite clearly that she would be receptive to his attentions. He had neglected to take her up on the offer. Lady Benedict's sultry charms seemed stale next to the breath of fresh air that was Deborah Stratton.

Richard grimaced. If neither Lady Sally nor Lady Benedict was the culprit, that only left Helena Lang, the vicar's vulgar daughter, or Olivia Marney, the cool and gracious chatelaine of Midwinter Marney Hall…

Or Deborah Stratton, of course.

There were other ladies who came and went from the reading group, but these five were the core. And one of them had to be the spy.

Richard sighed. Olivia Marney was enigmatic, for she wore her coolness as a barrier against the world. He could have sworn, however, that she was not a traitor. And as her husband, Ross, was a friend of his, it made matters even more difficult.

And then there was Deborah.

Richard knew that he was as averse to Deb Stratton being the Midwinter spy as Justin was unwilling to suspect Sally Saltire. There was a deep and irrational instinct that told him the Deb was not the woman they sought. Richard was accustomed to acting on logical sense rather than pure feeling and he found this state of affairs as amusing as it was bewildering for, despite Deborah's wariness, he knew he was drawn to her by something that went deeper than reason, something that was deep in the blood.

Richard picked up the copy of the *Suffolk Chronicle* that carried Deborah's advertisement. He was almost certain that it had nothing to do with the Midwinter spy, but even had he not had an interest in Deborah herself, it was something that he could not let pass.

He laughed to think of her wallowing in the mud of the duck decoy. No matter that she had refused his invitation. He would find a way to see her again, and soon.

## Chapter Five

'One reply?' Deb said incredulously, as she stood in the Bell and Steelyard Inn the following week. 'Only one? Are you sure?' She upended the mailbag and shook it hard. One letter dropped out on to the floor of the coaching inn and lay there amongst the wood shavings and scraps of paper. Deb frowned in disbelief.

'Are all the men in Suffolk slow tops,' she said crossly, 'that they are all so backward in coming forward?'

The innkeeper looked blank. 'Beg pardon, ma'am?' he said.

'It was a rhetorical question,' Deb said, sighing. 'Perhaps I should have advertised for a dishonourable man and then, no doubt, I would have been inundated with offers...'

As though in response to this thought, she heard a familiar, mocking voice from behind her.

'Good morning, Mrs Stratton. Is there some kind of difficulty?'

Deb scooped the letter up and stuffed it in her reticule. Lord Richard Kestrel was standing in the door of the mail office, a smile on his wicked, dark face. Today he looked immaculate in buff pantaloons and a green coat that Deb was obliged to admit suited him very well. Last week, in his riding dress, he had looked a man of action. Today, that power was held under tighter control. Paradoxically, it made him look even more dangerous. And, idiotically, all Deb seemed to be able to think about was the blissful pleasure that she had felt when she had been held in his arms. As she stared at him she saw his eyes widen and his mouth curl into a smile as he read her thoughts. He looked as though he was about to kiss her again, there in the Bell and Steelyard Inn. Blushing madly, Deb dragged her gaze from his.

'Good morning, Lord Richard,' she said, trying to speak through an odd constriction in her breathing. 'No, there is no problem at all.' Seeing his quizzical expression, she improvised wildly. 'I am merely trying to collect some mail on behalf of Ross, but it appears that the expected letters have not arrived...'

Lord Richard raised his brows. 'Surely there is no need for you to play the postman, ma'am? Does Lord Marney not have a private mail box at home?'

Deb felt the familiar rush of exasperation. 'Do you have an interest in the way in which the mail service operates, my lord? Perhaps you could recommend some improvements. I hear that they are always open to new ideas.'

Richard smiled and stood aside to allow her to go out on to Quay Street. Woodbridge was busy that morning.

'I have no interest in the mail service,' he said easily, 'but as always, I do have a great interest in you, Mrs Stratton. It is a pleasure to see you again so soon.'

'Usually we contrive to avoid each other for far longer periods of time than this,' Deb said. 'I cannot understand how we have managed to bump into each other again.'

'As to that, I engineered it,' Richard said easily. 'I warned you I would. I saw you entering the Bell, so I followed you.'

'To what purpose?'

Lord Richard looked amused. 'My dear Mrs Stratton, to have the pleasure of your company, of course! May I escort you somewhere?'

'No, thank you,' Deb said, determined to be strong.

Richard looked enquiring. 'Are you then intending to stay rooted to the spot here in Quay Street? I do believe that you are in the way of the other passers-by.'

'How absurd you are,' Deb said. 'I was not refusing to move, merely refusing your offer of escort, my lord.'

'Ah.' Richard took her arm and steered her expertly out of the path of a large lady with an even larger marketing basket. 'That is a pity, for I have a gift I wished to give to you.'

Deb was taken aback. She did not want to accept gifts from Lord Richard Kestrel. It seemed too intimate a gesture and she was sharply aware that if she were to give him any latitude he would take advantage with shocking speed. He had demonstrated that on more than one occasion. Yet despite her determination to withstand his advances, it felt rather as though they had already made the first moves in a game of chance and the game was becoming complex and unpredictable. She had no certainty that she could win.

Richard was proffering a brown paper parcel that was tied neatly with string. 'I remembered our conversation about poetry,' he said, 'and that you were studying the work of Andrew Marvell in Lady Sally's reading group. Please take it.'

Deborah reluctantly put out a hand. The parcel was the right shape and size to be a book. She enjoyed receiving books more than anything, and she felt a sudden rush of pleasure followed by a rather alarming urge to rip the paper off. She held the present stiffly out to him.

'I do not believe that I can accept this, my lord.'

'Please try, ma'am,' Richard said persuasively. 'I chose

it especially for you.' He waited, watching her. 'Are you not going to open it?'

Deb was in two minds and she knew that he could tell, for he was smiling at her. She tried to resist, but willpower had never been her strong suit. With a little sigh of abandonment she tore off the paper.

As she had thought, it was a book of poetry, with a marbled cover and a beautiful leather binding trimmed with gilt.

'Oh, how lovely!' She could not help her involuntary exclamation.

Richard looked pleased. 'I was anxious to demonstrate, Mrs Stratton, that my interest in seventeenth-century poetry was not merely assumed. There is a bookmark in the poem that is my favourite.'

Deb opened the book. The wind off the river riffled the pages a little and then the book fell open at the point where Richard had inserted the bookmark. Deb read the title of the poem, then looked up, caught between amusement and exasperation. 'I might have guessed!'

The poem was 'To His Coy Mistress' by Andrew Marvell.

Lord Richard spoke softly. '"Had we but world enough and time,"' he quoted, '"this coyness, lady, were no crime." How very appropriate, Mrs Stratton.'

Deb shut the book with a decided snap, knowing that she had to depress his pretensions here and now. 'There is nothing appropriate about it at all, Lord Richard.'

'How so? Do I not admire you, and you in turn spurn my advances?'

Deb frowned. 'I do not wish to debate literature with you.'

'No? Must I then join Lady Sally's reading group if I wish to have a literary discussion?'

Deborah's steps quickened. He kept pace with her easily

as she headed down the road towards the quay. 'I am sure that the ladies of the reading group would be happy to benefit from your literary insight,' she said. 'Alas that I am not so eager for your company.'

Lord Richard did not seem cast down. In fact, Deb could not help but notice that he seemed amused and encouraged by their apparent discord.

'Is that so? The other night you were persuaded to stay and talk to me, yet now it seems that you do not wish to discuss anything with me, Mrs Stratton, never mind literature. I wonder why that might be?'

Deb shot him an irritated look. 'It must be painfully obvious to all but the most limited intellect,' she said, 'that I do not wish to speak with you, Lord Richard, because I do not *trust* you. I do not trust you, I do not like you and I do not enjoy your company!'

Richard took her hand in his, perforce requiring her to stop walking. Deb was vaguely surprised to see that they had come as far as the waterfront and were now in the flower gardens that bordered the edge of the river. The air was keen here. The breeze tugged at the brown wrapping paper, making it crackle. Deb held on to the book a little more tightly to prevent it blowing away.

'Mrs Stratton,' Lord Richard said, 'at least two of those three statements you have just made are false.'

Deb looked at him. She raised her chin a little haughtily. 'Indeed, my lord?'

'Yes. If you must have me spell it out, you neither dislike me nor my company.' Richard paused, thoughtful. 'Probably it is true that you do not trust me.'

'And with good reason!'

'Ah, you are thinking about our kisses last week.'

'I am not!'

'Yes, you are. I saw it in your face when I came through

the inn door and was hard put to it not to kiss you again there and then.'

Deb bit her lip, trying to repress the jumble of words that were clamouring to escape.

'And I feel rather inclined to do it now,' Richard added, his gaze going to her mouth.

Deb took a hasty step away from him, pulling her hand from his grasp. 'Lord Richard—' She cleared her throat. Her voice did not sound convincing enough. 'Lord Richard,' she said again, more strongly, 'it seems to me that I have tried to be civil to you—'

'Have you?' Richard enquired. 'I confess that I had not observed it.'

'I have tried to be civil to you,' Deb soldiered on, 'but now I shall have to be more blunt. You are a scoundrel—an untrustworthy scoundrel—and I do not seek your company. What woman of sense would do? If you approach me again in future, I shall be obliged to cut you dead.'

'Will you?' Richard said with the greatest admiration. 'I shall look forward to that immensely.'

Deb wrinkled up her face with frustration. Why could the wretched man not take her point?

'You are not a stupid man,' she said wrathfully, 'although I am still unsure whether or not you are a shallow one. On this occasion, however, I am aware that you are merely being deliberately awkward! I do not wish to associate with you.'

Lord Richard did not look cast down. 'You associated with me last week and it was delightful.'

A tinge of colour crept into Deborah's cheek. It was monstrous difficult to summon up the resolution required to dismiss him. A part of her—a large and perfidious part—enjoyed his company immensely, and the more time that she spent with him the more attractive he seemed to become to her. It was like an inverse equation. Whilst she was telling him how little she cared for him, she found that she was making a liar of herself.

'You are a rake, my lord,' she said, rallying.

'My dear Mrs Stratton, I do not think that anyone disputes that. What is your point?'

Deborah glared at him. 'That *is* the point, my lord! I do not seek the company of rakes.' She took a deep breath. 'You have made no secret of the fact that you wished me to be your mistress last year. Your intentions were entirely dishonourable!'

Lord Richard smiled ruefully. 'I cannot dispute that either,' he said.

Deb felt a confusing mixture of emotions. Uppermost was the need to tell him to withdraw his attentions to her, but beneath that was a guilty sense of enjoyment. She knew that a respectable widow should not be having such feelings when speaking to a rakish gentleman. She pushed the feelings away.

'Let me construe for your further, my lord,' she said. 'I am a respectable lady and females of good reputation do not consort with rakes—not if they wish their reputation to remain intact, that is.'

'And you feel that neither your reputation nor your virtue could remain…intact…were you to spend some time in my company?' Lord Richard queried softly.

'Precisely!' Deb had agreed before she thought that one through properly. 'That is…'

'You do not think that you could withstand the onslaught of my charm?' Lord Richard asked whimsically and Deb blushed.

'I did not say that,' she said hastily. 'I did not mean to imply that I thought you could seduce me—'

'Would you care to wager on that?' Lord Richard asked.

Deb felt a surge of anticipation. Yes, she would like to wager on it. Very much. And she would like to lose…

She bit her lip. 'Certainly not!'

'Then you *do* have doubts over your ability to withstand my seduction. Otherwise why refuse the bet?'

'Because I do not gamble!' Deb said. 'You are the most provoking man!'

'And you prefer the companionship of more sober gentlemen, I assume?'

'No,' Deborah said. 'I do not seek male companionship at all.'

Now Lord Richard looked even more interested. Deb could have kicked herself for the unwary comment.

'Tell me why that is,' he said.

'No,' Deb said again. She was gripping the book so hard that her fingers cracked. 'You ask too many questions. In fact, you are impertinent, my lord.'

Lord Richard laughed. He thrust his hands into the pockets of the green jacket.

'And you enjoy crossing swords with me, Mrs Stratton. Admit it!'

'I…' Deborah hesitated on the very point of denying it. This was the perfect moment to dismiss him, to tell Lord Richard Kestrel that she did not wish to see him ever again. But the only problem was that it was not true and she had always had terrible trouble with lying. Even simple social untruths were a problem for her, such as telling her hostess that she had enjoyed an evening when in fact it had been a dead bore.

It was impossible to lie now, for Richard had drawn closer to her so that his body shielded her from the attention of those who passed by. His very proximity demanded the truth from her. Looking up, Deborah saw the expression in his eyes, dark and intense. It frightened her, but it also struck an answering chord deep within her and that she could not deny.

'There are some things,' she said, with difficulty, 'like… like riding too fast across country, or eating too many truffles, that are enjoyable but vastly dangerous. One should always try to avoid them. I would place you in the same category, my lord.'

She saw the hard light in Lord Richard's eyes soften into something more tender at her words and she felt as though her insides were trembling. He took her gloved hand in his and pressed a kiss on the back of it.

'Oh, Mrs Stratton,' he said, 'if you think that after that I could possibly withdraw my attentions to you, then…' he shrugged '…well, I cannot.' The laughter lit his eyes again. 'I am unreservedly looking forward to you cutting me dead at Lady Sally's ball tonight, for I fear I shall approach you once again.'

He let go of her hand, sketched a bow and sauntered off up Quay Street. Deb waited until she was sure that he would not turn around and then sank nervelessly on to the nearest bench. Damn her honesty and her runaway tongue! Why had she had to tell him the truth? Why could she not simply have allowed a lie to suffice this time?

She felt shaken and confused. Her elopement, which had ended in the most disillusioning manner possible, had led her to take a private vow never to entertain the thought of love again. Further, it was against all common sense to become entangled with a man who was a reprobate. Put the two together and she had the recipe for a full-scale disaster.

Deb knew that she was impulsive and fatally outspoken. She had worked very hard in the years of her widowhood to try and achieve a coolness and composure of which even Olivia would be proud. Feeling a treacherous affinity to a dangerous, rakish gentleman was in no way part of her plan.

She put her hand to her head. It was best to forget the entire incident and to concentrate on the reason that had brought her into town in the first place. The letter from the mail office was burning a hole in her reticule. But next to it was the book of poetry that Richard had given her and when she took it out it opened not at the work of Andrew Marvell, but earlier, with a quotation from Shakespeare: 'Then come kiss me sweet and twenty, youth's a stuff will not endure.'

With an exasperated sigh, Deborah stuffed the book under her arm. Was even the wretched book bewitched, that it had to taunt her with the same sentiments that Lord Richard had voiced himself?

She walked slowly up the road to the inn where she had left the carriage. There was no sign of Lord Richard Kestrel in Woodbridge's narrow streets, even though she had had a definite feeling that she would bump into him again. If she had, she knew that she would have to snub him. Even so, she searched the vicinity very carefully indeed and was disappointed that he was not there to ignore.

As soon as she reached home, Deb hurried into the study, threw herself down into a chair and opened the only reply to her advertisement. Dangling her bonnet from her hand, she read the letter once, frowned, then went in search of Mrs Aintree. She found her companion settled in the drawing room with her netting frame set up beside her. Mrs Aintree looked up and smiled. Deb handed the letter over without a word. Mrs Aintree fixed her glasses more firmly on her nose, cleared her throat and read aloud: *The odd conciseness of your style pleases and intrigues me. If I should like you as well as I like your advertisement, I think I could venture to help you. If you wish for further communication, address to Lord Scandal at the Bell and Steelyard Inn in Woodbridge.*

She put the letter down in her lap and looked at Deborah with great reproof. 'I knew you would not take my advice and tell your father the truth. But advertising for a gentleman—have you run mad, Deborah?'

'Never mind that!' Deb said impatiently. 'What do you think?'

'Saucy,' Clarissa Aintree said, shaking her head. 'Very saucy indeed. What character did you anticipate in your… um…betrothed, Deborah?'

'I thought of someone moderate, agreeable and open to my guidance,' Deb said. 'He would need to be quite biddable.'

Clarissa Aintree made a noise that was somewhere between a snort and a cough. 'Then Lord Scoundrel cannot be the man for you.'

'Lord Scandal,' Deb said.

'Whichever. He cannot be the right man for this role, for every line of his communication screams arrogance.' Mrs Aintree put the letter down on the little table beside her. 'Throw the letter in the fire, my love. Better still, throw the entire paper, advertisement and all, into the flames. Advertising for a fiancé indeed! Outrageous!'

'I need to find myself a gentleman most speedily,' Deb argued. She got to her feet and walked across to the drawing-room window. 'My father expects me to arrive at Walton Hall with my betrothed.'

'Really, Deborah, was there ever anyone like you for getting yourself into a scrape?' Mrs Aintree said, not quite managing to eradicate the reproach from her voice. 'Instead of solving the problem, you come up with a solution that creates a further difficulty!'

'You do not think that Lord Scandal could be the answer to the problem?'

'With a name like that?' Mrs Aintree enquired drily.

'I thought that it might be his real name.'

Mrs Aintree raised her brows. 'And are you called Lady Incognita?' she asked, drier still. 'Now I consider it, I do believe Lady Incognita to be the sobriquet for one of the most notorious courtesans in London. No wonder that you have Lord Scandal answering your advertisement!'

Deb sighed and pushed the curly fair hair away from her face. 'I suppose that you are right. No, I *know* that you are right. I was merely clutching at straws. Lord Scandal will not do. I shall have to wait a week or so for other replies to my advertisement.'

'No,' Mrs Aintree said calmly. 'I do believe that you should give up this silly notion of a temporary fiancé at once, Deborah. No good will come of it. No gentleman of respectable means would ever respond to such a notice. This is not like advertising for a butler, you know.'

Deb sighed again. She knew that Mrs Aintree, the epitome of common sense, was absolutely right. But she had hoped—expected—that there would be so many more replies from which to choose. She had been certain that there would be at least one sensible gentleman whom she might select from the crowd. Alas, it seemed that the gentlemen of Suffolk were far too conservative, too stuffy, to respond to an intriguing invitation. All except for Lord Scandal, who was clearly a rogue of the first order.

'You are correct, as always, Clarrie,' she said, slumping on to the window seat and propping her shoulders against the panelling in a deplorably hoydenish manner. 'It was a silly plan. I shall forget about it and go to dress for Lady Sally's ball. What do you do this evening?'

'I shall sit here and compose advertisements for the newspapers,' Mrs Aintree said calmly. 'They will read: *Mrs Prim requires new post as a lady's companion. She is utterly unable to cope with the demands of her current place and requires a quiet life with a sober, respectable, elderly lady.*'

Deb laughed and hugged her. 'You know that you would not care for a quiet life, dear Clarrie! You would miss my hoydenish behaviour. Come now, confess it. You would be quite lost without me!'

But as she went upstairs to dress, Deb reflected that it would not do to dismiss Lord Scandal quite yet. She had not completely relinquished her plan and, unless some other gentleman came forward, he was all that she had. An arrogant reprobate... Deb paused with her hand on the banister. She knew one such man already and if it were not for the fact that she doubted he ever read the local press, she would have sworn that Lord Scandal bore a strong resemblance to Lord Richard Kestrel. That was impossible, of course. Even if he did read the *Suffolk Chronicle*, Lord Richard would surely never respond to an advertisement.

At any rate, it did not matter, for she would not take Lord Scandal up on his offer. Soon she would have any number of respectable responses from which to choose and in the meantime she would go to Lady Sally's ball and greet Lord Richard Kestrel with a cool composure that would soon depress his amorous intentions. It was a good resolution, but she could not help wondering, with a little shiver of premonition, whether she would be able to keep it.

# Chapter Six

Promptly at nine, the carriage from Midwinter Marney Hall drew up on the gravel sweep outside Saltires. None of the occupants of the coach was in a particularly sunny mood. Olivia and Ross had been sitting in a simmering silence for the entire journey. Deb was torn between exasperation with them and a most unfamiliar nervousness on her own account. She felt as shy and awkward as a débutante at her first Assembly. In consequence she chattered even more than usual, until Ross had brusquely suggested she save her energies for the dancing. The silence had then become even more strained and it was with relief that they arrived at Lady Sally's ball and made their way under the arched portico and into the hall.

Many of Lady Sally's guests had already arrived and the air was thick with perfume and the scent of fresh flowers. The sound of a string quartet tinkled in the background and servants passed unobtrusively through the throng, offering glasses of champagne and lemonade.

'We have only an impromptu dance tonight, my dears,' Lady Sally said, as she ushered them through into the Great Hall. 'Society in the Midwinter villages seems sadly lacking these days, with Lord and Lady Newlyn gone to Cornwall on their honeymoon and the Duke of Kestrel and his brother up in London—'

'Richard Kestrel is gone to London?' Deb enquired. She felt a strange mixture of relief and disappointment. 'I thought that he had promised to be here tonight.'

'No, it is not Lord Richard who is absent,' Lady Sally said, laughing. 'Justin and Lucas Kestrel are gone, as you know. Richard remains in Midwinter for the time being.'

Deb bit her lip, annoyed to have betrayed an interest. 'Oh, how unfortunate,' she said. 'I keep wondering when he will be leaving.'

Lady Sally viewed her face with shrewd amusement. 'Would you prefer to exchange Lord Richard for one of his brothers, Deborah? A pity, when he told me that he was looking forward to dancing with you this evening!'

Deborah set her lips tightly. Lord Richard had given her fair warning, after all. The prospect of crossing swords with him again filled her with a shivery anticipation.

But even as she thought it, she saw Lord Richard through the crowd, chatting to Lady Benedict of Midwinter Bere. Lady Benedict was a most elegant woman and her exquisite gown of pale lilac with an overdress of pearl-sewn gauze made Deborah feel rather provincial in her own two-year-old rose pink satin. Lord Richard seemed very taken with his current companion and, although he met Deb's eye and inclined his head with studied courtesy, he made no move to leave Lady Benedict's side. Deb, who had never even entertained the idea of having a rival until that moment, and still less of feeling piqued if Lord Richard showed a lack of interest in her, was suddenly assailed by the alien emotion of jealousy. It seemed that in a short space of time she had begun to consider Lord Richard Kestrel her property. She stared at him for several seconds longer than she ought, saw him glance back at her with raised brows and realised that once again she had given her feelings away. She felt the red colour mantle her face and clash horribly with the pink satin dress. She turned abruptly away, wondering if she would ever achieve the town bronze that she desired.

'Allow me to introduce you to Mr Owen Chance,' Lady Sally said, smoothing over the awkward moment. 'Mr Chance is but recently come to Woodbridge to visit his uncle and aunt, the Jacksons of Church Place. Mr Chance, may I introduce the Honourable Mrs Deborah Stratton from Mallow House?'

Lady Sally smiled impartially on them and moved away to speak to some of her other guests, leaving Deb and Mr Chance looking at each other with a cautious friendship.

Owen Chance was a well set-up young man of about five and twenty, with an open, friendly face and a laugh that came easily. It quickly became apparent that he found Deb a charming companion, and although Deb discovered that her attention was inclined to stray to Lord Richard Kestrel with the same predictability of a compass swinging to north, with concentration she could keep her gaze riveted on Mr Chance instead. They enjoyed two dances together, a quadrille and a country dance, by which time Deb's card was starting to fill with other partners. Owen Chance then reclaimed her for supper in Lady Sally's artfully decorated conservatory, and they had the opportunity of furthering their acquaintance.

The conservatory had been decorated in a rustic style with coloured lamps hung from the ceiling and the water splashing into small rock pools amongst the greenery. Deb thought that Olivia should be in ecstasy to see such picturesque decoration, for horticulture was an interest that she shared with Lady Sally. Olivia, however, was still looking rather glum. As she chatted to Mr Chance, Deb watched her sister, who was taking supper with Mr Lang and his wife and daughter.

The vicar was a thin man who looked as though he were sucking on vinegar, and his wife was a plump woman with an aggrieved expression. No one in the party appeared to be enjoying themselves.

Ross Marney, in contrast, was dining with Lady Sally herself, and seemed to be having a splendid time. Deb noted that he filled his own and Lady Sally's wineglass with abandon, and at one point it seemed he was about to commit the somewhat questionable act of feeding his hostess with strawberries from his own spoon. Deb felt a little chilled at the sight, and embarrassed to see that Owen Chance had also observed it. In her opinion, Ross was behaving disgracefully and, whilst Lady Sally was gently restraining his wilder excesses, something simply had to be done. Deb decided to tackle Ross about his deplorable conduct.

Her opportunity arose when Mr Chance went to claim his cousin, Miss Jackson, for the polonaise, and Sir John Norton came to ask Lady Sally to dance. Deb was about to slip into Lady Sally's vacated seat when she saw Richard Kestrel come across and have a word in Ross's ear. Richard threw a smiling glance in Olivia's direction, and Deb saw Ross smile ruefully in return, run his hand through his tousled dark hair and get to his feet. To Deb's surprise, Ross then went across to the Langs' table and gave his wife a very creditable bow. The two of them headed towards the ballroom and Lord Richard Kestrel, smiling slightly, came across to Deb's table.

'Good evening, Mrs Stratton,' he said, with a bow.

'Good evening, Lord Richard,' Deb said coldly. She had forgotten her earlier vow to rebuff him, but she did remember how elegant Lady Benedict had looked hanging on his arm—and how pleased Richard had appeared to have her attention. Just the thought of it made her determined to freeze him.

Richard gestured to the empty seat beside her. 'May I?'

'If you wish.'

Richard sat. 'Your tone implied that that might be in doubt, Mrs Stratton,' he said, smiling sardonically. 'I assured you earlier that I was looking forward to our meeting.'

'So you did,' Deb said, feigning nonchalance and hoping that she could carry it off. 'I had forgot.'

Richard's smiled broadened and challenged the truth of her statement.

'Indeed?' he said. 'And I am disappointed that you have not yet delivered the cut direct, but perhaps you are saving yourself for a particularly acerbic set down?'

Deb smiled, despite herself. 'I am sure that I can come up with a suitable snub,' she said, 'if you will just give me a moment. You took me by surprise, my lord. I thought that Lady Benedict was your companion of choice for the evening.'

Lord Richard's sardonic smile deepened. 'I see. I hope that you felt suitably jealous, ma'am?'

'Jealous? Not I!' Deb said, with an airy wave of the hand. 'It would be too much to expect you to confine your attentions to one lady.'

'Oh, do you think so?' Richard looked vaguely offended.

'Of course,' Deb said. 'You are as fickle as the day is long, my lord. Everyone says so.'

'You should trust your own judgement rather than the observations of others, ma'am,' Richard said.

'Oh, I do.' Deb toyed with her glass, then looked up and met his eyes. 'When we met this afternoon I told you that I considered you faithless and unreliable and downright dangerous—' She broke off, realising that her tone demonstrated her feelings for him more clearly than any words. She looked down, vexed, and concentrated rather intensely on the leftover strawberries in the bowl.

A second later, Richard's hand covered hers and stilled her fidgeting fingers. 'You should give me the chance to show myself faithful,' he said. 'You might be surprised.'

Deb summoned up all her resistance. 'I *should* be surprised,' she said tartly. 'Very surprised.'

Richard's grip tightened for a second. 'Take a risk,' he said softly. 'After all, you also told me this afternoon that you were drawn to me.'

Deb set her jaw. 'I caught the measles when I was a child, my lord,' she said, 'but I recovered. It is in no way a fatal affliction.'

The warmth in Richard's gaze threatened to overset her.

'It is not a flattering comparison, ma'am,' he said, ruefully, 'but I take your point.'

His wry appreciation of her words made Deb feel ungracious. She almost apologised, but managed to stop herself in time. She cleared her throat and struggled to find a less personal topic of conversation.

'I was about to ring a peal over my brother-in-law when you intervened in my place just now,' she said. She frowned as she thought about it. 'Whatever did you say to Ross, my lord, to send him hurrying to solicit Olivia for a dance?'

Richard laughed and sat back in his chair. 'Why, I merely told him that if he did not snap up his beautiful wife, some other man would be there before him. It works every time.'

Deb looked enquiring. 'What does?'

'Challenging a man's possessive instincts,' Richard drawled. 'As soon as your brother-in-law knew that I wished to dance with his wife, he was there to claim his own before I could approach her.'

Deb smiled slightly. She could not help but admire his strategy and it had worked splendidly well for Olivia. One had to give Lord Richard credit where it was due.

'It was most kind of you,' she said. 'They have been at

daggers drawn all evening, so if you have manoeuvred a reconciliation I cannot but be grateful. At the least it spares me their bad temper in the carriage going home!'

Richard laughed. 'I am glad that I was able to be of service, Mrs Stratton,' he said. 'I would like above all things to see Lord and Lady Marney settle their differences.' He touched the back of Deb's hand lightly. 'However, I assure you that I would rather spend my time with you than with any of Lady Sally's other guests.'

There was a ring of sincerity in his voice, but Deb hardened her heart to it. She smiled reluctantly. 'You always speak very prettily, my lord.'

'And you do not believe a word of it.' There was a challenge in Richard's voice, but beneath it Deb thought that she could hear an unexpected note of regret.

'I believe one word in every two,' she said, and saw him smile.

'So you will not admit to jealousy, Mrs Stratton, and further you will not believe me when I say that *I* was suffering its pangs myself when I saw you with the charming Mr Owen Chance.'

'Oh, Mr Chance is entirely delightful,' Deb agreed, with deliberate obtuseness. 'I am so glad that he has come amongst us. He is indeed an asset to Midwinter society.'

'I rather doubt that,' Lord Richard said with a whimsical smile. He glanced towards the ballroom door, where the tall figure of Owen Chance could be seen conversing with Lady Sally Saltire.

'Did Mr Chance tell you about his profession?' Richard continued.

Deb raised her brows, slightly surprised. 'Should he have done? We did not speak of matters so mundane as business, my lord. We were far too busy chatting on things that were more interesting.'

'I see,' Lord Richard said. 'Well, perhaps he did not wish you to know. Mr Chance is a Riding Officer.' He turned back to look at her. 'And as such he is not welcome in many houses in these parts.'

'Because people are too snobbish, perhaps,' Deb observed sweetly. 'You surprise me, Lord Richard. I had not thought you a man to whom rank was important, but perhaps as the brother of a duke, you are conscious of such things?'

'You deliberately mistake me,' Richard said, smiling at her. 'I believe that Mr Chance's pedigree is as good as my own; if it is not, that makes no odds to me. What makes him an unwelcome guest is the propensity of the Riding Officers to frighten away our smugglers, Mrs Stratton. And then where will we get our brandy and tea and all our other commodities?'

Deb's lips twitched. 'Is smuggling then something in which you take a keen interest, my lord?'

'The purchase of good French brandy is certainly an ardent pursuit of mine,' Richard agreed feelingly. 'I am sure we are all wishing Mr Chance in Hades!'

Deb laughed. 'You are too harsh. A man should have a profession,' she added, giving him a sideways look. 'You said so yourself when you spoke to me about your time in the Navy. It is not beneficial to sit idly by all day with nothing to amuse oneself but brandy and a book of seventeenth-century poetry!'

Lord Richard gave a crack of laughter. '*Touché*, ma'am! Is that how you envisage I spend my days?'

'I have no notion,' Deb said lightly. 'I did not mean *you*, my lord! I have never given any thought to how you spend your time.'

This was transparently untrue and she could see from the look on Richard's face that he knew it. His dark eyes searched her face.

'It disappoints me that you never think of me,' Lord Richard said. 'Perhaps in speaking of brandy drinking and poetry reading you were describing the activities of the Midwinter reading group?'

Deb laughed. 'We do not care for brandy, my lord, although Lady Sally's port is a fine vintage. As for the poetry, I confess I have read some of the book you gave me, and very pretty the verse is too.'

'I am glad that you like it,' Lord Richard said. 'A great deal of it is very romantic, is it not?'

Deb's lashes flickered as she looked down. 'It may well be. However, I am more struck by the pastoral poems. I was reading the odes to the beauty of the sunset rather than Shakespeare's sonnets.'

'Perhaps you are afraid that too much romantic poetry would turn your own thoughts to love,' Richard suggested.

Deb fidgeted. 'Certainly not.'

Richard laughed. 'I remember—you do not look for male companionship. I have the feeling that it seeks you out all the same, Mrs Stratton. How could it not, when you are young and beautiful, and have such a zest for life? It is asking too much of a man not to view that as a challenge.'

Deb sighed. 'Your compliments are very polished, Lord Richard, but they fall on stony ground.'

Richard was looking at her thoughtfully and she felt a *frisson* of anticipation go through her. He leaned closer.

'What would you say if instead of a compliment I issued a dare, Mrs Stratton?' he said.

Deborah's eyes opened very wide. Her curiosity was caught. 'A dare, my lord? Of what nature?'

Lord Richard leaned closer still and beckoned her to draw near to him. After a second's hesitation, Deb complied. Immediately she was distracted by an entirely new set of sensations. Richard's lean cheek was close to hers and she could smell his sandalwood cologne. Her gaze focused on his lips and she blinked and hastily cast her gaze down. She felt his breath stir a tendril of hair.

'You told me earlier this afternoon that you did not believe I could seduce you,' Lord Richard murmured, for her ears alone. 'I dare you to let me try.'

Deb almost snapped the stem of her wineglass between her fingers, so great was her shock. Images, heated and provocative, raced through her mind. She looked up at Richard, saw the dancing flame in his dark eyes, and looked away quickly.

'No! I cannot accept that dare.'

Lord Richard covered her hand with his again. 'But you want to.'

Deb felt her fingers tremble beneath his and his grip on her hand tightened in response. She felt part-appalled, part-exhilarated. What was the matter with her that she was even considering accepting such a scandalous wager? This man was a rake and so dangerous that she should not even be giving him the time of day. He was particularly perilous to her, for a part of her responded to him in a manner that could only be considered reckless. And whilst these thoughts chased across her mind, she saw him watching her face and reading her thoughts as clearly as though she had spoken them aloud.

'No…' She could hear the reluctance in her voice and so could he.

'My dear Mrs Stratton, you are so close to capitulating…'

A shiver ran along Deb's skin, raising goose pimples. Richard was rubbing his fingers over her hand with gentle repetition, and this lightest of touches was enough to make her burn hot and cold at the same time.

'Admit you are tempted…'

'No, I am not,' Deb said, firing up. 'I am not in the least inclined to accept your suggestion.'

Richard released her hand and sat back in his chair. 'Well, you responded to that challenge, at any rate,' he said wryly. 'I must remember not to do that again, unless I wish to achieve the opposite reaction to the one I was wanting.'

He drained his wineglass. 'We should return to the ballroom, I believe. We are quite alone and no doubt the servants are waiting to clear the tables.'

Deb looked around and realised to her shock that all the other guests had finished supper long ago. The conservatory was deserted and, with its coloured lanterns and pools of shadow, it suddenly seemed a vastly different and very private place. The splash of the water mingled with the faint strains of music from the ballroom, but it seemed to Deb as though the silence was alive and waiting. The summer moonlight poured through the glass roof and sprinkled the tiled floor with silver. Richard stood up and offered his arm to her and she put her hand gingerly on it, as though just the touch of him might be unsafe, enough to trigger an elemental reaction. His arm was warm and hard beneath her fingers and it seemed a very long way to the ballroom door...

Her senses were concentrating so hard on Richard that she was not watching where she stepped. There was a patch of darkness between the pools of lantern light and she missed her step, catching her heel in the flounce of her gown. It was instinct on her part to hold more tightly to Richard's arm to steady herself. And no doubt it was also instinct on his part to slide his other arm about her waist, drawing her hard and sure against him.

She thought that he would kiss her, but instead he held her close, his mouth against her hair, the warmth of his hands a shocking, heated seduction through the thin satin of her dress. Deb's cheek was against his shoulder and the mingled scent of sandalwood and his skin made her head swim. She could hear the beat of his heart beneath her ear. She felt warm and safe and protected, yet alive in every part of her being. In some strange way it felt even more intimate than his kiss and such affinity shook her deeply. She looked up helplessly into his face, felt his arms tighten about her and saw the intense desire darken his eyes. She fought the devastatingly strong urge to hold him close and never let go. This was madness.

Deborah freed herself from his arms and moved away from him, as though mere physical distance could break the hold he had on her.

'Excuse me,' she said, with a superficial brightness that suggested they had been conversing on the weather or the state of the roads. 'I must go and mend my skirt.'

She made her way, a little blindly, to the ladies' withdrawing room and found herself standing before the mirror, leaning on the top of the chest of drawers as though for support.

She stood there, trembling, staring at her reflection and wondering what was the matter with her.

Richard Kestrel had held her in his arms and she had taken both pleasure and consolation in the experience. In that moment she had felt cherished and loved as well as desired. She had known that Richard wanted her. The touch of his hands on her body had conveyed the depth of his need. Yet he had not kissed her, but had held her with tenderness as well as desire. It had been frighteningly tempting to give herself up to the embrace. No doubt if common sense had not reasserted itself, she would still be clasped in his arms, oblivious to the world, for all to see.

Deb tucked a wayward curl behind her ear and noted that her hand was still shaking. She knew it was the force of her thoughts that raised this nervousness in her. For this was no mere attraction to a handsome man. What she felt for Richard Kestrel was far more insidious. He stirred longings in her that were buried very deep and had been denied for a very long time. He had awoken a need for the physical bond that she had expected from marriage but had never found, and he had stirred in her a longing for an emotional closeness that she had never experienced.

Deb folded her arms as though to protect herself from the coldness within. Until that moment she had not realised how vulnerable she was. For three years she had lived retired and imagined that she could spend the rest of her life in such a manner. And then Richard Kestrel had appeared and had made her face up to the folly of that particular belief.

So now she had a stark choice. She could abandon the precepts and principles that had governed her life so far in order to seek the delights of a love affair. She had no doubt that to become Richard Kestrel's mistress would be to experience a heady bliss, a dream of physical fulfilment. Yet she was afraid, afraid that the emotional intimacy she craved would still elude her and ever more terrified that she would want too much and end up being hurt more deeply than she ever had been by Neil Stratton.

Deb stared hopelessly at her reflection. She was afraid of marriage and yet she longed for the solace of true love. She ached for physical satisfaction and yet she could not imagine it without tenderness. She rejected the advances of a rake and yet she ardently desired for him to make love to her. She was a mass of contradictions and, that being the case, she must play safe. She had no choice after all. She must protect herself against Lord Richard Kestrel and the perilous attraction she felt for him. She must enforce her decision with iron determination. She must not see him again.

* * *

Richard Kestrel walked slowly into the ballroom. He saw Olivia Marney watching his progress with her eyebrows raised like perfect half-moons. No doubt she had already seen Deb erupt through the door that led to the conservatory and had drawn her own conclusions. She met Richard's eyes quizzically but with no censure. Richard smiled at her. He liked Olivia and thought Ross to be a complete fool when it came to the matter of his wife. Not that Richard was tempted to play Ross false. Olivia was lovely, but she lacked Deborah's passionate flame.

He took a glass of wine from a passing servant and stood with his shoulders propped against the doorway, waiting for Deb to return. He did not flatter himself that she would rejoin him. Very likely she would cut him dead. Very likely he deserved it. He had pushed her to act on her attraction to him, had prompted her to take it further by word and by deed. He had held her in a scandalously close embrace in a public place where anyone might have seen them. He had felt the softening in her body as it responded to him and the weakening of her defences. And now... He wanted to take Deb home and make love to her and instead he had to stand here and pretend to a cool interest in the proceedings at the ball.

Lily Benedict was smiling at him, but he did not cross the room to join her. He knew that there were plenty of women who would be more openly receptive to his advances than Deborah Stratton, but he did not wish for their company. He wanted Deborah, and that meant that he had to give her time, court her slowly. He sensed that in time he might be able to gain her trust and the prospect was more appealing than any quick seduction had ever been.

He gave an ironic smile. No one knew better than he that a true rake would not be troubled by such scruples. A true rake took what he wanted and be damned to the consequences. He did not deserve the name of rake any more. He had not been entitled to it from the moment he had set eyes on Deb Stratton and she had occupied his thoughts to the exclusion of all others. He had not been entitled to the name of rake from the moment he had decided that he wanted to marry her.

Briefly, Richard considered making Deb a declaration. It would assure her of his sincerity, about which she had patent doubts. On the other hand, it was a risky strategy. He had not given himself enough time to win her trust, nor convince her to put aside her fear of marriage. If he proposed to her now, she might well run from him and then he would lose all that he had gained. He would have to wait.

Richard finished his wine and put the glass down gently on a nearby table. Deb had returned to the ballroom now. Apart from a high colour and a militant sparkle in her eye, there was nothing in her behaviour to suggest that she was discomfited. As he had suspected, she ignored him and went over to join Olivia, who was chatting to Lady Sally Saltire.

Richard's smile turned wry. He had set himself a difficult task in courting Deb and there would be those who would advise him to turn from his pursuit to a more receptive quarry. Lily Benedict was still giving him a come-hither look, but it was about as appealing as a plate of leftover roast beef. Across the room Deb sparkled as Owen Chance came across to solicit a dance. Richard felt a tightening of something inside, which he recognised as a very possessive jealousy. He had pulled that trick on Ross earlier and now this was his reward. How appropriate.

He watched Deb take Owen Chance's hand and join the set of country dances that was forming up. He watched the play of light across her expressive face and the way that her irrepressible curls bounced on her white shoulders. He saw her smile and felt the tug of it deep inside him. He knew he was not going to disengage. He could not.

He watched her as she performed the complicated steps of the dance. He found that he could not take his eyes off her. The situation was filled with irony. Deb found it difficult to trust him because of his reputation as rake. He had ceased to be a rake from the moment that he realised he loved her. He could not control his feelings for her. Deb did not know it, but she had him utterly at the disadvantage.

## *Chapter Seven*

'Today, ladies, I thought that we might move on to discuss the poetry of John Dryden,' Lady Sally Saltire said, opening a copy of the same poetry book that Richard Kestrel had given to Deborah the previous week. 'We have plenty of poems to choose from. Would you prefer "London after the Great Fire" or "Farewell, Ungrateful Traitor"?'

There were groans from several members of the reading group. 'Must we read something so dry, Sally?' Lily Benedict besought. She gave Deb a sly, sideways glance from her slanting dark eyes. 'I am sure that the majority of us would rather talk about love poetry, would we not, Deborah? How about those faithless Cavalier poets—Rochester or Sedley?'

Deb flicked open her book. She felt a little self-conscious. She had spent quite a while reading through the poems and wondering whether they had also been Richard's favourites. She could picture him alone in the library at Kestrel Court, one candle burning at his elbow as he flicked through the pages. A lock of dark hair would fall across his forehead and in the pale light he would look like one of the poets of old, penning lines to his lady love…

' A line of text caught her eye. 'If I by miracle can be this livelong minute true to thee, tis all that heaven allows…'

Deb sighed. If anything was true of Richard Kestrel, then it was that. He would never be able to be constant to one woman for longer than a minute and probably not even that. She was foolish to imagine it could be so.

Since Lady Sally's ball the previous week, Deb had thought long and hard about Richard Kestrel—too long and too hard, probably. She had not been able to come to any conclusions other than that she was spending an unconscionable amount of time on him, which was unprofitable and made her heart ache. Her only hope was that the trip to Somerset for her brother's wedding would distract her thoughts—and that the appointment of a temporary fiancé would give her both purpose and interest.

She looked up to see that the other members of the group were watching her. Lady Benedict's eyes were bright with malice and Lady Sally Saltire looked shrewd, as though she had already divined the cause of Deb's trouble. Deb dragged up a bright smile.

'Why do we not read "The World" by Henry Vaughan?' she suggested. 'It is a very beautiful poem.'

Some half an hour later the discussion had flagged and Lady Sally encouraged them to put their books aside and come out into the conservatory.

'I am most excited,' she confided. 'You will recall that I had commissioned a watercolour calendar a few months ago? Well, I received my first copy from the publisher today. Only come and see. It is even better than I had envisaged. The ladies of the *ton* will be mad to buy it when I go up to London next month!'

When Lady Sally had first mooted the idea of a watercolour calendar featuring pictures of various local gentleman, the members of the reading group had been quite scandalised. Even though the project was for a charitable cause, it had seemed utterly outrageous to parade a group of eligible gentlemen simply to whet the appetites of ladies of fashion. The vicar, Mr Lang, on hearing of the calendar, had even taken to preaching against it from his pulpit, much to Lady Sally's amusement. Already her rakes' calendar, as she called it, had achieved exactly the effect that she desired. Anticipation amongst the ladies of the *ton* was extremely high and charitable causes would benefit!

The ladies crowded around the easel where Lady Sally had mounted the book. Helena Lang grabbed Deb's arm in a thoroughly overexcited manner.

'Oh, Mrs Stratton, I heard a rumour at the ball that Lord Lucas Kestrel had agreed to be sketched without his shirt!'

Olivia Marney, overhearing, could not help but laugh. 'I fear that is completely untrue, Miss Lang, although if anyone were likely to be so outrageous I suspect it *would* be Lord Lucas. In fact, I had it from Ross that he posed in army uniform, and very fine he looked too.'

Lady Benedict was pushing all the other ladies aside in her haste to be first to view the calendar. She pressed one white hand to her lips to stifle a peal of laughter.

'Oh, Sally—all our rakes, and in magnificent style!'

It was true. As Lady Sally turned the pages of the calendar slowly and the ladies viewed the pictures, it became evident that the conservatory at Saltires was one of the hottest places in the kingdom. The pictures were magnificent. There was the Duke of Kestrel, looking handsome and athletic mounted on his coal-black horse, Thunderer. There was Cory, Lord Newlyn, adventurer *par excellence* with the wicked twinkle in his eye that had melted the heart of every lady for miles around. Lucas Kestrel looked every debutanté's dream and every chaperon's nightmare in his army uniform, whilst Richard Kestrel was dark and dangerous in evening dress. Deb felt her breath constrict in her throat and turned the page quickly, to where Ross Marney was depicted, virile and good looking in navy uniform, with the wind ruffling his dark hair and his blue eyes smiling.

Deb saw Olivia put a hand up to her throat and saw the pink colour stain her cheeks and smiled to herself that, for all their difficulties, Olivia and Ross were not indifferent to each other.

'Good gracious,' Olivia said, her voice not quite steady, 'Mr Daubenay certainly knows how to present a gentleman looking his best. This book should make his reputation as a water colourist, Sally.'

'I hope so,' Lady Sally said, smiling. 'He did have remarkably good raw material to work on!'

Lady Benedict was fanning herself ostentatiously. 'I do believe that I need to sit down, Sally,' she said, 'and perhaps a cool drink, after that display of unabashed manhood. One scarcely knows where to look.'

Deb knew it was evident from the reaction and from Lady Sally's self-satisfied smile that the project would be a raging success. None of the ladies of the *ton* would be able to resist parting with their money for such a good cause—and for the benefit of ogling a dozen personable gentlemen.

'You will have ladies beating a path to your door to buy a copy, Lady Sally,' she said, with feeling.

Lady Sally laughed. 'I plan to hold a ball at the end of October to launch the book and I am trying to prevail on all the gentlemen to attend. I am hoping it will be quite a sensation. In fact…' she ushered them back into the drawing room and rang the bell for refreshments '…I had another idea. I thought to auction the original of the book as well as sell copies. I suspect there might be much competition for the original version.'

The ladies were much struck by this and whilst they drank

their cooling lemonade they discussed the plans for Lady Sally's ball. Helena Lang, whose father the vicar disapproved so heartily of the calendar, was extremely upset that she would not be able to attend the London ball, and Lady Benedict also expressed her disappointment that her husband's ill health kept her, as always, in the country.

'What would be simply marvellous,' she said, eyes lighting up, 'would be if you were to hold a special private view here, Sally, before auctioning the calendar up in London. It would attract a great deal of notice—why, the Hertfords and the Prince of Wales might even attend!'

Helena Lang clapped her hands. 'Oh, *please*, Lady Sally! That way I may persuade Papa to allow me to be present...'

Deb's heart sank. She felt peculiarly out of sorts at the thought of Lady Sally's calendar heroes displaying their undeniable physical prowess before the *ton*. However, since everyone else thought it a marvellous idea, she was obliged to concur and walked back to Midwinter Marney with Olivia in rather a bad mood.

'Is Lord Marney at home?' Olivia enquired casually of the butler as they went under the Doric portico and through the big front door.

'Yes, my lady,' Ford replied. 'Lord Marney and Lord Richard Kestrel returned a little while ago and are down in the stables.' He hesitated. 'Shall I ask them to join you for tea, madam?'

Deb pulled a face and shook her head, for the thought of Lord Richard's company was the final strain on her poor temper, but unfortunately Olivia was stripping off her gloves and appeared not to notice her sister's disapproval.

'Please do, Ford,' she said. 'We shall all take tea together.'

Deb sighed and went through to the drawing room, whilst

Olivia went upstairs to remove her bonnet. The maid was already laying out afternoon tea in preparation for their return. Deb reflected that her sister's household ran like clockwork. Olivia was so efficient. Nothing ever seemed to go awry in her life.

There was the sound of voices raised in the hall and the gentlemen came in.

'If you wanted to go to Newmarket this week, I should be delighted to accompany you, Ross,' Lord Richard was saying.

Although she had known that he was present, Deb found that she was so flustered to see Lord Richard again that she dropped her poetry book on the floor. It skidded across the polished wood and bumped against the leg of the rosewood table. She bent to pick it up and a sheet fell out. Cursing herself for her clumsiness in loosening the pages, Deb whisked the paper up and hoped that Lord Richard had not noticed her carelessness with his gift. She stuffed the loose sheet inside the cover and put the book under her arm.

'Good afternoon, Deb,' Ross said, coming over to kiss her cheek. 'Did you enjoy your meeting of the reading group?'

'It was quite pleasant,' Deb said. She could feel herself blushing under Richard's scrutiny with all the self-consciousness of a green girl.

'How do you do, Mrs Stratton?' he said. His tone was scrupulously courteous, but the message in his eyes was very different, warm and speculative, and it heated Deb down to her toes. 'Were you studying Christopher Marlowe this afternoon?'

'We were reading Henry Vaughan,' Deb said coolly. She knew that she had blushed; she could feel her face radiating the heat like a glowing fire. Life was going to be excessively difficult if she could not conquer this curious susceptibility she had to Richard Kestrel. It seemed to get worse every time she saw him.

Olivia came in and Richard turned to greet her, giving Deb the breathing space she desperately needed. She took the opportunity of surreptitiously trying to put her book back together again. However, when she looked at the loose sheet she realised that it was not poetry at all and could not have come from the same book. It was a curious page of printed symbols. There was an anchor and a seagull and a ship and some wavy lines that she thought must represent the sea. Deb frowned. Her first thought was that it looked rather like a coded message, with the symbols representing certain words…

'May I pass you a cup of tea, Mrs Stratton?' Richard Kestrel said, at her elbow. Deb jumped. She had not noticed his approach and now she put the book and the sheet aside on the rosewood bookcase and reluctantly allowed Richard to draw her over to the long French windows that looked out over the garden. Olivia and Ross were sitting on the sofa, conversing in low voices over the relative merits of chicken or lamb for dinner. Deb sighed. She supposed that she should be grateful they were talking at all.

Rather than accept a tête-à-tête with Richard as he so clearly wished, Deb spiked his guns by raising her voice to include the whole group.

'Did Olivia tell you that we saw a copy of Lady Sally's watercolour book this afternoon, Ross?' she asked. 'We thought that you looked very fine.'

Ross laughed. He looked pleased. 'Thank you, Deb. I imagine that Lady Sally's calendar will cause quite a stir.'

'It will cause a riot,' Deb agreed ruefully.

'You also observed that Lord Richard's picture looked most elegant, did you not, Deb?' Olivia said sweetly. 'I remember you commenting specifically on it on our way home.'

Deb bit her lip. It was true that she had made an un-guarded remark to Olivia on the subject, but she had hardly expected her sister to repeat it. Richard was laughing at her, his brows raised quizzically.

'I am flattered, Mrs Stratton.'

'I suppose you looked quite well to a pass,' Deb said ungraciously, fidgeting with her teaspoon, 'but then, Mr Daubenay is a very talented artist.'

She heard Lord Richard smother a laugh in his teacup. 'I imagine he must be, to make something of such unpromising material,' he agreed.

Deb frowned. It was difficult to try and depress a man's pretensions when he had no vanity to deflate. Despite the fact that Lord Richard Kestrel was one of the most handsome men of her acquaintance, it appeared that he actually had very little personal conceit. It was rather annoying when she so earnestly wished to take him down a peg.

'I am sure that you do not need me to add my praises to the positive cacophony of other ladies,' she said. 'If you wish for acclaim, then you need only wait for the private view, when I am persuaded you will be drowned in a sea of feminine admiration!'

In response, Richard put his hand on her wrist and drew her slightly apart. Her hand shook slightly; the teacup rattled and she placed it quickly on the windowsill.

'You mistake me, Mrs Stratton, if you think I wish for general acclaim,' he said in an undertone. 'Yours is the only good opinion I seek.'

Deb's eyes widened. 'I may lead a sheltered life, Lord Richard, but I recognise a line of flattery when it is spun for me.'

Richard laughed. He leaned closer so that his lips brushed

her ear and all the hairs down the back of Deb's neck stood on end.

'If you wished your life to be less sheltered, you could reconsider my dare,' he murmured. 'A private view of our own would be far more enjoyable...'

Deb gasped. She threw a hasty glance over her shoulder, but Ross was now moodily perusing *The Times* and Olivia was apparently engrossed in the *Ladies Magazine* and neither of them was paying their guests the slightest attention. Deb could not believe that they were so insensitive to the atmosphere in the drawing room when she felt as though she was about to spontaneously combust. Her head was buzzing with tension and awareness and Lord Richard was still holding her wrist lightly. The touch of his fingers against her bare skin was sufficient to send a prickly kind of sensation all the way along her nerves.

'Thank you,' she said, hoping that her voice was steady, 'but you have no need to repeat your offer. My refusal still stands.'

She saw Richard's lips curve into a wicked smile. 'And yet you kissed me as though you meant it. Several times, in fact...'

Deb met his gaze. This was a tricky statement to rebut since she was all too aware that she had succumbed to Richard's skilful seduction with what could be considered a certain amount of enthusiasm. In fact, she had succumbed not once, but twice, so there was no possible way that she could dismiss it as an aberration.

She burned to think of their kisses. She had enjoyed being in Richard's arms and wanted to be there again. Yet she remembered the comparison with eating the truffles. They seemed like such a good idea at the time. They were delicious, sinful, a wicked indulgence to which she knew she should not surrender. She was equally certain that she should not surrender to Richard. She gave him a cool smile.

'Remember that I have consigned you to the same category as drinking too much wine, my lord,' she said, 'the category of being very, very bad for me.' She spun away from him and turned towards the door. 'Excuse me, I must go home. I am promised to drive along the river with Mr Lang this afternoon and do not wish to be late.'

Richard smiled easily. 'My route takes me back the same way as yours. I will escort you.'

'No thank you,' Deb said. 'I enjoy walking alone. Besides, you know full well that Mallow is not on the way to Kestrel Court.'

'It could be,' Richard said, smiling engagingly. 'Besides, I feel that it would be safer for you to be accompanied.'

Deb arched her brows. 'Having an escort may be safer in general but in this specific case I do not require your company.'

Richard laughed. 'You are always refusing me.'

'I am.' Deb smiled sweetly. 'That should tell you something, I believe.' She called a hasty farewell to Ross and Olivia and slipped out into the hall, congratulating herself on her swift escape.

She had not gone more than a few paces before she heard Richard's footsteps behind her and he caught her up as she reached the main door, putting a hand on her arm.

'A moment, Mrs Stratton,' he said. 'You have left your book behind.'

Deb felt annoyed at her carelessness. She had hurried out, wishing to escape his troubling presence, but in doing so she had given him a genuine reason to follow her. Now she could hardly be uncivil as a result. She took the book of poetry and tucked it under her arm, reining in her exasperation as Richard held the door open for her and accompanied her down the steps and on to the gravel.

'Thank you,' she said, trying not to sound too grumpy. 'There really is no need for you to escort me to Mallow, you know.'

Richard smiled and fell into step beside her. 'No need other than to take pleasure in your company.'

Deb laughed. 'Why do you persist where there is no hope, my lord?'

Richard gave her a very straight look. 'Perhaps I am of stubborn disposition, like you yourself, madam.'

He held open the little white-painted gate that opened on to the path to Mallow and stood aside for her to precede him. To Deb's surprise he made no attempt to engage her in teasing repartee and even less to force his attentions on her. They spoke politely enough on a number of topics, from the state of the roads to the current invasion threat and the political situation. To converse with Richard in an entirely natural manner proved dangerously enjoyable to Deb, for he was a most interesting man to talk with. Occasionally he would hold a gate open for her or pull aside a spray of briars from her path with exemplary courtesy. Deb found it disconcerting, not because she had imagined him without manners, but because it made her feel quite ridiculously cherished. She was rather annoyed with herself for being so receptive to his thoughtfulness, but she could not deny that the walk, in the late summer sunshine, was a very pleasant experience.

The path joined the lane to Midwinter Mallow and from there another white-painted wooden gate led into the back of Deb's gardens at Mallow House. At the gate Deb paused, preparing to make her farewells and fidgeting a little with her book of poetry as she did so. She realised that she had pulled some of the binding loose and peered at it with dismay.

'Oh dear, I—' She stopped, staring. 'Oh—but this is not my book!'

Richard came across to her. Deb opened the book and flicked through it. Now that she was looking closely, she could see that this book was exactly the same as the one he had given her, except that it was a little older and more worn. The list of odd symbols that she had tucked carelessly inside the front cover was also missing now. She searched the pages, the frown deepening on her brow.

'Are you looking for this?' Richard enquired affably. He put a hand inside his jacket and retrieved a folded paper. Deb stared from it to his face. He was watching her, but with neither the speculation nor the admiration to which she had become accustomed. There was an unreadable expression in his eyes and a hard line to his mouth and Deb felt a sudden chill. She put out a hand for the sheet, but he twitched it out of her grip.

'Oh, no, Mrs Stratton,' he said, his voice pleasant but definite. 'It is scarcely that simple. I believe that you have some explaining to do.'

# Chapter Eight

'Are you saying that this is your property, Mrs Stratton?' Richard was still holding the sheet of paper out of Deb's reach and his intent gaze had not wavered from her face.

Deb looked at him, bewildered. 'No,' she said. 'I found it in the book. How did you get hold of it?'

Richard ignored her question. 'So you are claiming that neither the book nor the sheet of paper belongs to you?' he asked.

His high-handed manner lit a flicker of temper in Deb. 'I am not claiming anything,' she said sharply. 'I am telling you that that is not my book. You should know—you gave it to me yourself!'

Richard took the book from her hand and turned it over, scrutinising it. A shadow of a smile touched his mouth. 'It is certainly not the copy that I gave to you, but that does not mean it is not yours,' he said smoothly. 'Presumably you had a copy that you were using before you received my gift?'

Deb glared at him. 'I am not entirely sure of the purpose of your questions, Lord Richard,' she said cuttingly, 'nor by what right you are asking them—' She broke off as a cart came around the corner of the road, its wheels churning the dust, harness jingling. Richard gave one sharp glance over his shoulder, caught her arm and bundled her unceremoniously through the wooden gate and into the shrubbery, along the mossy path and past the tangled ranks of holly and laurel.

Deb was taken aback at the manoeuvre. It was not that she suspected him of any sinister motive, rather that his sudden action had taken her by surprise. As soon as they were out of sight of the road he released her arm and Deb sank down on to the stone bench that had once had a very pretty view across to the river, until her garden had grown so out of hand that it was now hidden from sight.

Richard remained standing. In the pale sunlight that was filtered through the leaves Deb saw that he was watching her with narrowed gaze. She rubbed her arm automatically and gave him back a defiant look, but under her bodice her heart was beating rather quickly. Whatever this was about, it was no game. She could sense that instinctively.

'I apologise for my actions just now,' Richard said, immaculately polite. 'I had no wish for us to be seen or overheard.' He glanced around. 'I take it that we are hidden from view here?'

Deb nodded. 'No one can see us from the house or from the road.' She looked at him. 'I do not understand.'

Richard paused for a moment, then came to sit beside her on the bench. He sat forward, turning the sheet of symbols over in his hand.

'Please, would you answer some questions for me?' he asked.

Deb nodded silently, her eyes fixed on his.

'Before I gave you a new copy of the poetry book, what were you using?' Richard asked.

Deb frowned. 'I shared Olivia's copy before,' she said. 'I do not have a great deal of money to spend on books.'

Richard's gaze searched her face. 'Tell me what happened today at the reading group,' he said.

Deb rubbed her forehead as she tried to remember. 'We studied "The World" by Henry Vaughan,' she said, 'then, after we had finished, Lady Sally asked us to go into the conservatory to have a look at the copy of the watercolour book.'

'Did you take your book of poetry with you?'

'No,' Deb said, wrinkling her brow as she marshalled her thoughts in order. 'I put it down on the table in Lady Sally's library and picked it up again as we were on our way out. Except...' she met his eyes '...I must have picked up the wrong book. We had all left our copies there. There was quite a pile of them. We all have the same edition and the books must have become muddled.'

'You all have the same edition,' Richard repeated. He was smiling ruefully.

'Yes.' Deb looked enquiringly at him. 'All five of us have this book.' She tapped the cover. 'Mine was the only new copy.'

Richard's gaze was intent on her. 'When did you know about this?' he asked, gesturing to the paper with the symbols on it that was still in his hand.

'I found it when we arrived back at Midwinter Marney Hall,' Deb said. 'I dropped the book and the paper fell out. It was folded over, as though it had been used as a bookmark.'

She saw Richard's eyes narrow thoughtfully. 'Had you ever seen it before?' he asked.

'No, never.' Deb shifted on the bench, increasingly uncomfortable. 'To what end do you question me like this, my lord? Please tell me.'

Richard sat back and relaxed his shoulders against the

stonework with a sigh. 'I beg your pardon. It must seem
most uncivil of me.'

'It does,' Deb said, determined not to be deflected, 'and
you have not answered my question yet.'

Richard laughed. 'No, I have not.'

There was a small silence whilst Deb waited and Richard
declined to elaborate. Deb could feel his gaze on her and
could sense the rapid calculation going on in his mind as
he weighed what she had said. She shivered a little in the
cool shade. She understood what was going on. He was
trying to decide whether he believed her. He was deciding
whether or not he trusted her.

'I thought it looked like some kind of code,' Deb said,
taking the bull by the horns.

Richard raised his brows. 'Did you?' he said.

Deb gave a sharp sigh. 'Will you stop being so evasive,
my lord? What is on the sheet of paper? And what—forgive
my bluntness, but I know no other way—does this have to
do with you?'

Richard hesitated, then looked her straight in the eyes,
meeting her candour with equal frankness. 'This, Mrs Stratton, is a coded letter.' He looked at her and said deliberately,
'A letter from a spy.'

Deb felt winded. She blinked at the paper in his hand and
then at his face. 'A spy's letter? You mean it is written in
code because it is a secret message?'

'Exactly that,' Richard said.

Deb felt a clutch of fear that she might have bitten off
considerably more than she could deal with here.

'And your part in this?' she whispered. She waited, holding her breath, whilst there was a small pause.

'I told you that I once worked for the Admiralty,' Richard
said, with a faint smile. 'In point of fact, I still do.'

Deb felt a curious rush of relief. She studied his face,

dark, impassive, a little grim. 'What are you—a spy catcher?'

'For want of a better word,' Richard said, grimacing.

Deb got to her feet and took a pace away from him. Her perceptions of Lord Richard Kestrel, which had already been shaken thoroughly over the last couple of weeks, underwent another shift.

'You have indeed perfected your disguise, my lord,' she said. 'I should never have thought it! The gambling wastrel of a rake, who cannot manage to remove his boots without the help of a valet.'

Richard winced. 'Thank you,' he said. 'I am sure I was never quite as bad as you describe.'

Deb stared at him, shaking her head. 'It seems impossible, my lord.'

'That there are spies in Midwinter or that I should be here to capture them?'

'Both!' Deb rubbed her forehead again. 'I cannot believe it—not here in Midwinter…'

'It is as possible for a spy to operate here as in any other place,' Richard said. 'It is more likely here, in fact, given the strategic position of the harbour and the proximity of the French coast.'

Deb stared at him, her face suddenly pale as she thought through all the implications. 'But if the secret message was in the book of poetry…' Her eyes widened. 'You thought the letter was *mine*?' she whispered. 'You thought that I was the spy?'

'I found the paper in your book,' Richard pointed out, with a slight smile. 'What was I supposed to think?'

'Yes, but—' Deb flung herself back down on the stone seat and let her breath out on a sharp sigh. 'I told you that it was *not* my book.'

'You did tell me that, yes. Am I supposed to believe everything that people tell me?'

Deb flinched as she took his meaning. There was no particular reason why he should accept her word and yet she found that she had assumed he would. She wanted him to trust her. It seemed excessively important to her. She bit her lip, fighting an absurd and unexpected desire to cry.

'I assure you,' she said with dignity, 'that I had nothing to do with this.' She met Richard's level, penetrating gaze. 'Do you still suspect that I did?'

There was a long, taut silence, and then Richard shook his head slowly. There was a smile in his eyes now. 'No, I do not believe you to be a traitor, Mrs Stratton. I never did, although I may well have let my feelings get in the way of sound judgement.'

Deb stared at him. His head was bent and he was examining the inside cover of the book intently. He glanced up suddenly and caught her gaze. His mouth curved into the shadow of a smile. 'Of course, you could be playing a deep double game!'

'Richard—' Deb said, on a note of entreaty. She felt very vulnerable. She coloured and corrected herself. 'I beg your pardon, my lord.'

'Richard will suffice,' Richard said, his smile deepening. His hand covered hers in a brief, reassuring grasp. 'Be easy, Deborah. I am only teasing you. I doubt you could deceive me, for you are one of the most transparently honest people that I have ever met.'

'I am forever cursing my inability to hide my feelings,' Deb said, a little shakily.

Richard smiled and for a second his hand tightened over hers before he removed it. 'Do not,' he said softly.

Their eyes met and held. 'Oh, dear,' Deb said helplessly, feeling all the attraction that she had worked so hard to repress rushing back, 'this is very unfortunate.' She frowned, trying to wrench her thoughts away from Richard Kestrel and back to the matter in hand. It was extremely difficult to concentrate.

'The spy,' she said. 'The person that you are hunting... If the message was in the book, the spy must belong to Lady Sally's reading group.'

Richard nodded. 'We think that she does.'

Deb shot him a troubled look. 'But it cannot be so. It is not possible.'

'What is impossible? That there should be a female spy or that she should be a member of your reading group?'

'Either. Both!' Deb made a wild gesture. 'There is only Olivia and me, and Lady Sally and Miss Lang and Lady Benedict!' Her voice sank to a whisper. 'It must be one of us, yet it cannot be...'

Richard's steady gaze did not waver from her face. 'It must be one of you,' he repeated implacably.

'Not Liv!' Deb said. Her gaze was pleading. 'I could never believe her a traitor!'

Richard shook his head. 'No. I doubt that Lady Marney is the one.'

'Then it must be one of the others.' Deb frowned. 'Miss Lang is silly and vulgar and I do not like Lady Benedict, but that does not make her a spy...' She gave a gusty sigh. 'There must be some mistake.'

Richard's face was still. 'There is no mistake, Deborah.' He shifted on the seat. 'Nor is this to be taken lightly. This person has killed more than once and may well kill again. She is passing secrets to the French that endanger the lives of thousands of innocent people. She has to be stopped.'

There was a silence. Deb's gaze fell on the book and she picked it up. It bore absolutely no distinguishing marks and, thinking back to the meeting of the reading group, she could

not think of any way of telling the books apart. She picked
it up and opened the pages at random. It smelled of a very
faint scent; not perfume or flowers or polish, but something
else. Deb sniffed at the spine. She could not place the smell,
but she knew that she would recognise it if she smelled it
again.

'How providential for you that I accidentally left my book
behind,' she said, 'or you might never have seen the letter—' She broke off as she caught the edge of Richard's
rueful grin. 'What is it?' she demanded.

Richard's grin broadened. 'That was no accident,' he said.

Deb stared at him, the hand clasping the book sinking
into her lap. 'What do you mean it was no accident? I left
Midwinter Marney in a hurry and forgot that the book was
on the table!'

Richard stood up and stretched. 'You may think that is
what happened, but the truth is rather different.' He slanted
a smile down at her. 'I saw the coded letter when I brought
you your cup of tea, Deborah. You were looking very ab-
sorbed and very furtive, and I knew I had somehow to persuade you to forget the book and give me the chance to
have a look at the code.'

Deb stared in amazement. 'Oh! You mean that you…
When you were talking to me…'

'I deliberately diverted your attention,' Richard confirmed. 'I needed to distract you.'

'You mean that all that outrageous flirtation was designed
to make me forget my book?' Deb's tone was stormy and
her feelings were not soothed when Richard nodded, still
smiling.

'It worked, did it not? You stalked out like an outraged
duchess and I picked up the book and followed you.'

Deb clenched her hands. 'Oh, you…you hateful wretch!'

'I know,' Richard said resignedly. 'I am a cad and a deceiver.'

'You are without a doubt the most odious man I have ever met!' Deb said wrathfully. She jumped to her feet. 'We have all seen you and your brothers, mingling with us all and flirting and inveigling yourselves into our good graces. Now I discover it was all a means to an end…'

Richard's gaze was dark and amused. 'I cannot deny that we set out to charm the ladies of Midwinter,' he said smoothly, 'but—'

'Oh, do not seek to make excuses,' Deb said, cutting him off sharply. She felt cheap and betrayed. 'How can there be any justification for the way you behaved?'

Richard had also got to his feet and, although he was not touching her, his gaze held her as still as though he was forcibly restraining her.

'I was about to say that my behaviour towards you was always sincere, Mrs Stratton,' he said. 'With you, I feigned nothing.'

Deb fought her emotions and the insidious instinct that told her he was telling the truth.

'You would say that, wouldn't you?' she retorted. She let her breath out on a huge sigh. 'I would be a fool twice over if I believed you!' she added bitterly.

Richard said nothing, but his dark gaze challenged hers and Deb was the first to look away.

'I do not know if I can trust a word you say,' she complained, in a more moderate tone.

'No,' Richard agreed levelly. 'I can understand that.'

He came to her and took her hand in his. When she tried to free herself he pulled her around to face him. Deb's breathing constricted.

'My lord—'

'I will let you go in a moment,' Richard's face was sud-

denly grim again, 'but this is important. You know far more
than is safe for you now, Deborah. I must beg you to keep
quiet about this. Tell no one. No confiding in your sister...'

The touch of his hand conveyed urgency and something
more personal that tugged at Deb's heart. She sighed. 'I
suppose I cannot speak to anyone.'

'Please,' Richard said, and Deb heard the insistent note
in his voice. 'Be careful, Deborah. With good fortune we
may trap this person soon, but in the mean time I must ask
you to be on your guard.'

Deb nodded. 'I understand.'

'I am not sure that you do,' Richard said, an edge to his
voice now. 'Whoever has lost this book will know that one
of the other members of the group must have it. You are all
in danger now and I do not want anything to happen to
you.'

Their gazes locked and all manner of unspoken feeling
passed between them. There was a moment of absolute still-
ness and then Richard pulled Deb close and lowered his
head to hers.

A quiver went through Deb. The kiss was soft and deliberate, but almost before it had started Richard was drawing
back and leaving her with an ache of disappointment. She
opened her eyes reluctantly and knew that he must be able
to see the longing clear in her face and know what she
wanted. His expression changed as he looked down at her.
Deb had time only to draw a quick breath before he pulled
her back into his arms and his mouth settled hard on hers
this time. His tongue coaxed her lips apart and slid deep.

This time the kiss was long and sweet and lingering. It
left Deb trembling all the way down to her toes. She clung
to Richard and responded to him with untutored passion and
he held her and kissed her back with a will and finally, when

they were both panting and breathless, he pressed his lips to her hair and stilled her shaking body against his.

'Deborah…' His voice was rough, but it held an undertone of laughter. 'I cannot quite believe how we have come to this, but we are in your shrubbery and up in the house you have a very proper lady's companion—'

'Mmm…' Deb rubbed a cheek against the smooth material of his jacket. She was glad of the strength of his arms about her for she felt distinctly light-headed.

'And you are late for your appointment to drive with Mr Lang—' Richard continued.

Reality returned. Deb's eyes flew open. 'Mr Lang! I forgot all about him.'

'Good,' Richard said, and Deb could hear the raw masculine satisfaction in his voice. She eased away from him and looked into his face a little uncertainly, suddenly recalled to where she was and what she had been doing. How was it possible to forget herself so completely in Lord Richard Kestrel's arms? His touch filled her with the most exquisite longing to take and hold and be possessed by a passion so fierce that she had never dreamed it could exist. She felt torn. Long-repressed desire—feelings that she had forbidden herself for so long—were threatening to triumph over rational thought and sweep her away. Another tremor shook her and she took a step back, pressing both hands to her cheeks in embarrassment.

'You make me forget propriety,' she said. 'I must go in…'

'Of course,' Richard said gravely. He took her hand away from her face and pressed a kiss on the back. 'Deborah,' he said. 'I shall call on you soon…' He sketched a bow and released her hand reluctantly, and when he reached the bend where the path was lost from sight, he turned and looked back at her and Deb's heart leapt to see the expression on his face. And then he was gone.

When Richard reached Kestrel Court there was an unexpected level of activity about the place. Servants were unloading baggage from a coach that was drawn up on the gravel sweep before the house, and from the direction of the stables Richard could hear upraised voices and the sound of laughter. He quickened his step and rounded the corner into the yard. His elder brother Justin, Duke of Kestrel, was standing there chatting to the grooms and holding the reins of a prime piece of horseflesh, a raking chestnut hunter that was showing its teeth and looked as though it possessed a thoroughly bad temper. Richard walked round the beast and gave a low whistle.

'What do you think?' Justin asked, grinning.

'What you gain in speed and stamina you lose in temperament,' Richard said.

Justin looked resigned. 'That's exactly what Hobbs said.' He gestured to the head groom. 'Told me I'd bought a pig in a poke.'

'I assume you rode him from London?'

Justin nodded, handed the chestnut's reins over to the groom and fell into step with his brother. 'Bought him at Tattersalls on Thursday and rode up to Chelmsford yesterday and on up here today.'

'How did he handle?' Richard asked.

'Like he wanted to break my neck,' Justin said ruefully.

They went across the gravel, where the coach was still disgorging huge amounts of luggage, and in at the front door.

'You travel with more of an entourage than Mama,' Richard said. He stopped dead and looked at his brother. 'Oh lord, don't tell me this *is* Mama's baggage?'

'Just the advance guard,' Justin said. 'Mama plans to spend the winter here and wishes to do so in comfort.'

Richard groaned. 'But it is barely October! Are we to see cartloads of luggage arriving by the week?'

'I imagine so,' Justin said.

Richard groaned again. 'Whatever has prompted her to come to Midwinter? I thought she detested the place as a little provincial backwater.'

'She heard that Cory Newlyn had found himself a bride here,' Justin said with an expressive lift of the brows, 'so now she thinks to find one for each of us.'

Richard shot him a look and pushed open the door of the study. 'You had better be careful then, Justin.'

Justin closed the door behind them and threw himself down in one of the *fauteuils*.

'Not me, old fellow!' he said. 'Thought you might appreciate the help, though. You seem to be making a bit of a ham fist of it yourself. How is the divine Mrs Stratton, by the way?'

'Divine,' Richard said, trying and failing to repress a smile. 'I was with her just now.'

Justin laughed. 'And you are totally *épris* again?'

'Not again,' Richard corrected. 'I never stopped.'

Justin grinned unsympathetically. 'How very frustrating for you.' He gave his brother a sly look. 'So Mrs Stratton is still the epitome of virtue?'

'Mind your own damned business,' Richard said. He was astonished how protective he felt towards Deborah.

Justin's grin deepened. 'It must be serious if you are refusing to talk about it.' He flicked the three-day-old copy of the *Suffolk Chronicle* that was resting on the table. 'Plus you are reading the local papers,' he observed. 'Next thing you'll be telling me you have taken up tea drinking.'

'Splendid idea,' Richard said, reaching for the bell. 'You'll take some?'

Justin looked scandalised. 'No, thank you. What happened to my fine French brandy? Have you drunk it all?'

Richard nodded towards the decanter. 'Help yourself.' He put a hand in his jacket pocket. 'Take a look at this, Justin.'

He tossed the sheet of code down on the table between them. Justin glanced at it casually, looked again and drew his breath in with a soundless whistle. He looked at Richard, his dark eyes alight.

'At last! Where did you find it?'

Richard laughed. 'In Mrs Stratton's copy of the seventeenth-century poets.'

Justin frowned, opened his mouth to speak and closed it again. 'Explain,' he said economically.

Half an hour and two glasses of brandy later, they had talked the matter through.

'So the spy is using a pictorial code,' Justin said thoughtfully, 'where the symbols represent groups of words rather than letters, you think?'

Richard nodded. 'I think it would be good to ask Cory to take a look at this. He has done a lot of work with Thomas Young on hieroglyphs. He may have some useful ideas about breaking pictorial codes.'

Justin nodded. 'We should send it directly.' He swung the brandy glass gently between his fingers. 'As for the members of Lady Sally's reading group... I cannot believe it, but we are no further forward in finding the spy.'

'No, but our field of suspects has narrowed,' Richard said.

'Only if one discounts Mrs Stratton.' Justin hesitated, then took a deep breath. 'She could be playing you for a fool, Richard. You are scarcely impartial in this.'

There was a moment of tension and then the lines of Richard's body relaxed. 'She could. But she is not.'

Justin did not say anything; he merely looked a question.

After a moment Richard said slowly, 'Mrs Stratton is transparent as water, Justin. She finds it impossible to dissemble. She would have to be a damnably good actress to carry this deception through. I am certain that neither Mrs Stratton nor Lady Marney is the one we seek.'

Justin nodded slowly. 'Miss Lang?'

'The least likely option of the three remaining. I cannot believe she has the coolness or the intellect to carry it off.'

'So it is Lady Sally Saltire or Lady Benedict.' Justin looked thoughtful. 'What do we do?'

'Watch them.'

Justin gave him a crooked grin. 'I infer that you have been watching Mrs Stratton a little too much, Richard?'

'A great deal too much.' Richard laughed. 'So I leave Lady Sally and Lady Benedict to you.'

Justin sighed heavily. 'Leaving you free to pursue your interest in Mrs Stratton, I suppose.'

'Precisely.'

Richard went over to the desk, drew the inkpot towards him and started to pen a quick note to Cory Newlyn. Justin got up and sauntered over to the door. 'Mama always hoped that Papa's example of faithlessness would lead her sons in the opposite direction and breed uxorious men,' he said. 'She will be glad that one of us at least will not disappoint.'

Richard laughed. 'Fate has a manner of thwarting our plans, Justin,' he said. 'Unless I can find a way to convince Mrs Stratton of my good intentions, she will never trust me enough to marry me. As for you and Lucas…' He shook his head. 'Parson's mousetrap will catch you in the end.'

Justin took a guinea from his pocket and tossed it idly in his hand. 'Care to wager on that, Richard?'

'No,' Richard said, bending his head over the letter once again. 'I never wager on a certainty.'

# Chapter Nine

Olivia Marney was lying in her bed, eyes wide open, staring at the ceiling. The design of her bedroom had been a particular triumph for Olivia, who had taken the floral theme she loved so much and transformed her house into an extension of her garden. The domed starfish ceiling was patterned with trelliswork in delicate green and floral sprays of pale rose, and there were flower stands and brackets attached to the wall, from which cascaded a riot of ivies and miniature, scented limes. There were mirrors inset in the walls and the morning light was soft and ethereal. It was by that pale light that Olivia had noticed the finest of cracks in the bedroom ceiling, cracks which probably no one else would ever see but which quite spoiled her enjoyment of her pastoral surroundings. She would have to do something about the plaster. Perhaps it was the exceptionally dry summer that had made it fracture into a spider's web of fine lines. She would need to send to London for a plasterer of sufficient skill to make the repairs. The last time she had tried to use a local craftsman, the fool had completely filled in an alcove that she had intended for a cinerary urn…

She became aware somewhat belatedly that something had changed. It took her several seconds to work out what had happened and then she realised that Ross was not moving any longer. In fact, he was propped on one elbow above her, his cynical blue gaze scanning her face.

'Would you care for me to hand you a magazine?' he said. 'That might help you to pass the time.'

He did not wait for any reply, but swung himself off the bed and reached for his dressing-robe. Olivia averted her gaze from his hard, well-muscled body. She could not remember a time when she had permitted herself to look openly on Ross's nakedness.

'Naked men look *so* untidy,' she remembered her mother, Lady Walton, saying to her on her wedding night. 'It is best to lie back, close one's eyes and think about something pleasant. The menus for the week, perhaps, or what one might wear for church on Sunday. You will find that your husband will soon finish and you will have the added benefit of having planned the food for an entire seven days.'

Olivia had often reflected that Lady Walton's words had been all too true. With Ross, the moment had passed all too quickly. They had been virtual strangers when they had married, in a match that was a long-standing arrangement between their two families. Olivia had wanted to please her parents and had not objected to Ross as a husband. He seemed kind enough and she knew, in the instinctive way that one did, that he admired her. She was pretty and obedient; she thought that she should have been the ideal wife. It therefore caused her great pain when she realised that Ross found her lacking in some way. He almost seemed bored with her. And she, in turn, could not reach him. There was a part of him that had been locked away since she had first known him; the part that had gone to sea at fifteen and had seen naval action around the world, had fought and suffered and inflicted suffering on others. Ross never spoke of his experiences of war. It was other people who told her that he had been a hero.

They had fashioned a compromise in their marriage over the past six years, but occasionally that compromise was upset, as it had been when Ross had overheard her speaking to Deborah the previous week. She had known then that he would come to her and make love to her, almost as though he had something still to prove. Almost as though he still cared. And now he *had* come to her and she had been thinking about decorating the ceiling... If only she could be more like Deb—more open, more spontaneous, more capable of saying how she felt...

Olivia swallowed a sharp lump in her throat. Ross had his back to her as he tied the sash of his robe, but she could see his reflection in one of the inset mirrors. He was tanned from all the time that he spent outdoors, and his thick black hair tumbled across his forehead. There was a heavy frown on his brow. He looked up abruptly and his narrowed blue eyes met Olivia's in the mirror. She hastily covered herself with the tumbled bedclothes and saw a parody of a smile touch Ross's firm mouth.

He turned towards her and his gaze swept comprehensively over her as she huddled beneath the coverlet.

'Do not worry, my dear,' he said. 'There is no enjoyment to be had from making love to a piece of statuary. I shall never trouble you again.'

He went through the painted door into his dressing room and closed it with studied quiet. Olivia's bedroom resumed its bucolic peace. For a long moment she stared at her reflection in the mirror—the tumbled fair hair about her shoulders, the thin pale face that looked so bereft, the slender body that *should* still be desirable to her husband. She felt dreadfully lonely.

Rolling over, she rang the bell beside the bed to summon

her maid. Her mind seemed strangely blank, but she was
aware that if she did not get up and do something, she would
probably cry. So she would go out. She would go out and
see Deborah and her sister's irrepressible spirits would cheer
her. It was no great matter if she was not on intimate terms
with her husband. Most people rubbed along together tol-
erably well without being madly in love. A sob caught in
her throat and she gulped, taking a deep breath as the maid
came in, and turning a smiling face in her direction.

'Jenny, is it not a beautiful day? I shall go out to see my
sister at Mallow. She is in need of some advice on her
garden. I fear it is in a sad state of decay, but then Deb only
ever wanted those plants that would flower immediately...'

And chattering inconsequentially, she made her toilette
and shut out the knowledge in the maid's eyes that said that
she and the entire household knew that Lord and Lady Marney were estranged and that Lord Marney would shortly be
seeking consolation elsewhere.

Deb was trying to write a letter that morning. It was a
strange business, but she had found that since she had spent
more time in Lord Richard Kestrel's company, she seemed
to have even less inclination to hire herself a temporary
fiancé. It was odd, and she could see no direct connection
between the two facts, but it was undeniable. To become
betrothed, no matter how briefly, no matter how practically,
seemed some sort of betrayal of her feelings. She was out
of all patience with herself.

She sighed and re-read the missive.

*Dear Lord Scandal, I need to be certain that you are a
man of honour before I agree to a meeting. Though I have
adopted so strange a mode of proceeding, I mean to be
cautious in my choice. I confess that I am undecided. I shall*

*write again to you shortly, and if you are still interested in
rendering me assistance, perhaps we may meet...*

Deb sighed and crumpled up the paper, throwing it inaccurately in the direction of the fire grate. It was her fifth
attempt and it still was not quite right. The first had been
too coy, the second too vague, the third too bold. She had
had no idea that this business of advertising for a fiancé
would be quite so difficult, nor that she would be so short
of choice. She had visited the Bell and Steelyard Inn again
the previous day and there were still no more replies to her
advertisement. It seemed inexplicable.

Deb paused at the sound of a step in the corridor outside,
for she had not told Mrs Aintree that she was pressing ahead
with her plan. She felt a little ashamed of this, but she had
lain awake for a long time into the night whilst she puzzled
the whole matter out. She could find a fiancé or she could
confess all to her father and accept his reproaches as her
due. If it would end there, then perhaps she might have
taken it on the chin. But it did not. Lord Walton was of
choleric disposition and Deb knew that once he was aware
that she had no matrimonial plans, he would compel her to
return to live in Bath. If she refused, he would cut off her
allowance. There would be no discussion.

Deb rested the quill pen on the inkpot and pushed the
paper away from her. After three years away it would be
impossible to go back and to live at her parental home. It
had been bad enough before she had run away with Neil.
The atmosphere there had been stifling. Her father had ruled
with a rod of iron and her mother had practically pushed
her into the lap of any eligible man who passed by. So,
before her parents tried to marry her off again, she had to
find her own fiancé.

*Dear Lord Scandal, you simply must help me. I have told
my father that I am engaged to be married, but unfortu-*

*nately this is not the case. I do not have a betrothed and
most earnestly seek a gentleman who can fulfil the duties of
a fiancé during the period of my brother's wedding. This is
crucial to me if I am to avoid the ignominy of being dragged
home to live with my parents again…*

Deb ran a hand through her disordered honey-coloured
curls. She could not help but wonder what Lord Richard
Kestrel would make of her attempts to hire herself a fiancé.
Although it was the merest business arrangement, she felt
the same wave of disloyalty sweep over her again. She
groaned. This was ridiculous since she owed Lord Richard
no loyalty at all. For all her affinity with him, she did not
know whether he was trifling with her or not, although her
blood burned to believe him faithful.

Both reason and observation were against Lord Richard
Kestrel. Deb had heard of his conquests and seen him flirt
with a great many ladies. For all his fine words, she suspected that he had tried to fix her interest in order to discover more about the Midwinter spy. All in all, he was not
to be trusted, no matter what her instincts told her. And he
was not a marrying man. Since Deb considered herself not
to be a marrying woman, this should not have mattered, and
yet, unaccountably, it did. Her feelings had been made
starkly plain on the subject when Lily Benedict had cornered
her at Lady Sally's soirée a few days before and helpfully
whispered that *did she know* that Lord Richard Kestrel had
once been engaged to a lady who had found him in the arms
of a Cyprian on the night of their betrothal ball…

'Malicious cat!' Deb said now, aloud. Even so, she knew
that Lord Richard was a man one might flirt with or even
take as a lover, but that marriage would be out of the question. And she told herself that she had no desire to enter
that state again after her experience with Neil. She knew
exactly how unfaithful, unreliable and downright cruel a

man could be and she would not put herself in that position again.

She was about to pick up her quill with renewed energy to frame her letter to Lord Scandal when there was a commotion in the corridor outside and Olivia erupted into the room. Her face was flushed pink, her eyes bright, her hat tilted askew on her flyaway curls. For a moment it was almost like looking at a mirror image of Deb herself. Deb got up, smiling, and then she saw the expression in her sister's eyes and her smile turned to a frown of concern as her insides turned to ice. Something was dreadfully wrong.

'Liv?' she said. 'What has happened? What's the matter?'

And then Olivia did something that Deb had never seen her do in her entire life. She burst into tears.

'I am sorry, I am so very sorry…' It was ten minutes later and Olivia was finally able to speak again, although not in any coherent way. Her words were making no sense to Deborah at all.

'I cannot help it. I cannot stop crying!' Olivia gulped. 'Oh, Deb, you would not believe what has happened this morning…I simply *have* to tell someone. I cannot bear it any longer!'

She stopped and looked at Deb with tear-drenched eyes, as though daring her sister to contradict her. Deb waited. Olivia took a deep breath.

'Ross was making love to me,' she said. 'Ross was making love to me and I was thinking about decorating the ceiling. The ceiling, Deb! I was entirely engrossed. So Ross stopped and looked at me and I realised what had happened and how angry he was, and I felt ill—quite *sick* with fear and misery—and Ross stormed off and I believe this is the end for us, the absolute end, Deb—'

'Wait!' Deb besought. She noticed that Olivia's nose was

running, so she rummaged around in her sleeve but could not find a handkerchief. Instead she was obliged to give her sister the small cambric cloth from the table instead. Olivia blew her nose heartily and did not even notice the unorthodox nature of the handkerchief.

'Wait,' Deb said again, as her sister dabbed at her reddened eyes and seemed about to burst into renewed speech. 'Give yourself time to draw breath.'

Olivia sighed and Deb looked at her curiously. She was very shocked by Olivia's outburst, for she would never have believed her sister capable of such strong feeling. She was also fascinated to see that Olivia did not cry in a pretty way at all. Somehow she had expected her sister to look pale and interesting with tear-wet eyes. Instead, Olivia's nose had turned red and appeared twice its normal size. Deb felt a great rush of affection for her. She slid along the sofa and put an arm around her.

'Now then, Olivia,' she said calmly, 'I am afraid that you will have to explain yourself more clearly. What it all this about Ross and the ceiling?'

'I told you,' Olivia sniffed. 'Ross was making love to me and I was not paying attention.'

'You mean actually making love, or…?' Deb waved her hands about vaguely.

Olivia looked irritated. 'Actually making love as opposed to—what, Deb?'

'As opposed to kissing, or…' Deb shrugged, trying to look knowledgeable. She hoped that her exceptionally limited knowledge of the ways of the world would not let her down here.

'Yes,' Olivia sounded ruffled. '*Making love*, Deb! Please do not interrupt me again!'

'I am sorry,' Deb said. 'Do go on.'

'Whilst Ross was busy, I was lying there, gazing at the

ceiling,' Olivia said, clearly unable to stop talking even had she wanted to do so, 'and I noticed a hairline crack in the trellis work painted above the bed, so I started to plan how I might have it mended…'

'Oh, dear,' Deb said.

Her sister cast her a sideways look. 'Indeed. So I was intending to call a decorator from London, and really I was quite carried away by my plans, and after a little while I suddenly returned to the present and realised that Ross had paused in what he was doing—'

'How long?' Deb asked.

'I beg your pardon?' Olivia wrinkled up her reddened nose.

'How long do you think your mind was on other matters?'

'Ten minutes?' Olivia guessed. 'Perhaps fifteen?' Her voice faded. She looked stricken. 'I cannot be certain. Once Ross starts, you see, he can sometimes go on for quite a while because he likes to—'

'Please do not tell me the intimate details!' Deb spoke hastily. 'I would never be able to look Ross in the eye again.'

Olivia gave a watery giggle. 'No, I suppose you would not. Oh, dear, I am being very indiscreet. I do not seem to be able to help myself!'

'Never mind that,' Deb said. 'You have been discreet enough in the past six years. I expect it will do you good to be indiscreet for a change.' She frowned. 'Olivia, there is something I must ask. When Ross makes love to you, do you not join in at all?'

Now it was Olivia's turn to frown. She looked at Deb in a puzzled way. Deb looked back.

After a moment Olivia said uncertainly, 'Mama never said anything about joining in. Is one supposed to?'

Deb's frown deepened still further. She fidgeted and

avoided her sister's bewildered gaze. 'I think one is. I mean, I do not know. I thought that *you* would know…'

'I don't know,' Olivia said, her forehead wrinkling. 'I do not know anything about the way one is supposed to behave in the marriage bed. That is what I have been telling you, Deb. I feel completely stupid.'

They looked at each other again and then Olivia clapped a hand to her mouth. Above it, her eyes were very bright but with laughter this time, not tears.

'Oh, how funny! I cannot believe that we are both so utterly without a clue…'

'At least you had the benefit of Mama's talk about the duties of a wife,' Deb pointed out. 'I never had that. I ran away and so she did not have time to warn me about what to expect.'

'Mama never said anything about participating,' Olivia said, torn between incomprehension and laughter. 'It was all about gowns and menus—'

'*Menus?*' Deb stared. 'How on earth could that possibly be relevant?'

Olivia smothered another snort of amusement. 'That was Mama's suggestion of a topic to think about whilst your husband was busy. The only other mention she made was of how untidy naked men look…' She gave an unladylike guffaw. 'Which they do, of course, all dangling bits and—'

'Liv!' Deb blushed scarlet. She put both hands over her ears. 'Oh! You are shocking me!'

'Isn't it splendid?' Olivia said, giggling. 'Do you want to hear what happened after I realised that Ross had stopped?'

'No!' Deb shrieked.

'Well, I shall tell you anyway! We looked at one another and then Ross offered to find me a magazine to help pass the time!'

Deb could not help herself. Her natural curiosity overcame her scruples. 'Was he still…I mean, were you still… conjoined at this point?'

'Yes!' Olivia shrieked with laughter. 'But after that he dwindled away…'

Deb could not help but give a snort of laughter herself and, once she had started, she could not stop. The sisters fell into each other's arms, still laughing uproariously, and hugged each other hard.

'I was so upset!' Olivia gasped, between huge guffaws. 'And now I find it so terribly amusing! Is it not strange…?'

There was gentle tap at the door. The sisters fell apart, Deb pressing a hand to her side. 'Oh! Do not make me laugh any more. It hurts!'

Clarissa Aintree put her head around the door with an enquiring look. 'Is everything quite all right, girls?'

'Oh, yes thank you, Clarrie!' Olivia said, gulping. 'Everything is very fine! Would you care to join us for tea?'

'I would not dream of intruding,' Mrs Aintree said, her blue eyes twinkling, 'but I will send in a pot.'

She closed the door softly behind her. Olivia wiped her eyes on the tablecloth and looked at Deb. She sobered slightly.

'I am sorry, Deb,' she said, 'That was very funny and you have made me feel much better, but it was monstrous thoughtless of me to raise this subject with you. Forgive me?'

Deb shook her head slightly. 'There is nothing to forgive,' she said, but she knew her face betrayed her.

Now that her hysterics had subsided, the familiar mix of blame and misery returned like a shadow to her mind. Mrs Deborah Stratton… She had no real claim to the name, nor to the status that her supposed widowhood gave her. She had never been properly married.

She knew why Olivia felt guilty. Her sister had assumed

that she would understand about her difficulties in the marriage bed and Deb *did* and that was the precise problem. Very few people knew that Neil Stratton had already been married when he had eloped with Lord Walton's younger daughter. With good fortune, no one would ever find out. And yet Deb felt haunted by the truth and even more troubled by her seduction at the hands of so skilled and callous a man.

It had been Olivia who, in the painful weeks after Deb had discovered herself betrayed, had pointed out to her gently and beautifully that Deb should never consider herself dishonoured because she had given herself to Neil in good faith, thinking him her husband. Deb had wept for days, knowing that Olivia spoke a logical truth, but also knowing that it made no difference to her feelings. She blamed herself. If only she had not been so impetuous, so quick to be persuaded into an elopement, so foolish in thinking that what she was doing was romantic... It had never crossed her mind that Neil might be a fortune hunter intent on catching a larger dowry than the one he had originally married. She had aided her own downfall by playing into his hands and, if anyone ever discovered the truth, she would be ruined.

She had not been married to Neil Stratton when she had made love with him, even though she had thought herself to be his true wife at the time. It was only after his death that Deb had discovered about Neil's wife and child, and she was left feeling used and tainted, both by her faith in his love for her and by his casual taking of her body. She could not see how she could ever conquer the feeling of dishonour. She could not see how she could ever trust a man again.

Olivia was watching her and put out a sympathetic hand. 'Oh, Deb, I am sorry...'

'Do not be.' Deb gave her sister a quick smile. 'It was a long time ago. These days, I scarce think on it. And at least I know that *you* understand why I could not contemplate marriage, no matter how Papa presses me…'

Olivia looked stubborn. 'With someone else it might be different.'

Deb shook her head. 'No, no marriage.' She cleared her throat, anxious to push her worries back into the dark corner where they belonged. 'I thought we were talking about you, Liv, not about my difficulties in that respect.'

'I think that we have done quite enough talking on that subject,' Olivia said, trying to regain her previous composure. 'It is not in the least genteel of me to divulge so much intimate detail. I cannot think what possessed me.'

'Yes,' Deb said, 'but since you have done, what is to be done about Ross, Liv? You cannot carry on like this.'

Olivia blushed slightly. 'No, we cannot. I suppose that I must talk to Ross and try to build up some sort of understanding with him. And next time that he comes to my room I will try to…to join in…'

'Do you want to?'

Olivia blushed harder. 'I can try. It might be quite nice.' She looked up at Deb, a smile still lurking in her eyes. 'I do not wish to spend the rest of my married life in a passionless desert,' she said. 'And after all, Ross is quite an attractive man.'

'He is prodigiously attractive,' Deb said drily.

'Yes. And I would not wish someone else to think so and offer to console him. It is not that I dislike him, Deb.' Olivia frowned. 'It seems that there is a huge gulf between us that we do not understand how to bridge. The only problem is that Ross swore he would not trouble me again.'

There was a pause whilst the maid bustled in with tea, but once the door was closed again, Deb jumped to her feet.

'If you truly wish to attract Ross, then I have just the thing for you,' she said. 'I received a letter from Rachel Newlyn this morning—'

Olivia's face lit up. 'Oh, how is she?'

'Very well,' Deb said. She gave Olivia a dry look. 'I think that she may be enjoying married life rather more than you or I did!'

Olivia giggled. 'Would you not, with Cory Newlyn? He is devastatingly attractive…' Olivia waved her hands around descriptively.

'I know,' Deb said meaningfully.

She passed her sister the letter and went across to the desk in the corner on the room. Rachel's parcel was still there, where Deb had unwrapped and left it earlier in the morning.

Olivia read aloud: 'I am sending a pot of balm for Lord Marney's collection of rare breeds, for I hear from your sister that the pigs have a skin complaint—'

'No, not that bit,' Deb said hastily as Olivia gave her a curious look. 'The next paragraph.'

'I am also sending a pot of my own rose-scented face cream, made from a recipe discovered by Mama in an ancient Egyptian text. It is certainly extremely good for the complexion, but I have to counsel you not to use it unless you wish to attract a great deal of masculine attention!' She paused and raised her eyebrows.

'Read on,' Deb said, laughing.

'It contains a special ingredient that the Egyptians swore was an aphrodisiac—*oh, my!*—so I am warning you to use it sparingly, unless you wish to bewitch Lord Richard—'

'Quite so!' Deb said, snatching the letter. She had forgotten the last bit and felt herself colouring up. 'So if you wish to borrow it—'

'Not so fast,' Olivia said, laughing at her sister. 'Are you sure that you do not wish to use it yourself?'

'For what purpose?'

'To attract Lord Richard Kestrel,' Olivia said. She eyed Deb with amusement. 'On reflection, however, I do not believe that you require any artificial assistance in that task, not when you appeared out of the conservatory at the ball looking as though you had been thoroughly kissed!'

Deb smiled reluctantly. 'Actually, that was the one occasion on which Lord Richard did not kiss me!'

Olivia opened her eyes very wide. 'The one occasion he did *not*? You mean on every other occasion—'

'Almost,' Deb said.

'When he escorted you back from Marney a few days ago?'

'Yes.'

'And before that—at the musicale?'

'Yes.'

'And in the wood—'

'Yes, but you knew about that already. I mentioned it to you myself that afternoon we took tea.'

Olivia looked riveted. 'And?'

Deb shrugged a little awkwardly. 'I do not know, Liv.' She frowned and smiled simultaneously. 'It is quite absurd, but I find that I like him...I cannot seem to help myself.'

'It was bound to happen sooner or later,' Olivia said gently, 'and Lord Richard is very likeable.'

'Yes, but...' Deb gave her sister a guilty, sideways look. 'I have been thinking of him a great deal, Liv. I do not understand myself. On the one hand I feel I simply have to avoid him, and on the other I would like... Well, you know what I would like! It is the most appalling and wanton thing. I cannot trust a man, I have no desire for marriage and yet

I long for the fulfilment of a physical relationship. I am quite shocked at myself.'

There was an unhappy silence.

'It is most understandable,' Olivia said, after a moment. She patted her sister's hand. 'Do not be so hard on yourself, Deb. You have been cheated of every natural emotion and every good experience that you might have expected to find in marriage. Yet you are young and full of life, and you feel things passionately. You are starving yourself of love…'

'I know,' Deb said shakily. She got up and walked over to the window. The tears blurred her eyes and thickened her throat.

'There was no tenderness in your relationship with Neil,' Olivia said, after a moment, 'and since then you have been the very pattern-card of respectable widowhood. It is only natural that you feel the way that you do. Do not reproach yourself for it.'

'Almost you convince me,' Deb said unhappily. 'But why have I fixed upon Lord Richard? I have a lowering feeling that it is simply because he is there.'

Olivia looked at her for a long moment and then she shook her head. 'No, Deb. You do not believe that. Do not demean your feelings like this. If you were only looking for an *affaire*, then you might have chosen any of the personable gentlemen who have been in Midwinter this year past. Sir John Norton, for example—'

Deb shuddered. 'Never!'

'Exactly. Whereas you have known Richard Kestrel for several years and, despite your protestations, are most attracted to him. There is an affinity between you whether you like it or not.'

Deb shook her head. 'It is an affinity that can come to nothing. I cannot compound my previous folly by entering into a relationship like this with my eyes open. What, am I to indulge in not one but two relationships outside the bond of marriage? I should be nothing but a wanton!'

'It is not like that,' Olivia said, 'and you know it. Neil—'

'Oh, very well, I acknowledge that I was tricked by Neil!' Deb raised her hands in a vehement gesture. 'The fact remains, Olivia, that I have never been truly married and yet I have given myself to one man and I *will not* compromise my own honour by giving myself to another. I cannot!'

Deb realised that she was shaking, and when Olivia came across to her and put her arms about her she allowed her sister to hold her like she had done when they were children comforting each other.

'I am sorry,' Olivia said, after a moment. 'It was wrong of me to offer advice. You must do what you believe is right.' She laughed a little bitterly. 'Hark at me! And I am the one reaching for the *Ladies Magazine* when my husband makes love to me! It is always easier to give guidance than to take it.'

Deb laughed too. She went over to the desk and pushed the pot of hand cream towards Olivia. 'At least one of us may yet get this right. So take this with my blessing, Liv. I wish you luck.'

'What about the ointment for Ross's pigs?' Olivia asked, tucking the pot of face cream in her reticule.

'Oh, yes!' Deb jumped up and hurried over to the window seat, where she had left the rest of Rachel's parcel half-unpacked. 'Here you are!'

Olivia took the second pot and pressed a kiss on her sister's cheek. 'Thank you,' she said softly. She paused in the doorway. 'If you do decide to act on your feelings, Deb, then I wish you every happiness.'

After Olivia had gone, Deb went across to the grate and removed one of the scrunched up pieces of paper. Sitting at her desk, she rested her chin on her hand and bit the end of the quill pen. Forget Richard Kestrel, she instructed herself sharply. Her task was to find a discreet and reliable gentleman to be her fiancé, not a disreputable knave to be her lover, no matter how her body ached for him. She tried to concentrate.

*Dear Lord Scandal…*

She put the pen down again. Damnation, Deb thought, as well ask a rake to be her fiancé as a man with such an alias.

*Dear Lord Scandal, are you a trustworthy and honourable gentleman? I suspect not, with a name like yours. However, my need for assistance is acute. I should therefore deem it a kindness on your part if you were prepared for us to meet…*

A day later, Lord Richard Kestrel pocketed the letter that was waiting for him under the alias of Lord Scandal at the Bell and Steelyard Inn, and passed two guineas to the innkeeper, one for the safe delivery and the other for the suppression of all the other missives addressed to Lady Incognita. He went out and climbed straight back into his carriage, waiting until the vehicle was on the move before he broke the seal. Resting one elbow against the window, he perused the contents. An appreciative smile touched his mouth. Lady Incognita certainly had a way with words. And she wanted to meet him. Sensibly, she had chosen a public place for their tryst, but one that gave them the opportunity to be alone if they wished to talk in private. He wondered whether she would bring a chaperon to meet him. He tried to imagine the look on the chaperon's face, and on Deb's face, when they saw him.

The assignation was arranged for the following day. He would certainly be there. In fact, he could barely master his impatience.

# Chapter Ten

Deb had arranged to meet Lord Scandal at the Customs House in Woodbridge that Wednesday afternoon. She had read in the paper that there would be an auction of smuggled goods held that day and it had struck her that the sale would provide the perfect circumstance for an assignation. There would be a great many people about, thereby providing security, yet once the initial contact was made it would be possible for her to step aside with Lord Scandal if she wished.

She had also taken the additional precaution of asking Ross to escort her to the sale so that she should not be alone when the contact was made. There was, however, one small difficulty. She had not told Ross the true purpose of their errand to Woodbridge for she had known that he would cut up rough about it. Now, however, they were approaching the rendezvous and she realised that the moment of truth had come.

'Ross,' she said, as her brother-in-law held open the Customs House door for her, 'there is something that I should tell you.' She hesitated, for Ross did not look very receptive. A black frown had settled on his forehead and he waited for her to continue with weary patience. Deb took the plunge. 'You see, I particularly needed your escort today as I am meeting a gentleman here and I—' She broke off as someone hushed her from inside the auction room. 'I need to be sure that he is reliable…'

Deb slid into one of the seats at the back of the hall and pulled Ross down beside her.

The auction was in full swing, but the room was only half-full. The sale of items taken by the revenue usually drew quite a crowd, but seizure of smuggled goods had been light recently and there was no brandy on sale today so none of the town's publicans had turned out. At the front of the hall sat the usual bunch of gawpers who always attended an auction but never bought anything. Further back sat a sprinkling of Woodbridge citizens including Mr Rumbold, who was a collector of items such as snuffboxes and jewellery.

Ross's frown had not lightened whilst he waited for Deb to explain herself further. Now he started to whisper crossly in her ear.

'Do I understand you to be saying that you have made an assignation with a gentleman, Deborah?'

'Yes!' Deb whispered back. 'And just in case he is not trustworthy, I need you here to protect me—'

Ross muttered some imprecation, fortunately under his breath. 'You mean that you have arranged to meet a stranger? What the devil are you about, Deborah?'

'It is not as it seems,' Deb hissed back. 'Allow me to explain.'

'By all means,' Ross said, scowling.

The auctioneer pointed his gavel at them. 'Sold to the gentleman!'

'Now you have cost me five guineas,' Ross complained, 'and gained me a set of engraved glasses that I did not want.'

'Oh, stop complaining,' Deb grumbled. 'Give them to

Olivia—it would be nice for you to give her a present for once!'

She heard Ross give a bad-tempered sigh and was grateful that the progress of the auction prevented him from asking her any further questions. Explanations would simply have to wait until later. She felt a little guilty. She knew that she was taking advantage of Ross's good nature. She should have told him more of the business first, instead of springing it on him at the last moment. But if she had done that, he would have forbidden her to attend and then she would have no chance of meeting Lord Scandal…

She sat bolt upright, clutching her reticule on her lap. Seldom had she felt so apprehensive. Lord Scandal might already be in the room. The thought made her feel breathless with nerves. She had come this far in her quest for a fiancé, but now she had a very strong urge to turn tail and flee. Had it not been for Ross's reassuring if irritable presence beside her, she probably would have done so.

A hasty scan around the hall revealed that it was unlikely that Lord Scandal was already among them. The Tide Surveyor was sitting a little way away to her left, and next to him was Owen Chance, the Riding Officer whom Deb had met at Lady Sally Saltire's ball. Mr Chance saw her glance in his direction and a smile lit his eyes. He inclined his head politely. Deb smiled back, although she thought it might have come out a little lopsidedly. Her nerves were not diminishing as she made an inventory of the people in the hall. In fact, they were increasing.

There were two ladies who had come in after Deb and Ross and were now sitting whispering through the auction, the plumes in their hats nodding as they gossiped. They could be discounted. Deb's gaze moved on. The only gentleman in the room was Sir John Norton of Drybridge, who was currently bidding for another set of fine engraved wineglasses. Deb felt a clutch of horror. She hoped that Lord Scandal was not Sir John, for she did not care for him very much. How unconscionably embarrassing it would be to discover that her respondent was someone she already knew and did not like. That would be far worse than having to dismiss the application of a stranger.

The door opened behind her. Deb heard it but could not see anything, for she had just realised that she had chosen the worst possible place to sit to watch for anyone coming in. Her back was to the entrance and in order to see the door she would have to turn around and crane her neck. That would draw too much attention so she would simply have to sit tight and wait…

She tensed. There was a swirl of fresh air, a burst of sunlight, and then the door closed and the hall was quiet again, but for the drone of the auctioneer's voice as he drove the price up on a packet of Dutch mantua silk. Deb sat still as a mouse, her nerves stretched to breaking. She could hear measured footsteps coming closer. She could see nothing, but she knew that someone was standing just behind her, and suddenly, disconcertingly, she could tell who it was.

The air stirred and then a voice she recognised very well said softly in her ear, 'Lady Incognita, I presume? And with a stalwart chaperon! How do you do, ma'am? Shall we step outside and talk?'

Deb was mortified. She sat on the bench outside the Customs House and watched Ross and Richard Kestrel as they talked. They were some distance away, but she could follow the conversation fairly well by watching her brother-in-law's expression. Ross was looking furious and Deb did not really blame him. It was doubly mortifying, however, that Richard was obliged to accept the censure that should by rights be vented upon her. Now she felt even more at a disadvantage.

Deb looked out across the River Deben and wondered why on earth she had never imagined that Lord Scandal and Lord Richard Kestrel could be one and the same.

It seemed so obvious now that she knew. Mrs Aintree had commented that his letter was arrogant, just like the man himself: arrogant, authoritative under that deceptively lazy air, and given to command. Deb remembered that she had even mused at one time that they might be one and the same person, and then she had dismissed the idea because she had thought that Lord Richard would never take the local newspaper, nor answer a chance-placed advertisement...

She glanced back at the gentlemen. Whatever it was that Richard was saying to Ross was evidently quite persuasive. Deb saw Ross's forbidding expression ease slightly, saw him nod once, shake his head twice, and finally look in her direction. Richard shook hands with him and Ross, with one hard, backward glance at Deb, headed away up Quay Street. Deb took a deep breath as she watched Richard approach. Now that the moment—and Lord Scandal—was here, she did not really know what to do. She thought it best if they ended the interview as quickly as possible. Clearly it was impossible for her to appoint Lord Richard Kestrel as her temporary fiancé and the quicker the matter was settled the better.

Richard was standing before her. He took one look at her scarlet, mortified face and said, 'Shall we walk a little, Mrs Stratton? Your brother-in-law has very kindly given us a half-hour together in which to discuss this matter.'

Deb took his arm, feeling slightly dazed. 'What did you say to Ross?' she asked. 'I did not think that he would leave us alone.'

'I said very little,' Richard looked rueful. 'Since I did not wish to betray your confidence and could not be sure whether you had told him about your advertisement, I made no mention of it. Instead I merely said that you and I had a matter to discuss and asked him to grant me a little time with you.'

Deb nodded. She felt even more distressed as she realised the extent to which Richard had most chivalrously drawn Ross's fire away from her and to himself.

'Thank you,' she said.

'You are welcome.' Richard scanned her face. 'I was assuming, of course, that you still wished to speak with me. If you have changed your mind, you need only say the word. Ross has gone to the gunsmith's and we may meet him there.'

Deb hesitated. Richard waited. There was nothing in his face to sway her opinion, but even as she was poised on the edge of calling the whole thing off, she was surprised to feel a strong urge not to dismiss him. He was, after all, her only hope.

'Perhaps,' she said cautiously, 'I could decide what to do once we have spoken.'

She saw a ghost of a smile touch Richard's lips. 'Of course,' he said.

They walked a little way along the path, Richard waiting politely for her to take the initiative.

'I should have guessed it was you, I suppose,' Deb said wryly. 'I cannot imagine why I did not. Probably—' she stole a sideways look at her companion '—because I did not want to. Lord Scandal, indeed!'

Richard laughed. 'I thought it peculiarly appropriate.'

'No doubt it is. But it is not at all appropriate for the role that I had in mind.' Deb sighed. 'I knew all along that it was a poor idea, but it was the only thing that I could think to do.'

'Why do you not tell me all about it?' Richard asked encouragingly. 'Since you do not have any alternative applicants to interview, Mrs Stratton, you might as well see if I would fit the bill.'

'There is no possibility that you would be suitable—' Deb broke off, looking at him with narrowed eyes. 'Just a moment. You said that I do not have any alternative applicants. How would you know that? Did you know that I was the one who had placed the advertisement?'

Richard looked at her, brows raised quizzically. 'I confess that I did.'

'How? How could you possibly know that?'

Richard did not prevaricate. 'I met with your gardener's boy on the road, the morning that you placed your advertisement. I…happened to see the letter addressed to the *Suffolk Chronicle*, and when the advertisement came out I guessed that it was you.'

Deb regarded him stormily. Certain issues that had puzzled her were beginning to make more sense. 'Oh! I do believe that you deliberately asked Mr Strawbridge to throw away any other letters addressed to Lady Incognita!'

Richard grinned. 'You should be flattered, Mrs Stratton, that I wanted to help you so much that I was prepared to go to any lengths to do so.'

Deb gave a long, angry sigh. 'Flattered? I am no such thing. For all I know there could have been a whole host of meek and helpful gentlemen prepared to offer me their assistance—' She broke off as she heard Lord Richard's unmistakable guffaw.

'Meek and helpful?' he repeated incredulously. 'You are looking for a gentleman who is meek?'

'Yes!' Deb said, thoroughly ruffled now, 'so you may see why you do not fit the bill *at all*!'

'In that respect I should have to concur,' Richard said, 'but I am still anxious to offer you my aid, Mrs Stratton. Especially as I have denied you the chance of assistance from other gentlemen.'

Deb shook her head. She felt wretched. 'There is no point in my relating the whole story to you, Lord Richard. No point at all. It was a stupid plan and now I shall simply have to reconsider.'

They were walking slowly along the path that wended its way beside the River Deben. The breeze off the river was cool but it did nothing to calm Deborah's frantic thought processes. She could see no way out of the coil. She knew she would have to call off the plan she had made to hoodwink her father and come up with some other ideas. The only difficulty was that at present her mind was a complete blank.

'I feel very guilty for preventing you from finding your meek and…er…helpful gentleman,' Richard said presently, the quiver still in his voice. 'Are you sure that I may not help you, Mrs Stratton?'

Deb looked at him. She felt hot and frustrated—frustrated because she could see no way out of her dilemma now and hot because merely looking at Lord Richard Kestrel seemed to have that effect on her. Had she been advertising for a lover, then she might be looking at the right man. She had to remember, however, that that was not the role she wished to fill.

'No, Lord Richard,' she said, 'you may not help me. When I tell you that I was advertising for a temporary fiancé you will understand why.'

Not a muscle moved in Richard Kestrel's face. Deb had

to admire the coolness with which he took her announcement.

'You require a fiancé?' he queried.

'No,' Deb corrected, 'I require a temporary fiancé. Now you may see why you would be the very *worst* person for the role.'

'I do not see that at all.' Richard sounded quite hurt. 'Why am I not suitable?'

'Why not?' Deb looked at him closely, trying to work out if he was teasing her. The handsome face was quite impassive and she could not tell.

'Where do I begin?' She said. 'I need someone who is biddable, reliable and—'

'Meek?' The betraying quiver of humour was back in Richard's voice.

'Precisely,' Deb said. 'You, on the other hand are reckless, dangerous and a rake.'

'In your advertisement you asked for a man of honour, discretion and chivalry,' Richard pointed out.

'Yes?'

'I possess all of those qualities.'

Deb bit her lip. 'I do not believe so.' She paused, feeling that this was a little harsh. 'I suppose that you are discreet,' she allowed. 'You did not march into the Customs House and announce your business in front of everyone. And you were most chivalrous just now in drawing Ross's anger away from me.'

'Thank you,' Lord Richard said ironically. 'You do not seem so certain about my honourable qualities.'

'Your behaviour to me has been far short of honourable,' Deb pointed out. She remembered guiltily that she had entertained some decidedly dishonourable thoughts about him herself and had connived at his activities with a certain degree of enthusiasm. She did not wish to appear a hypocrite. She fidgeted.

'A rake's behaviour is by definition dishonourable,' she amended.

*'Touché,'* Richard agreed. 'It is, of course. But do you at least concede that I can behave with honour if I try?'

'I have no notion.' Deb gave a little shrug. 'I should say, if pressed, that probably you could not. However, the question does not arise since you do not fulfil my other requirements.'

'The…er…biddableness and the meekness?'

'Indeed.'

Richard squared his shoulders. 'No, I am certainly not that, and what is more, I should not even try.'

'You would not do what I told you?' Deb looked at him and decided that the question was pointless. Was this a man who would be obedient to a woman's dictates? She thought not—unless they coincided with his own.

'No, I would not do as I was told,' Richard said, confirming her thoughts.

'There, then.' Deb spread her hands. 'You are quite unsuitable to be my short-term fiancé.'

They had reached the place where the path narrowed and became a rough track leading down to Kyson Point. There was a seat in the sun, with a fine view across the river to the parish of Sutton beyond. Deb made to turn back, but Richard put out a hand to stop her.

'Perhaps you could tell me a little about why you need a fiancé in the first place,' he suggested. 'Who knows, I may at least be able to provide an alternative suggestion to solve your difficulties. May we sit? I find perambulation unsuited to serious conversation.'

Deb looked at him suspiciously. 'Are you seeking to make fun of me?'

Richard looked hurt. 'Not the least in the world! No sane person advertises for a temporary fiancé unless they have a very powerful reason to do so.' He gave her a smile. 'I can testify that you are not insane, Mrs Stratton, therefore you must have your reasons. I confess that I am keen to discover them.'

Deb frowned. On the one hand Lord Richard Kestrel was hardly the person she would have chosen as a confidante, for such a role seemed too intimate. The previous time they had met, they had exchanged confidences that had made her feel very vulnerable. To open her heart to him again was surely a mistake. But on the other hand he spoke a great deal of sense and she was in a tight corner now. If he had any proposals that might solve the problem, then she wanted to hear them. After a moment she sat down and opened her parasol to shade her both from the bright sunlight and Lord Richard's perceptive gaze. He waited patiently and after a moment Deb started her story.

'I require a temporary fiancé because I have told my father that I am engaged to be married,' she said. 'We are to return home for my brother's wedding in less than two months and Papa has commanded that I bring my betrothed with me.' She picked at the seam of her gloves. 'I am in the suds because I pretended to be engaged when I was no such thing. Papa was demanding that I return to live in Bath and I could not bear to do so—' Once she had started, she found that the whole foolish tale tumbled out. She told Richard of her father's concerns about the dangers of invasion in Suffolk, of his desire to see her living back at Walton Hall and his determination to promote the match she had rejected when she eloped with Neil Stratton. On the one hand she was mortified to be exposing her folly to Richard Kestrel, but on the other it was oddly soothing to talk to him. To her surprise, she found that he was a good listener.

He did not interrupt and only asked a few questions for clarification.

'I can perfectly comprehend,' he said as she finished. 'why you feel you cannot return to live under your parents roof after three years away. If Lord Walton plans to arrange a match—'

Deb shuddered and he broke off, covering her hand briefly with one of his. His voice had dropped. 'You would not feel able to marry your cousin Harry, I assume?'

'No,' Deb said wretchedly. She tried to keep the pain from her voice, but could not quite succeed. 'There is nothing wrong with Harry, my lord, other than the fact that we could never be happy together. I may sound selfish, but I have already made one improvident match in my life and have no wish to be miserable a second time.'

She glanced at Richard's face and saw that he was watching her with both shrewdness and sympathy, and she gave him a shamefaced smile.

'I am sorry that your first choice was so unhappy,' he said.

'I...' Deb blushed and looked away from his searching gaze. She did not feel comfortable revealing too much to him. 'I thought that I was in love with Neil,' she said, with difficulty. 'It was only on mature reflection that I realise that I had been rather hasty.'

'You were only married a short time, were you not?' Richard asked.

Deb nodded. 'We had five weeks together before he was posted abroad and he died of a fever two months later.'

'Those five weeks must have been quite dreadful to have left you with such harsh memories,' Richard said. Deb could sense his eyes upon her, but she did not look up. She could not. All her bitterness and misery had fused into a tight pain in her chest and she could not speak.

After a moment, Richard sighed and said, 'Forgive me. I realise that you do not wish to speak of it.'

Deb shook her head dumbly. She did not wish to say any more whilst her feelings were in such confusion. She knew that she could not countenance losing her relative independence by returning to Bath, and that another marriage was quite out of the question after the fiasco that had been her first. Making a business arrangement to employ a temporary fiancé had seemed a relatively safe way to thwart her father's plans and maintain her independent existence.

Yet now that had become far more complicated. The only candidate for the role of fiancé was a man to whom she was drawn by intense feelings that she did not understand and could barely accept. Until her recent wayward thoughts on the subject of taking a lover, she had imagined that she did not wish for male companionship at all. Her attraction to Richard Kestrel had given the lie to that and, though Olivia had made her see that there was nothing unnatural in such feelings, she was still on edge and uncertain what to do. To confide in him now brought a new level of intimacy to their relationship. To accept him as her fiancé, albeit temporarily, would draw them even closer.

'I am not quite sure how we came to discussing this topic,' she said, striving for an even tone. 'What I require is a fiancé acceptable to both myself and my family or—' she looked at Richard '—some other alternative. Perhaps you can help me there?'

Richard shrugged. 'I can see no alternative.' He smiled. 'Fortunately the solution is close at hand. I will be your temporary fiancé.'

Deb jumped up in agitation. 'I have already told you, my lord. It is quite impossible for you to fulfil the role!'

Richard got to his feet. 'It is not so foolish. Think for a moment, Mrs Stratton! What could be more acceptable to your family than a betrothal to man who is already an acquaintance of long standing—and a friend to your brother-in-law? It is far more credible than that you produce some stranger for approval, like a magician whipping a rabbit out of a hat. No one would be taken in by that!'

Deb bit her lip. His logic so far was faultless. 'I cannot believe that my family would approve of you,' she said slowly. 'Your reputation precedes you.'

Richard did not seem unduly perturbed. 'There is not a matchmaking mother on earth,' he said cynically, 'who cannot overlook a rake's reputation if he is rich and titled.'

Deb could not argue with that either, although she tried. 'I cannot believe that Papa would be so sanguine,' she said.

'Oh, he will,' Richard said, the cynical light still in his eyes. 'I guarantee it.'

Deb pressed the palms of her hands together. 'Then there is Liv and Ross. They would never believe that ours was a genuine betrothal. I have told Liv—' She broke off, biting her lip. She could hardly repeat to him the conversation that she had had with her sister.

*'I told Olivia that I wanted to take you as a lover not a husband'* would start them on an entirely different conversation, and one that would be even more perilous. Which was what made it madness even to consider Lord Richard Kestrel in the role of her fiancé. She was already far too susceptible to his charms as it was.

Richard took her hand. He smiled a little. 'You have told your sister that you think me a reprobate and want nothing to do with me?'

Deb blushed. 'Not precisely, but those are the sentiments I should be holding.'

'Ross would very likely call me out if he knew what we planned.' Richard's smile turned rueful. 'However, I think that it would still probably be worth it.'

Deb did not miss his use of the word 'we'. Her heart skipped a beat. It seemed that the betrothal plan was suddenly moving rather swiftly.

'I am persuaded that you are correct,' she said. 'Ross may be a friend of yours, but he would never countenance our betrothal, nor the deceit involved in misleading my father.' She freed herself from his grip, 'Oh, I wish I had never started this! There must be a dozen reasons why it would never work. You will not do, my lord. I wanted someone deferential. You are too…too forceful and too high-handed…'

She turned away. There was far more to it than that, of course. There was something about Richard Kestrel that made her respond on the most instinctive and feminine of levels, something male and dangerous. To accept him as her fiancé, temporary or not, to agree to spend more time with him, to allow him insidiously to grow closer to her… These were all such foolish ideas that she had to put a stop to them now.

Richard was standing close to her, unnervingly close. 'I think that we are approaching the crux of the problem,' he said softly. 'Your other protestations could be overcome. You are using them as a distraction. What you really object to is me personally. Why is that, Mrs Stratton?'

He was so near to her that Deb felt utterly overwhelmed. She made a slight, nervous gesture. 'I have already told you the answer to that, my lord. You are the opposite of all the qualities that I require in a fiancé, temporary or otherwise! You are also an untrustworthy rogue.'

Richard caught her wildly waving hands. 'You object to me because you are attracted to me,' he said.

Deb gasped. 'You go too far, my lord.'

'Frequently. It is true, though, is it not?'

'I do not feel comfortable with you,' Deb prevaricated.

'It would be ridiculous to try to convince anyone that I was betrothed to you when I feel so ill at ease in your company.'

'We could overcome that,' Richard said, 'if you could trust me.'

Deb's heart jumped. A part of her, a deeply instinctive part, wanted to do just that. It was extraordinary. Her head was telling her that she was making a mistake but her intuition was telling her that she could depend on him.

He leaned closer to her. 'Deborah—' she caught her breath at his use of her name '—my impression is that you are accustomed to living alone and relying on your own resources, but that, in this one matter, you need some help.' His gaze trapped and held hers. 'Why else come up with this unorthodox solution to your difficulties? It might go against the grain with you, but you need a strong man who can protect you, not someone meek or compliant. Whilst I am with you, you will be safe. I swear it.'

Deb stared into his dark eyes. The vision was so seductive. Her father had never offered to protect her, and neither had Neil Stratton in the short time that she had known him. Rather the reverse, in fact, for he had done everything in his power to ruin her. And now Richard Kestrel was offering her his protection. She wanted to accept it, and everything that it entailed. She struggled against the temptation.

'Ross will help me—' she began.

Richard shook his head. 'Ross cannot prevent your father from forcing you to stay in Bath, nor can he prevent him marrying you off if he so chooses. I can.'

Deb closed her eyes. She knew that he was right. If she arrived at Walton Hall with some nonentity of a man or, worse still, alone, there would be no one to stand between her and a betrothal to her cousin.

'Papa is not cruel,' she said, thinking of her father and wanting Richard to understand. 'It is merely that he is not accustomed to opposition and he wants to see me safely married off. None of the others—Liv, Michael, Guy—has ever done anything to thwart him…'

'You do not need to explain to me,' Richard said swiftly. 'I understand.' He smiled at her. 'Is it agreed, then? Are we betrothed?'

Deb looked at him. Betrothed to Lord Richard Kestrel. She was not sure if she was mad or dreaming.

'We are betrothed,' she confirmed, adding hastily, 'temporarily.'

Richard's smile made her feel warm deep in her bones. 'Temporarily,' he said. 'Of course. May I kiss my fiancée?'

'No!' Deb said. She felt a little panicked. 'Before we go any further, my lord, there are a number of conditions I should like to clarify.'

'Of course.' Richard sat down on the bench again and drew her down beside him. He sounded obliging, but Deb had the impression that her difficulties might start right here.

'There is to be no kissing or intimate behaviour,' she said, 'unless—' She stopped, appalled at the way her thoughts had almost run away with her tongue again.

Richard was looking very interested. 'Unless?' he queried softly.

Deb fidgeted. 'I was going to say…unless we are required to give each other a chaste kiss on the cheek to maintain the fiction.'

'You were not going to say that,' Richard said. 'You were going to say something along the lines of unless you change your mind.'

Deb stared at him, shocked by his perception. Did she wear her emotions on her face, that he was able to read her so easily? Or was it that he was so instinctively attuned to what she was thinking that he knew it almost before she did? Either way it was not a reassuring thought.

'I have other conditions,' she said, thinking it safer to ignore his remark. She saw him raise his brows sardonically, as though he were prepared to let it pass—for now.

'Please continue,' he said.

'You must be guided by me.' Deb looked at him. Even as she spoke she could sense his instinctive resistance. This man would make his own decisions. He might be influenced, but he could never be coerced. She moderated her tone. 'I hope that you will defer to me on all matters relating to my family, where I have the greater knowledge.'

This time he nodded, to her immense relief. 'That seems sensible.'

Deb took a careful breath. 'It is also to be understood that our engagement lasts only for the duration of the visit to Bath. After that, it is over.'

This time Richard laughed. 'We shall see,' he said.

Deb shot him a suspicious look. 'What do you mean?'

'You might find that by then that you do not wish our engagement to be at an end,' Richard pointed out.

His arrogance took Deb's breath away.

'I do not think that there is any likelihood of that,' she said stiffly.

Richard shrugged, as though he knew better. Deb's temper fizzed. Taken all in all, the response to her conditions had not been all that she would have wished.

'I have some prerequisites of my own,' Richard said. 'I will escort you back to Ross now and I shall call on you tomorrow to discuss this further.' He did not wait for her reply. 'We are to announce our engagement immediately after that. And we are to spend the next few weeks furthering our acquaintance, so that when we travel to Bath, no one will be in any doubt that we are genuinely in love.'

Deb stared. She had not been expecting this.

'I cannot accept that,' she said, her throat tight. 'There is no requirement for us to appear to be in love! Marriages are made for plenty of other reasons.'

'Not this one,' Richard said.

'Why not?'

Richard held her gaze. 'Because it is important that you convince people you are in earnest. Your father might well force you to break the engagement if he senses you are half-hearted about it.' He took her hand. 'Trust me. It will not be so bad, Deborah.'

'What, to pretend to be in love with you?' Deb felt extremely hot and bothered. She scrambled to her feet to put some distance between them. 'It is impossible that I should do such a thing!'

An expression crossed Richard's face, so fleeting she wondered if she had imagined it and when he spoke there was nothing but faint amusement in his voice.

'Why so?'

'Because I…' Deb flailed around as she tried to explain herself. 'It is dangerous…'

'In what way?'

Deb could see the trap yawning at her feet. She prevaricated. 'I am not very good at acting.'

'Then do not act,' Richard said. 'I am sure we may be convincing, nevertheless.' He got up in a leisurely fashion and, before Deb could move, his arms went about her and his lips came down on hers in an embrace that, despite its brevity, lit a sharp flame all the way through her body.

He let her go a second later. 'I am sorry,' he said, amusement in his voice. 'I could never keep any promise not to touch you, Deborah, though I do swear not to do anything that you do not want.' He stepped back. 'The decision must be yours. If you can accept me on my terms…then I am yours to command.'

Deb's heart was beating rapidly. Although her mind was

telling her that she was about to commit another impulsive act of folly, she knew her decision was already made. She had no real choice.

'Yes,' she said. 'I accept your offer and I thank you for helping me, my lord.'

Richard's transforming smile took her breath away. 'Then you are welcome, Deborah. Do you think that you might call me Richard, though? You will give the game away if you persist in addressing me as "my lord".'

Deb nodded. 'I can try. It feels…unfamiliar.' It was not the only thing that felt strange. The whole situation felt shaky and perilous. She was conscious of Richard watching her, a slight frown on his brow.

'Is something else troubling you, Deborah? You seem very tense.'

Deb hesitated. 'I feel very nervous,' she said.

'Of me?' Richard's expression was unreadable.

'Of our situation.' Deb's gaze faltered as it met his. 'I know that I should not say this,' she said. 'It is scarce modest in me, but I cannot be coy…'

Her voice wavered at the tenderness she saw come in to Richard's face. He waited.

'You were correct before,' she said, in a rush. 'I wish to keep my distance from you because I like you. I told you when we met here by the river—' Her breath caught. 'I like you, Richard Kestrel, but you are dangerous to me and this masquerade of ours…' her gaze touched his '…this just makes you more dangerous still. I must be monstrous foolish to allow you so close when you have a reputation for being the greatest rake between here and London and when it seems…' she sighed '…it seems that I cannot resist you.'

Once again she saw the flare of emotion in his eyes and felt her heart rate increase by several notches. What might have happened she could not say, but then Richard turned his head sharply, and over his shoulder she saw that Ross was approaching.

'A reprieve,' Richard said as he took her hand. 'Ross is coming to rescue you.'

Deb shrank. She wondered just how much Ross had seen of their recent encounter. 'I had no notion our half-hour had expired.' Her hand clung to his. 'I do not quite know what to tell him about this.'

Richard kissed her fingers. 'I shall speak to him tonight. And I shall call upon you tomorrow.' He smiled at her. 'Good day, Deborah.'

Feeling strangely shaky, Deb watched him go. He shook hands with Ross, exchanged a few words and then strode away. Deb watched his tall figure out of sight. She knew that she had a tiger by the tail now. From the moment that she had agreed to the betrothal she had lost control of the situation. She had gained a fiancé, but not the type of man that she had wanted in the role. She was obliged to admit that it was quite another service that she wished Richard Kestrel to perform for her, and that brief but passionate kiss had confirmed it. No precepts of modesty of respectability could hide the truth. The principles that had kept her life so barren of love were crumbling. She wanted a rake. She wanted Richard to be her lover and she was not at all sure how long common sense and propriety could govern her actions.

# Chapter Eleven

'You seem mightily distracted this evening, old fellow,' Ross Marney said, ushering his friend Richard Kestrel into his study and closing the door firmly behind them. 'Never seen you lose so badly at whist. Lucky the ladies only play for pennies or you'd be in River Tick by now.' He gave Richard a searching look. 'Is there anything that I can help with? Anything that a glass of brandy could improve?'

Richard laughed and accepted the invitation, taking one of the wing chairs set before the fire and waiting whilst his friend poured for both of them. He had attended Olivia Marney's card party that evening more in the hope of seeing Deb than in anything else, but in the event she had not been there and Richard had found himself bored and inattentive. He had lost badly, to the great pleasure of all the ladies, who had fleeced him mercilessly.

He had also known that he had to talk to Ross. His friend had been more generous than he had deserved earlier in the day, when Richard had turned up at the Customs House under the guise of Lord Scandal. Had it not been for the long history between them, Ross might well have called him to account. The least he deserved was an explanation.

Richard looked up with a smile of thanks as Ross passed

him the drink before settling himself in the other chair. For a while there was the companionable silence that often existed between old friends. Richard and Ross had served together on the *Valiant* and had shared more mess room debates than either cared to remember, both in and out of their cups. When Richard had come to Midwinter, the slight formality remaining from their professional relationship had deepened into friendship. Never before, however, had Richard proposed to marry Ross's sister-in-law, and whilst he hesitated on how to broach the topic, Ross looked at him directly and said, 'It is to do with Deborah, I suppose. Can it be that you wish to marry her?'

Richard jumped and spilled his brandy. 'Devil take it, Ross, can you not give me due warning before you pull such a trick? This brandy is too good to waste.'

Ross laughed. 'Sorry, old chap. Thought I'd move the conversation along a bit as you seemed lost for words. Do I take it that my wild stab in the dark was somewhere near the mark?'

Richard did not answer immediately. He turned the brandy glass round in his palm. 'Pretty close,' he said. 'Mrs Stratton and I pledged our troth today.'

Now it was Ross's turn to choke. When he had recovered his breath he said mildly, 'Didn't think you'd be able to persuade her. Nor did I think you were the marrying kind, Richard. Thought that you proved that when the betrothal to Lady Diana Elliot went awry?'

Richard pulled a face. In his long and frequently reprehensible history as a rake there was no episode more discreditable than the engagement to a duke's daughter that had ended almost as soon as it had begun, when she had discovered him pleasuring a Cyprian on the terrace at their betrothal party. It was many years ago, but Richard could not remember the episode without a wince of shame because he could see, with the benefit of hindsight, that it had been an act that had shown contempt towards a lady who had done him no wrong. Lady Diana had given him his *congé* in arctic terms:

'*You are clearly unsuited to the state of matrimony and I am not so desperate for a husband that I would bind myself to a man who shows me so little respect…*'

God help him, at the time he had thought it amusing. The incident had confirmed his outrageous reputation and he had played on it to the full. Yet after a couple of years the empty life of a rake about town had become too barren to sustain him and he had chosen to join the Navy, to his father's utter fury. He had enjoyed life at sea and had acquitted himself with valour, but when he had been invalided out, his old way of life had beckoned him as surely as a devil tempting him from the path of virtue. Until he had come to Midwinter and seen Deborah Stratton, and felt his heart seize in his chest. In one second she had achieved what the French had failed to do, and shot him down. It was rich retribution for a rake.

He did not intend to make any further mistakes. Deb had given him the advantage now and he would not let her escape him. It was marriage—or naught.

Richard stretched his long legs out to the warmth of the fire. He had already decided to tell Ross the whole truth, for he could see no way that he and Deb could sustain a masquerade beneath the noses of his friend and her sister. He rested his chin on his hand and sighed.

'I shall tell you the whole matter, Ross, and then you may have me horsewhipped from the house if you please.'

Ross paused. 'Is that a likely outcome?'

Richard sighed again. 'I cannot be certain. Suffice it to say that your sister-in-law recently advertised for a gentleman of honour to come to her assistance.' He saw the arrested look in Ross's eyes and added hastily, 'I need hardly tell you, Ross, that I am relating this in confidence. I have no wish to make further difficulties for Mrs Stratton. She was in urgent need of a fiancé and I offered my services.'

There was a very long silence.

'What form did this advertisement take?' Ross said, after a while.

'It was a notice placed in the *Suffolk Chronicle*.' Richard looked at him. 'Under a pseudonym, of course.'

'And you answered it,' Ross said.

'I did.'

'And you also paid to suppress all the other replies?'

Richard grinned at that. 'I did. How well you know me.'

'Hmm,' Ross said. 'Did you know from the start that it was Deb who had placed the notice?'

Richard hesitated. 'I…guessed.'

'Extraordinary,' Ross opined.

Richard smiled ruefully. 'I do have rather a strong instinct where your sister-in-law is concerned, Ross.'

'My dear fellow, we have all observed it,' Ross said. He reached for the decanter and topped up Richard's glass. 'I suppose it is the nature of your impulses towards Deb that have always concerned me. I have to admit that I had not expected chivalry to be one of them.'

Richard's mouth twisted wryly. 'Thank you, Ross.'

'I beg your pardon.' Ross laughed. 'I do not mean to imply that you would seduce Deb, merely that you might want to.'

'You give me too much credit.' Richard's conscience stirred. 'Until recently I would have seduced Deborah with the greatest of pleasure had she encouraged me to do so.'

Ross's eyes narrowed. He looked torn between amusement and disapproval. In the end he merely said, 'And now?'

Richard shifted. He was thinking of the incident the previous year when he had asked Deb to be his mistress. He had mistaken her then. Misled by her widowed status and also by her vivacious nature, he had assumed her to be a high-flyer like Lily Benedict, or, if not that, at least an experienced woman of the world such as Lady Sally Saltire. He had also assumed that once he had made love to her, her power over him would wane. Now he could see that both assumptions were groundless, for Deb was an innocent in matters of love and that very innocence captured and held him as surely as if he were bound with silken ties. He could ignore what was on offer from a practised flirt like Lady Benedict and prefer the infinitely more difficult prospect of wooing Deborah Stratton.

And that wooing would lead to marriage. If he wished to keep the friendship and respect of Ross Marney he could not simply take Deb to his bed. He did not even want to. He wanted Deb, but he did not wish to make her his mistress. Somehow that had become insufficient. He wanted to protect Deb and gain her trust. He was acting on an instinct that had never previously stirred in his relationships with women. He wanted more. He wanted everything. Once she was his, he would never let her go.

He spoke slowly. 'Now I want to marry her. Genuinely marry her, I mean. Not connive at a pretence.'

Ross nodded and moved on to another difficult question. 'What was it that prompted you to assist Deborah in this matter, Richard?'

Richard smiled. 'I felt that she had presented me with a perfect opportunity to woo her.'

Ross looked thoughtful. 'That is true, of course. She has played into your hands. But what of your other, more altruistic motives?'

Richard shifted a little uncomfortably again. Ross could never accept things at face value and he was usually correct.

He spoke slowly. 'I had the distinct impression that Mrs Stratton's need was acute. She tells me that her father is insisting that she return to live under his roof, and that she feels unable to comply.' His took another mouthful of brandy. 'She also implied that Lord Walton intended to marry her off to her cousin and that she had no desire to wed ever again. She seemed very distressed by the entire matter, which was one of the reasons why I offered my aid.'

Ross nodded. He hesitated. 'It is certainly true that Deb is set against marriage. She was very unhappy with Neil Stratton. She has frequently expressed the view that she would rather starve than marry again. It seems a shame, but she is quite adamant.' He gave Richard a look of acute perception. 'I should warn you that there are matters there which are very painful to her.' Ross looked away. 'But that is Deb's story to tell, not mine. Suffice it to say that I would have killed Stratton if the fever had not beaten me to it.'

Richard's head snapped up sharply. 'That bad?'

'Worse.' Ross took a moody sip of his drink. 'The man was beneath contempt.' He looked up again, his mouth a hard line. 'And as such, he gave Deb such a disgust of men in general that I believe you will have your work cut out to make her change her mind and accept you in earnest.'

Richard frowned. 'You do not think that I could persuade her?'

Ross looked rueful. 'I cannot say for sure, but I feel it only fair that you should be forewarned.'

'Deborah is not in a strong position to oppose her father alone,' Richard said thoughtfully. 'She needs some protection. I understand that her husband left her without much substance?'

'Penniless,' Ross confirmed. His mouth thinned. 'Though that was the least of his sins.'

Richard grimaced at the confirmation. It was no wonder that Deb Stratton was wary of men if her only experience of love had been with a man like that. The memory of the unhappiness he had seen in her eyes made him feel angry.

'So Mrs Stratton is dependent on the allowance her father makes her and…' he looked at Ross shrewdly '…your generosity, I suspect.'

Ross shifted in his chair. 'I help her a little.'

Richard let that pass. He knew that Ross's liberality to his sister-in-law was likely to be far greater than that but his friend would not thank him for prying.

'I know that you cannot like this temporary arrangement, Ross,' he said feelingly. 'God knows, if it was my sister Bella or Henrietta, I would feel much the same.' He looked up and gave Ross a very straight look. 'I can only give you my word that I shall do nothing to hurt Deborah.' He smiled wryly. 'My intentions are all that is honourable, damnable as it is for a rake to admit such a fact!'

Ross moved the decanter in a precise circle. 'I wish you luck,' he said, a little bitterly. 'And if you succeed, I hope that you find more joy in your marriage than I have in mine. How odd that Deb and Olivia look so very similar and yet temperamentally they could not be more different.'

Richard hesitated. He sensed that Ross needed to talk but in his experience, passing comment on another man's wife was fraught with danger. One always said the wrong thing and gave offence. He was prepared to take a risk though, for Olivia and Ross. If there was anything that he could do to help their situation, then he was willing to try.

'I think that both Lady Marney and Mrs Stratton may have some of the same spirit,' he said carefully.

Ross looked horrified. 'Good God, do you think so?'

'I did not mean,' Richard qualified hastily, 'that Lady Marney is as impulsive as her sister.'

'Thank the lord!'

'But from something that Mrs Stratton told me, I do believe that it may be a question of Lady Marney hiding her real feelings under what she sees as her duty. Parents are notoriously more strict with the elder than the younger daughter,' Richard continued, feeling his way and half-expecting an explosion at any moment. 'I have seen it myself with Bella and Henrietta. Bella always complained that Henrietta could get away with everything and she with nothing.'

Ross looked intrigued. 'You mean that Olivia might behave the way she does because Lord and Lady Walton expected it of her and so she conformed?'

Richard nodded. 'Precisely, old fellow. Deborah told me that Olivia and her brothers always did as they were told and never dissented, whilst she was the rebel. How would it be if Olivia secretly wished it to be different?'

He saw a flash of expression in Ross's eyes, the unmistakable sign that Viscount Marney thought the idea of a secretly rebellious wife to be rather fascinating.

'By George!' Ross said. 'What a thought!'

Richard hid his smile. Ross Marney had always had a short fuse, but in other respects he was steady, reliable and the antithesis of a rake. Who would have guessed that he wished for a show of spirit from his bride rather than cool compliance? Certainly Olivia was unlikely to have known. Most young ladies of aristocratic lineage were told that their husbands would expect conformity, not originality. It took a rebel like Deborah to break through those restraints and tell the world to go hang.

'Thank you for your tolerance in the matter of my betrothal to Mrs Stratton,' Richard said now, his thought returning with warmth to his temporary fiancée. 'I appreciate your support, Ross.'

'What? Oh…' Ross waved his hand vaguely. 'You are very welcome, Richard.'

Richard could tell that his thoughts were still on Olivia and he had no idea what they were talking about. Smiling a little, he thanked his host, excused himself and showed himself out, noting with interest that Ross went straight to the card room, where Olivia was hosting her party, as though he wished to test Richard's theory immediately. The night air held a chill edge of autumn and the faint scent of wood smoke. Richard breathed it in and realised that he felt more alive than he had done in months. No boredom dogged his steps now, no painted devil tempted him back to his old life and its debauchery.

He was to call on Deborah in the morning and discuss the details of their betrothal. His lips curved into a smile at the thought of seeing her again. So far matters were progressing with pleasing smoothness. He had persuaded Deb to give him a chance and he had gained Ross's support for his suit. Now all he needed to do was to proceed gently towards his goal and make sure that he did not frighten Deb into reneging on the plan. He had to woo her carefully. He was sure it would be a pleasure. Whistling softly under his breath, Richard drove his hands into his pockets and walked off into the night.

As soon as they met the following morning, Richard could tell that he had given Deb too much time to think and that those thoughts were not positive. She was looking pale and nervous, and much of her natural good spirits seemed depressed. Richard had a horrid suspicion that she was about to call the entire betrothal off.

Remembering his resolution to woo her gently, he decided to proceed with the utmost caution. She might well be regretting her frankness the previous day and have her defences firmly in place. So instead of kissing her properly he kissed her hand with deference and allowed her to usher him into the drawing room. The house seemed very quiet. She did not send for a servant and poured his glass of sweet sherry herself. She was drinking a cup of tea, which she was gripping so tightly he feared the china would crack.

'I have been thinking about this betrothal and I believe that we should change some of the terms,' Deb began. From the faint violet shadows underneath her eyes Richard suspected that she might have been thinking about it all night. 'This was not at all what I had planned. This is...' she gestured a little wildly and the tea slopped '...becoming quite out of hand.'

Richard had been expecting something of the sort, but although he was prepared to be soothing he had no intention of allowing Deb to back out now. If he did there was no guarantee she would not end up asking some other gentleman to act the role of protector, and Richard disliked that thought intensely.

'You cannot change your mind about the betrothal now,' he said. 'Last night I asked Ross's permission to pay my addresses to you.'

Deb's eyes flew to his face. She looked shocked. 'Was that necessary?'

'If I am to do this,' Richard said, 'I do it properly. As Ross was present at our meeting at the Custom House, I thought that he deserved a full explanation.'

'Yes, but...' Deb looked confused. 'You told Ross the truth? About it being a temporary engagement?'

Richard made a split-second decision. 'I explained the situation to him.' He saw the relief vivid in her face and smiled ruefully to himself. Mrs Stratton's reluctance to

countenance his suit was not flattering. It had obviously not
occurred to her that many young ladies would use this opportunity to persuade him into making the pretend betrothal
a real one. Her instinct was to do the reverse, and escape
him as quickly as possible.

'Please do not worry,' he said soothingly, taking her hand
in his. 'Ross understands. Before I left, he suggested that
you visit Olivia this afternoon to discuss the matter with
her. Then we may announce our betrothal formally tonight
at Lady Benedict's ball.'

He felt Deborah's hand tremble in his. She tried to withdraw it, but he held on to her, rubbing his fingers gently
over the back of her hand. Her head was bent, a tiny frown
wrinkling the skin between her brows. She looked very
young.

'I had not anticipated that we would make a public announcement,' she said. 'Surely that is not necessary? This
was to be for my family's benefit only.'

Richard nodded. 'I understand that, but consider for a
moment the questions that might arise if your parents were
to have an acquaintance in this neighbourhood.'

Deb's frown deepened. 'I am sure that they do not.'

'You cannot know for certain,' Richard pointed out. 'It
is better not to take the risk. If everyone hereabouts is aware
of our engagement, then there is no difficulty.'

He sensed that he was pushing too hard. A flame of resistance burned in Deb's eyes. 'I am sure that there is no
such necessity,' she said. 'I would prefer to keep the matter
secret.'

Richard let go of her hand and sat back in his chair,
feigning unconcern. 'If you wish. I should tell you though,
Deborah, that one of the first things that I learned when I
was involved in counter-espionage work was to prepare the

ground carefully. If you do not, something is bound to go wrong.'

He saw that the frown was back in her eyes. 'I suppose so. Yes, I can see that there is always the possibility of something going awry.'

It was a minor victory and Richard followed it up at once. 'That being the case, I believe we should spend a great deal of time together over the next few weeks,' he said. 'We need to make it apparent to everyone that we are comfortable in each other's company. No one will believe our betrothal otherwise.'

Deb's brow was still puckered. 'You have decided a great many things,' she said.

Richard smiled impudently. 'Did you expect me not to do so?' he asked.

'Oh, no,' Deb said, 'I expected it. It was just…not as I had planned.'

'And you will spend time with me?' Richard pressed. 'I thought that we could go riding tomorrow afternoon.'

He saw by the flicker in her blue eyes that the idea held appeal.

'I own that it will be pleasant to ride with someone who is so good at it,' she said, with a small smile.

'Good,' Richard said. He kissed her hand. 'Unfortunately I am engaged for the rest of the day or I would certainly ask you to spend it with me. I will see you this evening at Lady Benedict's ball?'

Deb nodded. He had seen from the slight droop to her shoulders that she was disappointed they would not be spending the day together. The knowledge encouraged him. Although she had been initially resistant to his plans, he could feel her softening with each step. He allowed himself to be cautiously optimistic that with time and careful wooing he might persuade her to his point of view and gain her agreement to their marriage. He drew her a little closer and after an initial hesitation, she came. Richard scanned her face, noting the shadow that was still reflected in Deb's pansy-blue eyes.

'Are you in agreement that we announce our betrothal tonight?' he asked softly.

Her lashes swept her cheek for a moment as she looked away. Richard fought a strong urge to kiss her. Repressing his most fundamental urges, he tried to concentrate. He knew that he could override her resistance, knew that she would respond to him, for she had been scrupulously honest about her attraction to him. That was not the way to succeed, however, for whilst he might gain a response from her body, emotionally she would slip further away from him. He took a deep breath and kept his eyes locked on hers and in a moment she looked up at him again.

'I…yes, I am in agreement,' she said.

Richard gave a silent sigh of relief. 'Thank you. I am honoured.'

A shy smile lit her eyes. The urge to kiss her became stronger, so powerful that Richard had to take a step back.

'I shall see you this evening,' he said. 'You have no idea how I look forward to it.'

He saw Deb take a breath as though she were about to speak. Richard frowned. He could sense some tension in her, some unresolved problem.

'Is there something else that you wished to discuss?' he asked.

Deb moved away from him and picked up her teacup. It rattled in her hands. Her face was averted from him, pink and feverish.

'There is something that I wish to say but I find—' she glanced at him, a fleeting look from those lavender blue eyes '—it is a little difficult…'

Richard took the teacup from her—she had not drunk any of it anyway—and placed it gently on the table before leading her back to the sofa and taking both her hands in his. Deb's blue eyes were huge and apprehensive now and he leaned closer.

'You are trembling,' he said gently, 'and you look terrified.'

'That is because…' she licked her lips nervously '…there is something I need to say to you and I am not accustomed to being in such close proximity to a gentleman.'

Ridiculous pleasure coursed through Richard at her words. He did not seem able to help himself. But the nervousness in her eyes puzzled him. He wanted to draw her into his arms and comfort her. He wanted to kiss her. Richard tried to concentrate.

'Deborah,' he said, 'if you are wanting to change your mind because you still do not trust me, then I must remind you that I promised to do nothing that you did not desire and I will keep to that.' His voice came out more roughly than he had intended and her gaze flew to his. Had she realised the difficulty he was having controlling his impulses? If she even guessed at the iron control he was exercising, then she would probably be so nervous she would not come near him again. He moderated his tone. 'You have not reacted to my presence like this before,' he said. 'What is the matter?'

Her gaze touched his face and skittered away. 'You do not understand,' she said.

'Then tell me,' Richard said bluntly. 'What is it?'

He was still touching her and now she looked down at their joined hands and swiftly away. There was high colour in her cheeks.

'I have been trying to pluck up the courage to tell you,'

she said. 'When I said that I wished to change the terms of our betrothal you misunderstood me—'

She broke off.

'Yes?' Richard said.

Her gaze met his with all the straightness of a sword thrust.

'I want you to make love to me,' she said. 'For the duration of our betrothal, I want you to be my lover.'

As soon as the words were out Deb was ready to sink with mortification, but she also felt a huge relief. She could scarce believe what she had just done. She had spent the entire night plagued with erotic thoughts and dreams until in the pale morning light she had finally admitted that matters could not carry on as they were. She wanted Richard Kestrel desperately. She wanted to give herself to him and experience the sensual bliss of physical love with him. She had starved herself of love and desire for so long that she was burning up. And if that made her a wanton who gave herself up to a man without the blessings of the church, then so be it. She had gone far beyond modesty and moral principle. She could not help herself.

Nevertheless, she was terrified. She knew that all the pretty phrases she had devised beforehand had deserted her and she had ended up speaking baldly and without finesse. It was no wonder that Richard was looking so stunned.

'No.'

He got to his feet abruptly, dropping her hands in her lap. He thrust his fingers through his hair violently, then strode over to the window, where he turned and looked at her with incredulous eyes.

Deb drew on all her courage.

'Do you mean no you will not do it?' She asked.

'No.' Richard shook his head slightly. 'I mean no, I do not believe this.'

'Oh.' A small smile touched Deb's lips. He had not rejected the idea out of hand, then. There was still a chance.

She noted that Richard's face was grim. Perhaps there was not a chance after all. Perhaps she had made a dreadful error and also made a complete fool of herself. She hoped not. She looked at him, her brow puckered. 'I thought that you would agree,' she ventured.

Now he looked absolutely furious and sounded cuttingly sarcastic. 'Did you? You thought that I would agree to teach you about love *for the duration of our betrothal only*?'

Deb's breathing caught. She did not dare explain that if she let him closer than that, if she let him into her heart, she was afraid that she would never be able to let him go again.

'I thought that if it was for that short while only then I might understand about the pleasures of physical love without any further obligation,' she said. 'I had no wish to constrain you in a relationship when our association is to be so fleeting…'

Richard looked suitably disgusted. 'So you thought to order me up for a few weeks, like a servant? Good God, you have it all worked out!'

Deb got to her feet. She could feel the whole thing slipping away from her. This was not how she had imagined it at all. Perhaps she had been naïve, but she had thought that a rake like Richard Kestrel would not need much encouragement. But then, she did not know a great deal about rakes and she had clearly misunderstood this one.

'It was not like that!' She got to her feet and put a hand on his arm, desperate to ease the situation. 'I do not understand… I thought that you wanted me.'

She saw him draw a sharp breath. His gaze searched her

face, hard and furious. Behind the anger she saw the desire
and felt her heart flip. So he did want her, but for some
reason this had all gone wrong. She put a hand to her head.
She was starting to feel humiliated. 'Oh, dear. I think I have
made a mistake.'

'I think you have.'

Now he sounded as stuffy as a church elder. It made Deb
quite annoyed. She forgot the embarrassment in a wash of
anger.

'Well, it is not surprising if I mistook you!' she said,
firing up. 'You are experienced and you have made no secret
of your attraction to me.'

'That is true, but I prefer to do the asking myself.'

Deb felt another rush of annoyance. 'I see that I have
offended your male pride! That is what this is about!' She
made a gesture of disgust. 'If it comes to that, you did ask
me. You asked me to be your mistress a year ago!'

'Yes, and you turned me down.' Richard's tone was
clipped. He came across to her and seized her arms above
the elbow. 'You have been fighting your attraction to me
every step of the way, Deborah. Why change your mind
now?'

Deb stared up into his face. There was a pain lodged
inside her, but there was also a shimmering need. She could
see the reflection of it in his eyes. 'I have been fighting
*myself* every step of the way, not you,' she whispered. '
wanted to know—'

'What you were missing?'

He still sounded angry, but she sensed that he was weak
ening. She shook her head.

'No, not that. I told you that I was…married…but a short
time and that it was unhappy.' She blushed slightly. 'I had
never experienced passion. I thought that I should neve

want to, but with you I am forced to admit that the possibility intrigues me…'

Richard shook his head, as though trying to clear his mind. He was still holding her, but lightly now. Even so, she could sense the tension in him, tight as a spring.

'You are not thinking straight,' he said. 'What you need is a fiancé, not a lover. You need someone who can protect you from your father's plans and act the role of your betrothed, not someone to acquaint you with the delights of love.'

Deb took a step closer, until her body was touching his. Her heart was hammering. 'Perhaps I need both,' she said.

She raised her hand and rubbed her fingers gently against Richard's cheek. She saw him close his eyes as though to blot out the effect of her touch.

'So what do you say?' she whispered.

When Deb had first spoken, Richard had thought that he had misheard her request. His mind had been full of the pretend betrothal, the strategy they should adopt, and the necessity of persuading Deb that they should spend considerable time in each other's company. He had noted her reluctance to his suggestions and had assumed that she had had second thoughts about their engagement. It had never occurred to him that her nervousness had sprung from a completely different source. And when she had propositioned him, told him that she wanted him to be her lover, it had seemed absurd, outrageous. He was certain that he had misunderstood.

Once he was over the initial shock, however, Richard's second feeling was one of disbelief. He considered himself a good judge of character, but evidently he had been sorely misguided over Mrs Deborah Stratton. She was as brazen as all the rest. She had been playing a game with him and for once his finely-honed instincts had let him down. He had thought her innocent. He had been deceived.

Such reflections did not stand up to one moment of observation. He had looked at Deb and seen that her nervousness had not dissipated. Her bottom lip was caught between her teeth, a mannerism he had noticed she affected only when extremely disturbed. There was a stricken look in those pansy-blue eyes. Only a fool could imagine that she was an experienced woman. He had felt a savage, purely male satisfaction as he realised the stunning truth. Deborah Stratton had never done this before. She was petrified.

Her utter vulnerability filled him with tenderness as well as desire. Although her invitation was terribly tempting, he knew that he could not take her up on it, at least not yet. When she had said that she had never experienced passion, he had felt a huge gentleness as well as a strengthening of desire. He wanted to take her and show her all the things that she asked, teach her the truth about love with a sweetness and a fervour that was as intense as it was unexpected. But there was a problem and it was an ironic one for a rake to confront. He wanted to marry her before he took her to his bed. And she was about as receptive to the idea of marriage as oil was to mixing with water.

She was so close to him now that he could smell the scent of her skin. Her gentle touch against the roughness of his cheek was disturbing. It distracted him at the moment that he most wanted to keep a clear head.

'I still say that what you need is a fiancé, not a lover,' he said.

'And I still say that I want both,' she said.

His arms came about her and this time he did not even try to resist his feelings. He raised one hand to skim her jaw, running his fingers into her hair as he tilted her head to kiss her fiercely. Hunger and desire slammed through him with devastating power as soon as their lips touched. The heat raged through his veins. He wanted to take her there and then on the velvet sofa. For long, shattering moments they stood locked in each other's arms, Richard plundering her mouth with his kisses, Deb responding with all the fervour of long denial.

He felt her shudder slightly and eased back, tracing his thumb over the fullness of her lower lip, swollen from the violence of his kisses. Her eyes were dark inky blue and full of longing as he bent to kiss her again, gently this time.

'Deborah…' he said.

Her eyes widened as they held his. 'Does that mean…can that possibly mean…yes?' she asked.

Richard scanned her face. She looked innocent and hopeful and utterly desirable. His stomach clenched. He smiled at her. 'Perhaps,' he said. 'Yes.'

He felt the shock go through her. She blinked. 'I thought that you would refuse,' she said.

Richard sat down on the sofa and drew her down on to his knee. 'Deborah…' he said again.

'Mmm?' She sounded dazed. He wanted to keep her that way because he was not at all sure that he could refuse her if she turned demanding. He sprinkled tiny kisses across the soft skin of her face. Immediately she turned more fully to him, tilting her face up like a flower to the sun. Her eyes were closed, the lashes fanned across her cheeks. Richard was stunned by the latent passion in her. It made it incredibly difficult for him to concentrate. Tracing a path of kisses down her throat, he spoke softly. 'Deborah, you still require a fiancé.'

'Uhuh…' She sounded intoxicated. Richard smiled against her throat.

'So,' he said, 'I accept both your commissions. I will act

the role of your fiancé and I shall also be your lover.' And
your husband, he added silently, in the fullness of time.

Deb opened her eyes and looked at him. 'Thank you,
Richard,' she said sweetly.

She sounded as though he had just picked up her glove
for him rather than agreed to be her lover, but he knew that
that was because she was so adrift with sensual longing that
she scarcely knew what she did. He also knew that this was
not the time and the place for such an encounter. If—
when—he became Deborah Stratton's lover, he wanted all
the time in the world to introduce her to those passionate
delights that she so longed for. He wanted to bind her to
him heart and soul, so that she would never want him to let
her go. He moved slightly.

'I do not wish us to hurry matters, however,' he said. 'We
must wait a little.'

'I do not understand,' she said.

'You will find,' Richard said, deliberately blunt, 'that anticipation heightens one's pleasure enormously.'

He smiled inwardly as he saw the colour fizz beneath her
skin. 'I see,' she said slowly.

Richard smiled gently. 'I have to leave you now,' he said
regretfully. 'I am sorry, but I really do have another appointment.'

Deb made a soft little noise in her throat that conveyed
regret and disappointment. She pressed her yielding body
closer against his. Richard's senses tightened. Unable to resist, he bent his head and took her parted lips with his once
more. She pressed closer still, her breasts soft against the
hard wall of his chest. Richard was within an inch of forgetting all his good intentions and carrying her upstairs to
bed. With a huge effort, he pulled back from the brink.

'Deborah, we must not. Not here, not now.' He tilted up

her chin so that he could look at her properly. 'When I make love to you for the first time, I want it to be perfect.'

Her lips turned down again in a disappointed moue and her lashes fluttered. She pressed a soft kiss on his lips and he felt it all the way through the rest of his body. She was naturally passionate and Richard thought ruefully that she was learning rather too quickly for his comfort. His breeches were so tight he was afraid he might burst. He got to his feet with a wince of pain.

'Sweetheart…' He kept an arm about her waist and drew her towards the door. 'You will go to visit Olivia later?'

'Mmm,' Deb agreed. She sounded sleepy.

'And I shall see you this evening at Lady Benedict's ball, when we shall announce our engagement.'

Richard held her at arm's length, scanning her face. She was waking up now, the dazed light fading from her eyes, but she still looked charmingly ruffled and frighteningly seductive. Richard summoned every ounce of self-control he possessed and put her firmly away from him.

'I must go,' he said again.

'You said that already,' Deb pointed out. A very feminine and satisfied smile touched her lips. 'Can you not tear yourself away?'

It was too true. Richard sighed sharply and pressed a kiss on her hand before going quickly outside and running down the steps to retrieve Merlin from the mounting block. He swung himself up into the saddle. He found that that was painful too. And even when he was halfway down the drive he could not help but look back at the house. Deb was still standing in the doorway, watching him. He could have sworn that she was smiling.

Richard kicked Merlin to a gallop. Deb had tasted her power now, and he had a sudden suspicion that, for all her inexperience, this would not be so easy a business to manage as he had hoped. He had set out to control the situation and had almost ended in losing his head. She was too tempting, too seductive, and he wanted her too much. But the one thing that their encounter had confirmed was that he had to marry her. Nothing less would do. He was not yet her lover, but he would be before he was finished. And not merely for the duration of the betrothal. He would prove to her that a few weeks were nowhere near enough and a lifetime would barely suffice.

He would be her husband. Of that he was determined.

# Chapter Twelve

'Engaged to Lord Richard Kestrel,' Lady Benedict said, her narrowed gaze scanning Deb from her satin slippers to the diamond slide in her curls. Her venom was barely concealed by her cold smile. 'How you are going up in the world, Deborah! Sister-in-law to a duke! And what a sly puss you are, trapping our most eligible bachelor. Still, I suppose that he has run through half the ladies in the neighbourhood and had to settle down at some point.'

Deb smiled politely. 'Was it only half the ladies?' she enquired. 'Why, Richard told me that it was at least three-quarters.' She put her head on one side. 'I do not believe that your name was on the list, however, Lady Benedict.'

Lily Benedict closed her fan with a sharp snap. Her lips thinned. 'Let us hope for your sake that he has truly reformed,' she said. 'Ladies love a reformed rake, but are not so sanguine when he relapses. Excuse me, I must attend to my other guests.' And with an angry slash of her satin skirts she turned on her heel.

'That woman is a spiteful cat,' Olivia said in Deb's ear. She put her hand on her sister's arm. 'Are you quite well, Deb?'

'Yes, thank you.' Deb dragged her gaze away from Lily

Benedict's retreating back. She was a little surprised to find
that now the encounter was over, she felt rather shaky. She
had seldom encountered such malice and had not expected
it from Lady Benedict, who had been a neighbour for the
full three years that Deb had been in Midwinter.

'There was a time when I liked Lady Benedict,' she said,
her brow wrinkling. 'I thought she was rather nice.' She
heard Olivia's smothered laugh and gave her sister a look.
'What? What have I said?'

'Lily Benedict,' Olivia said, taking Deb's arm and steering her away from the other guests, 'is the most spiteful
tabby in Midwinter, Deb! I am amazed that you had never
noticed.'

Deb frowned, raking her memory. 'I suppose there have
been times when she has made sharp remarks.'

'And do not forget what she said when she heard Rachel
was to marry Cory Newlyn.'

'What, that she had thought he was the adventurer, but it
seemed that Rachel matched him in more ways than one? I
thought that she meant they would enjoy travelling together!'

Olivia laughed. 'Well, now you know better. She never
liked Rachel because Cory Newlyn paid her no attention
and she cannot bear to play second fiddle. And now you
have prevented her from indulging in her favourite pastime.'

'Flirting with Richard?' Deb looked across the room to
where Richard was chatting with Ross and John Norton. He
looked elegant, distinguished and handsome. She found that
just looking at him made her want to smile and yet she felt
a strange ache in the region of her heart. 'Richard and Lady
Benedict…' she said. 'Do you think that they—?'

'No,' Olivia said decisively. 'That is why she is so cross
with you, Deb. She thought that she had a chance and now
she sees that there is none.'

Deb felt the heartache melt away and a little smile curve her lips. 'Oh, I see.' A shadow touched her. 'But she said that Richard had run through half the ladies of the neighbourhood.'

Olivia laughed. 'She would say that, wouldn't she? Wake up, Deb! Not everyone is as straightforward as you are.'

'I suppose not,' Deb said. She felt a little naïve. 'Poor Lady Benedict. I suppose it cannot be pleasant for her to have a bedridden husband.'

'And to be denied the pleasure of flirting with the most attractive man in the neighbourhood,' Olivia said. 'Do you really feel sorry for her?'

Deb examined her feelings. 'No, not at all. How horrid I am! Still...' she lowered her voice '...I must remember that this is merely a pretend betrothal, Liv, not the real thing.'

Olivia drew her down to sit on a rout chair in a quiet alcove. 'I know you explained this to me this afternoon,' she said softly, 'but are you sure that is all there is to it, Deb?'

'Of course.' Deborah fidgeted with her gloves, evading her sister's gaze. 'Richard and I have made an arrangement. I thought you understood.'

'I understood what you told me,' Olivia said drily, 'but, if I am to believe the evidence of my own eyes, I find it difficult to credit that this is only a business arrangement.'

She put one hand over Deb's clasped ones. 'Deb, are you sure that your feelings are not involved?'

Deb blushed. She looked across at Richard again. As though aware of her regard, he glanced up and smiled at her, his wicked, heart-stirring smile. Deb's blush deepened.

There was nothing remotely businesslike about the feelings that Richard had awakened in her that morning, nor was the arrangement that they had made a practical one. She felt wicked and wanton and lighter than air.

'Deb,' Olivia said, 'your thoughts are wandering.' She looked thoughtful. 'Perhaps that is the answer to my question.'

Deb blinked and dragged her scattered thoughts into some kind of order. 'I beg your pardon, Liv. My feelings—' She stopped and looked at her sister. 'I am not sure.'

'Ross and I were saying,' Olivia said, with studied casualness, 'that Richard seems to like you a great deal. Enough to wish to make the betrothal a reality.'

Nervousness clutched at Deb. Marriage was a different matter entirely. The thought of it terrified her. It had taken all her courage to ask Richard to be her lover and even now she could not quite believe the risk she was prepared to take.

'I do not wish to marry again,' she said quickly. 'You know that, Liv! Besides, I do not believe Lord Richard seeks marriage.'

Olivia was soothing. 'I understand how you feel, but you may find your feelings are quite the opposite when you have had the chance to grow to know Richard better.' She smiled. 'He has been a rake, but perhaps now he wishes to lead a more settled life? If you could trust him sufficiently—'

'I do trust him,' Deb said. 'That is, I trust him not to deliberately hurt me the way that Neil did. What I do not trust is myself! I believe my aversion to marriage goes too deep to be overcome, no matter Lord Richard's feelings.'

'Perhaps I am reading too much into this,' Olivia said placidly. 'It is, as you say, foremost a matter of business.'

Deb looked suspiciously at her sister. She knew Olivia well and was not taken in by her insouciant air. In addition, there was Ross's peculiar behaviour. Her brother-in-law had been surprisingly complaisant when Deb had broken the news of the betrothal to him earlier in the day. Deb had been expecting both Ross and Olivia to express their disapproval in the strongest possible terms and had been amazed at their reaction. Olivia had said mildly that although a pretence of a betrothal was not the sort of thing she could encourage, she understood her sister's reasons for wishing to avoid their father's plans. Ross had said that he never could follow Deb's logic, but he wished her luck. Deb had been so astounded that she had challenged him.

'I am betrothed to Richard Kestrel,' she had pointed out. 'Richard Kestrel! Surely you must disapprove, Ross?'

'Would you like me to?' her brother-in-law had asked mildly. 'I could object if you wish, but Richard is the greatest of good fellows, and my only opposition, Deb, springs from the fact that this is not a genuine engagement.'

With that he had kissed her cheek, exchanged a meaningful look with his wife, and strolled out of the room.

And now Olivia was contemplating the same betrothal with something approaching complacence. It made Deb wonder what it was that they knew that she did not.

She glanced back at Richard. The only thing she could think of that could account for Ross's good humour was if he knew Richard's intentions were honourable and that was manifestly absurd. Richard had told her that he had told Ross the truth about their betrothal agreement, so there could be no misunderstanding. For a moment Deb thought about what might happen were Richard to make her a declaration. The cold fear of marriage that had held her in its grip for years had not diminished, yet alongside it was a small but tantalising glimmer of hope. Deborah crushed it. She had thought very carefully about her proposal to Richard. She ached to experience the passion that she had starved for all these years. Yet even in that she had limited the risk she was taking by specifying that it would only be for the duration of the fictitious betrothal. She had no wish to tumble headlong in love with Richard and be at the mercy of her feelings again. She had to be able to let him go.

'How has the Duke greeted the news of his brother's betrothal?' Olivia enquired, glancing across to where Justin Kestrel partnered Helena Lang in the country dance.

Deb fidgeted with her fan. 'He has been everything that is charming to me, though Richard says that he teases him mercilessly in private.' Deb shifted slightly and the rout chair squeaked protestingly. 'Truth to tell, Liv, I cannot like it that Richard's family now know of the betrothal. It was only intended as a private arrangement and now I feel a little trapped…'

Once again Olivia looked so blandly unconcerned that Deb started to feel quite irritated.

'If you have agreed with Richard that you may break the engagement when it has served its purpose, then I do not see that you need be concerned,' she said.

Deb frowned. 'I know that. It is merely…' She waved her fan vaguely. 'It makes it more difficult for me to end it…'

'Because you do not wish to appear heartless?'

Deb frowned harder. 'It is not only that. People have been so kind. Most people,' she amended, thinking of Lady Benedict. 'The Dowager Duchess of Kestrel will hear of it soon and then no doubt she will write to me. The Duke tells me that she has been wanting her sons to marry this age, and will be *aux anges* to hear the news.'

'Perhaps you should consider telling them that it is only a convenient arrangement,' Olivia suggested. 'That way there would be no misunderstanding when you jilt Lord Richard.'

Deb winced. She had deliberately avoided using that word in both her thoughts and her conversation, for it made her feel rather tawdry. Yet she had to accept it. That was exactly what she was planning for Richard once he had served his purpose—and not merely his purpose as her short-term fiancé, either. She deliberately turned her thoughts away from her plan and the strangely mixed feelings that it was starting to arouse in her and thought about the other arrangement she had made with Richard, which involved neither plights of troth nor benefit of clergy.

What would happen during their nights of passion? Deb shivered as a wave of heat started at her toes and swept over her entire body as she considered what it might entail. Seduction by a rake... The thought was both delicious and terrifying. She almost shivered. Once she had tasted the pleasure that she knew Richard could give her would she really be able to turn her back on it? Her body craved the sensual delight that she had never experienced before. Starved of physical love, she longed for Richard's touch. Her mind whispered that she craved more than that and she firmly ignored the thought. This was all that she dared afford.

She looked up to see Olivia watching her, a wry smile on her lips.

'Whatever it is that you are drinking,' Olivia said drily, nodding at her glass of lemonade, 'I would like some. You look like a girl in love, Deb, for all your protestations of pretend betrothals! You are burning up with excitement.'

Deb smiled. 'No, you are quite mistaken. I was merely wondering, rather improperly, whether Lord Richard is indeed the rake everyone claims.'

'No,' Olivia said decisively, 'I think not.' She turned her amused blue gaze on her sister. 'You look disappointed, Deb! But only consider—how could he be? In the time that he has been in Midwinter I do not think that he has seduced a single lady! His reputation is all hearsay and no substance.'

Deb laughed. 'He tried to seduce me last year,' she pointed out.

'You are the only one and now you are betrothed to him.' Olivia raised her brows. 'So perhaps it is for you to find out.'

'Liv!' Deb exclaimed at this frank echo of her own thoughts. She changed the subject quickly. 'Have you tried the face cream that I gave you yet?'

'Yes,' Olivia said, blushing. 'I did not think it smelled much of roses but it was delightfully smooth and I was careful to use only a small amount.'

'Good,' Deb said. 'You mentioned earlier that you and Ross had been talking?'

'Oh, yes, we have.' For a moment Olivia looked young and charmingly ruffled. 'We had quite a long conversation about your betrothal, and another about our plans for this autumn, and on both occasions we managed not to quarrel.' She looked a little perplexed. 'It is odd though, Deb... Ross keeps looking at me in a particular way, as though he is expecting me to say something or do something...yet I do not know what!'

Deb raised her brows. 'Does he? How intriguing!' She laughed. 'Has Ross come to your bed again, Liv?'

'Deb!' Olivia looked quickly over her shoulder to make sure that no one had overheard. She drooped a little. 'No, he has not.'

'Well, never mind,' Deb said bracingly. 'Unless I miss my guess, he is about to ask you to dance and that is a good start. This aphrodisiac cream must be potent!'

'Hush!' Olivia said, blushing scarlet. She turned a becomingly pink face to her husband as Ross strolled across and smiled down at her. Deb was intrigued to see an unmistakable spark of masculine interest in Ross's eyes. It was just as Olivia had said—he was looking at his wife as though he had not really seen her before.

'They put the most remarkable ingredients in face cream these days,' she said mischievously.

Olivia kicked her ankle. 'Deb, hush! Ross…' She smiled very sweetly. 'Are you enjoying the evening?'

'Not as much as I shall be once I have persuaded my beautiful wife to dance with me,' Ross said. He took Olivia's hand, turned it over and pressed a kiss on the palm. 'Shall we?'

Olivia's mouth formed a small, astonished 'o' of pleasure. 'I should be delighted,' she said.

Even Deb stood staring at this unlikely sight. She had not expected the face cream to work quite so quickly or effectively. She was so surprised that she did not even see Richard approach her until, most reprehensibly, he slid an arm about her waist. His lips brushed the sensitive skin of her neck and Deb shivered pleasurably. She turned within the circle of his arm, her hand against his chest.

'For shame, sir! We are in a public place…'

Beyond Richard's shoulder she could see the dancers dipping and swaying, but she scarcely registered them. Her whole attention was focussed on Richard, the hard warmth of his chest beneath her hand, the intensity in his eyes, the wicked smile on his lips.

'And I am enjoying myself,' he said, 'so do not stop me, I beg you.'

Deb's lips twitched. 'Was enjoying oneself a part of the plan?' she asked.

'Surely. If we are to be betrothed, then we should make it as pleasurable as possible, though this is nowhere near as pleasurable as what will happen soon…'

Deb's heart leapt in her chest, her blue eyes wide as they scanned his face. The laughter within her died, banished by a heated excitement. She saw the corner of his mouth lifted in a smile.

'Unfortunately it will not be tonight, sweetheart, unless you continue to look at me like that, in which case I may well carry you straight out of the ballroom and make love to you here and now.'

Deb hastily recalled herself to their surroundings. 'Come and dance,' she said. 'I believe that, rather than anything else, is the appropriate activity for a ballroom.'

It was a quadrille, which gave no opportunity for intimate conversation since Deb was obliged to move away from her partner swiftly and chat with a variety of gentlemen as she walked through the steps. She ended with Owen Chance, whom she had not seen since the day at the Customs House. He gave her a charming smile as he took her hand, and once the dance was ended, was swift to draw her to one side so that they could speak further. Deb, aware that Richard had been dancing with Lady Benedict and was yet to leave her side, saw no reason to excuse herself from Mr Chance.

'I hear I am to congratulate you,' Owen said, smiling in the open and friendly manner that had made Deb warm to him when they had met at Lady Sally Saltire's ball. 'Or, more properly, it is Lord Richard who should be congratulated since he has gained a treasure beyond price in persuading you to be his bride!'

Deb smiled. 'Thank you, sir. That is a pretty compliment.' She took his arm for the customary turn about the floor. 'Now that you have been here a little while,' she said, 'how are you enjoying Midwinter?'

Owen laughed. 'It is an odd, secretive place, Mrs Stratton. On the surface everything is charming and bright—' he waved his hand descriptively about the ballroom '—but beneath the surface all manner of currents flow.'

Deb raised her brows. 'How very mysterious! Whatever can you mean, sir?'

Owen shrugged a little uncomfortably. 'Why, merely that

while we dance here there are probably smugglers dragging their cargo up a beach not five miles distant, or privateers ploughing the ocean close to shore…'

'And should you not be out there catching them, sir?'

Owen laughed, his teeth very white in his dark face. 'I should, but I would rather be here dancing with you, ma'am!'

Deb shook her head in mock reproach. 'Tempted from your duty by other distractions, sir?'

'I admit it. There are other occupations far more attractive than chasing smugglers.'

Deb raised her brows. It was flattering to be the object of Mr Chance's admiration, but even as she enjoyed his attentions she was aware that they stirred nothing deeper in her. There was not the clutch of excitement that she felt when Richard so much as looked at her, nor the quiver of feeling that ran through her at the touch of his hand.

'You are an accomplished flirt, sir,' she said, smiling. 'I had no notion that the Revenue Service trained its Riding Officers in the art of flattery, but now that I think of it I imagine it must be a very useful accomplishment. You will wheedle all manner of secrets from the ladies.'

Owen Chance's eyes lit with laughter. 'I do believe you have divined my strategy, Mrs Stratton!'

They were still laughing when Lady Benedict slid up to them and insinuated her slender body between the two of them.

'Mr Chance…' she slanted a look up at him, her expression sultry '…I do believe you are monopolising Mrs Stratton. Let me take you away and…dance…with you…'

Deb saw the flash of expression in Owen Chance's eyes and felt a little shock go through her as she registered how much he disliked Lady Benedict. Fortunately, however, her ladyship did not appear to have noticed, for she was busy admiring her reflection in the long ballroom mirrors. And when Owen Chance spoke, it was so smooth and polite that Deb wondered whether she had made a mistake.

'With the greatest of pleasure, Lady Benedict,' he said, taking her arm and leading her towards the nearest set.

Deb frowned as she watched them walk away. She had intended to ask Richard what he thought about Mr Chance's opinion of Lily Benedict, but when he came to claim her for another dance she forgot about Owen Chance almost immediately and did not give him another thought for the rest of the evening.

It was late when they returned to Marney. Deb had agreed to spend the night there rather than require the coach to take her on to Mallow, but when they reached the house it was to find it in uproar. Whilst they had been away at the ball, the drawing room had been ransacked and some items stolen, chief amongst them Olivia's engraved glass vases.

'The most extraordinary thing,' Olivia said, as she and Deb surveyed the damage the following day, 'was that so very few items were taken or spoilt. It is only the glass really. I suppose that Ford interrupted them. He was making his rounds to check that all the doors and windows were locked and surprised the thief in the act.'

Looking around, Deb was a little puzzled. There was none of the chaos and untidiness that normally accompanied a burglary. There were no papers scattered over the floor, the desk had not been emptied and the valuable collection of china that Ross's mother, the late Viscountess Marney, had collected throughout her life, remained pristine and undamaged.

'How shocking for Ford,' she said. 'How is he this morning?'

Olivia was looking at the cherry-wood display case, her face wrinkled in perplexity. 'Oh, he is much recovered, thank you. Mrs Hillman dosed him up with milk laced with Ross's best whisky and honey for the shock, and the poor man was unconscious before they could even carry him to his bed! Ross was not too pleased either! I have told Ford to rest today, though I have no conviction that he will obey me. He does not like to think of the household running without him.' She touched Deb's sleeve lightly. 'Come and look at this, Deb. Do you see how they forced the lock on my display cabinet? It is almost as though they were looking for something specific.'

Deb ran her fingers over the rough wood about the splintered lock. 'Did they take everything from here, Liv?'

Olivia shook her head. 'No, for they were interrupted before they could empty it. Some of the glasses that Ross purchased at the Customs House auction are still here. They are very pretty, but they have no real value. I cannot understand it…'

Deb opened the lid of the case and picked up one of the remaining glasses. She had never seen them properly since it was only by accident that she had bid for them in the first place and it was Ross who had paid and brought them home. Now she turned the object over in her hands, admiring the quality of the crystal and the delicate engraving of a seagull on one side. It was beautifully executed, caught in full flight, with the wind beneath its wings.

'The glass is very fine and the workmanship exquisite,' she said. 'I imagine they must be worth far more than Ross paid for them.'

'I expect they are worth a lot to a collector,' Olivia agreed, taking out the second of the six and examining it. 'Ross said that John Norton approached him with a view to buying them, but as I had already expressed an interest in starting a collection, Ross would not sell.'

Deb frowned. 'But Sir John was at the auction. He could have purchased them then.'

'Maybe he was caught by surprise when you outbid him,' Olivia said drily. 'Look at the engraving on this anchor, Deb! Is it not the most delicate thing? An artist must have great skill to create such work.'

Deb bent her head and studied the picture. There was something about it that stirred a memory, although she could not place it. She looked at the engravings on the other glasses. They all carried two pictures, one on each side of the glass. The one with the seagull had a tree on the other side. The one engraved with an anchor had the sun on its reverse, and there was another with a ship, that also bore a picture of a small cottage.

'That one is rather attractive, is it not?' Olivia said, with a smile. 'The cottage looks very pretty... I cannot recall the pictures on the other glasses but they were all very finely drawn. There were twelve glasses originally, but the thief must have got away with six of them.'

Something clicked in Deb's memory and instead of the glass in her hand she saw a sheet of paper with cipher symbols on it. She put the engraving down quickly and turned to her sister.

'Liv—' she began.

The door opened.

'Lord Richard Kestrel has called to see you, madam,' Ford announced. His tone was slightly more quavering than normal, although whether that was due to the shock of the previous night, or the whisky still coursing through his blood, Deb was unsure.

Olivia was smiling. 'Oh, show him in, Ford! And pray send to the long paddock to tell Lord Marney that Lord

Richard is here. Lord Richard!' She advanced towards him, hand outstretched. 'How kind of you to call. You can see that we are not in as parlous a state as last night's reports may have led you to believe.'

'I am glad to see that the experience has not overset you, ma'am,' Richard said, a twinkle in his eyes. He bowed to her and then came across to Deb, taking her hand.

'Good morning, Deborah. How are you?'

'I am very well, thank you, my lord,' Deb said, feeling a quite-out-of-proportion pleasure that now they were betrothed, albeit fictitiously, he could address her in so personal a manner. 'It is fortunate that you are here,' she added, 'for there is something I need to speak to you about. Urgently. In private,' she amended, for good measure.

Richard gave her a quizzical look. 'Is there?'

'Yes,' Deb said. 'Perhaps you would care to come with me to the conservatory and inspect Olivia's collection of *Buxus sempervirens*? They are very fine.'

'Are they?' Richard said. 'Then I cannot wait to see them.' He turned to Olivia. 'If you would excuse us, Lady Marney?'

'Of course,' Olivia said, smiling widely. 'Since you are betrothed, there can be no objection to you spending a little time alone together. I had no notion that you were so interested in my horticultural work, Deb!' she added. 'You must let me show you my cuttings from the *Campsis radicans*.'

Deb managed to look suitably grateful. 'Dear Liv, I should be delighted. Just now, however, I do not wish to delay Lord Richard, who is no doubt anxious to be away to discuss horseflesh with Ross.'

'Of course,' Olivia said sweetly.

Deb grabbed Richard's arm and hurried him out into the hall, closing the door behind them. 'There is something that I need to tell you about the burglary,' she said.

She looked around. One of the housemaids was polishing the big windows by the front door, her hand moving slowly as she gawped through the glass at the groom who was leading a horse through its paces on the gravel sweep outside.

'We cannot talk here,' she added. 'We had best go and see these miniature box trees, or whatever it is that Olivia has in the conservatory.'

'That sounds like the sort of invitation I would issue,' Richard said, with a grin, but there was a keen expression in his eyes as he took her arm and they walked down the corridor into the cool green space of the conservatory beyond. Deb unlatched the door and drew him inside, taking a seat on the rustic wooden bench and gesturing to Richard to do the same. All pretence of indolence had dropped from his manner and he watched her with acute interest.

'What is it you have to tell me?' he asked softly.

'Olivia has a collection of glasses that are engraved with the same symbols that were on the secret message,' Deb said, trying not to allow the disturbing effects of his proximity to distract her from her tale. 'I saw them for the first time this morning and recognised the symbols at once—' She broke off at a soft oath from Richard.

'Tell me the entire story, please,' he said tersely.

Deb did so, trying conscientiously to relate it in order and leave nothing out. She told him how she had accidentally bid for the glasses at the Customs House auction, how Sir John Norton had bought a second set and tried to purchase the first from Ross and how half of them had been stolen the previous night. Richard listened and ventured no comment, but Deb could tell he was weighing her words with sharp perception.

'But I cannot understand the connection with the cipher,' she finished. 'Why were the same symbols on the glasses as on the message? It makes no sense.' She spread her hands. 'No one would use engraved glasses to pass secret messages! It would be far too cumbersome a process and take too long.'

Richard nodded. 'That's true. Most messages are undoubtedly written and passed by hand, like the sheet you found in the book. A spy network might, however, use engraved glasses as the master cipher.' He drove his hands into his pockets and got to his feet, pacing the floor thoughtfully.

'I do not understand,' Deb ventured, after a moment.

Richard shot her a look. 'In a written code, the letter A, for example, might in reality represent the letter P. You would go through your secret message substituting all the As for Ps and the same with every other pair of letters, to spell out the message. But this is a pictorial code and until today we had no idea what the pictures meant. But it could be very simple.' He ran his hand through his hair. 'You said that each glass bears two pictures. Suppose, for example, that this is the master you need to break the code. A glass with a picture of the sea and a picture of the sun…'

'Oh!' Deb's face cleared. 'You mean that in the message, the symbol of the sun might represent the sea.'

'Precisely. The pictures are in pairs. If we went back to our secret message and saw that the first symbol was of the sea, we could conclude that the sign we need to replace it with is that of the sun.'

Deb pulled a face. She was struggling. Cryptography evidently was not her strong point. 'It still does not make sense, however,' she complained. 'What does the picture of the sun actually mean?'

'Daylight?' Richard hazarded. 'There might be a corresponding one of the moon to represent night-time.'

'There is!' Deb said excitedly. 'There was a crescent moon and a full moon!'

Richard smiled at her enthusiasm. 'How gratifying. I do believe that we may at last be close to understanding the code.'

'Except that we only have six of the glasses,' Deb said, deflating, 'and no way of knowing how many there were in the first place.'

Richard's eyes narrowed. 'Perhaps that is something we could work on from the other end,' he said. 'Find the engraver. I doubt it can be anyone locally, for that might draw too much attention. London seems more likely. I shall send word to Lucas.'

Deb laughed. 'Or we could find the other glasses! Procure invitations to all the houses in Midwinter and see who is using engraved glasses for their wine!'

Richard's face was grim. 'I suspect that that is exactly what they *are* doing—right under our noses! It would be typical of the damnable arrogance of these spies, drinking toasts to the King with glasses that proclaim their treason. It is a trick that has been used before. The Jacobites did it last century.'

'Raising their glasses to the King across the water,' Deb said, remembering Mrs Aintree's history teaching.

'And inscribing coded messages on the glass as well.'

Deb was frowning. 'There are still many questions. What were the glasses doing at the auction? And who was responsible for the burglary? It cannot be John Norton or Lily Benedict, or Lady Sally, for they were all at the ball last night. I suppose there must be someone else in the Midwinter spy's employ…'

Richard shook his head. 'I confess that that is one of the things that puzzles me,' he said. 'The greater number of people involved, the greater the risk of exposure. It makes sense to keep the matter between as small a group as possible.' He frowned. 'I wonder if there is someone we have overlooked…'

'There is no one else,' Deb pointed out. 'At the least, there is no one else connected with the reading group.'

'No.' Richard straightened. 'I had better go and take a look at those remaining six glasses. I would like to know what pairs of symbols we do have.' He took Deb's hands. 'For goodness' sake, be careful, Deborah. I mislike your involvement in this.'

He pulled her to her feet. They were standing very close together. Richard caught her up in his arms and planted a hard, swift kiss on her mouth.

'Be careful,' he repeated, as his lips left hers.

'I understand,' Deb said. She rubbed her fingers over his lapel. 'You do not want anything to happen to me—'

'No,' Richard said. He looked so fierce that Deb almost flinched. 'I could not *bear* it if anything were to happen to you.'

Their eyes met and held. Deborah took a short, shaken breath. She felt even more dazed by his tenderness than by the kiss, for there had been so much intensity in his eyes that it frightened her. She realised that he was about to say something else. Nervousness gripped her.

'Go,' she said. 'Ross will be awaiting you.'

'Deb—' Richard said.

Deb felt terrified, as though she was on the edge of a precipice, with insufficient courage to carry her through.

'Please,' she said beseechingly. 'I will speak with you later, Richard.'

She saw the stubborn determination on his face and felt almost suffocated by feelings that she could not begin to understand. She turned on her heel and left him standing there, and she knew even as she went that once again it was herself she was running away from, and not he.

## Chapter Thirteen

During the week that followed, Deb was obliged to admit that there was something very pleasant about being affianced to Lord Richard Kestrel. It was all too easy to forget that this was only a pretence of an engagement. Richard was extremely attentive to her in company; on the occasions that they were alone together, his behaviour towards Deb did not alter, which made it even more seductive to imagine that the betrothal was real. Never by word or deed did he imply that they were only involved in a deception. Fortunately also for Deb's peace of mind there was no repetition of the scene in the conservatory. Richard's mood seemed as light as hers and he made no difficult demands on her emotions.

Ross and Olivia watched the courtship with indulgent eyes and even Mrs Aintree was heard to say that Lord Richard had hidden depths. After a while it seemed to Deb that she was the only one who remembered that they were playing a game, and even she was having difficulty quelling the little voice inside that told her it would be pleasant if the betrothal was more than a charade.

Richard escorted her to the theatre in Woodbridge, took her boating on the River Deben and danced with her at the assemblies and private balls. He never once paid the slightest attention to another woman, other than out of courtesy. Deb marvelled at it. Olivia seemed unsurprised when she confided her surprise.

'I always told you that you were misjudging the man,' she said, with a smile. 'He has eyes for no one but you, Deb.'

It was disconcerting to Deb to realise that this was true. Either Lord Richard Kestrel was an extremely accomplished actor who had no trouble in sustaining the impression that he was in love with her or… But Deb refused to contemplate the alternative. Richard had spoken no words of love and just the thought that he might was enough to create a fear and a longing in her that threatened to overset all her careful plans. The engagement was to be of short duration only; it was a pretence; she had no wish to lose either her head or her heart over such a man. And yet Deb knew that she was already in danger and that every moment she spent with Richard just made that danger more acute. The more she tried to ignore it, the more dangerous it seemed.

'It is no wonder that you never catch any spies,' she said one evening, when they were sitting together on a knoll overlooking the Winter Race at sunset. The sky was an angry red that evening and it felt as though there was thunder in the air.

'You have spent all your time with me these two weeks past, Richard, and given nary a thought to your work. The whole of Midwinter could be bursting with nefarious characters for all the attention that you are paying. You must be the poorest spy catcher in the government's employ.'

Richard laughed. 'Justin and Lucas are working on the case,' he said lazily. 'It keeps them out of trouble and gives me the chance to do what I like best.'

Deb turned her head slowly to look at him. They had been discussing Shakespeare, for Lady Sally's reading group was currently studying *The Winter's Tale*. Deb's ancient Shakespearean primer was lying between them and they had had a lively debate in which Richard had defended Leontes for his suspicions about his wife's infidelity and Deb had argued hotly in favour of trust. In the end they had been obliged to beg to differ, but it had been a stimulating discussion and Deb had been vaguely surprised. It was one thing to buy poetry books and quite another to defend one's opinions with such wit and clear knowledge.

'Is spending time with me one of the things that you like best?' she enquired now, and saw Richard smile at the artless honesty of the question. He answered her quite seriously.

'It is. And one of the things that I enjoy most about our situation is that, now we are betrothed, I may spend time alone with you.'

A shadow touched Deb's heart. It was three weeks until they were set to travel to Bath, four weeks—five at the most—before the betrothal was over. Lately she had been thinking about that more and more. She shivered suddenly in the sharp little breeze off the river that heralded a storm.

'It grows oppressive,' she said. 'Let us go back.'

They walked back up to the house in silence. When they reached the door, Richard handed her the book of Shakespeare and bent and gave her a very proper kiss on the cheek.

'I will call on you tomorrow,' he said. 'We are to go riding, I believe.'

Deb nodded slowly. She was at a loss to explain the sudden lowering in spirits that she had experienced there on the riverbank, almost as though something that was starting to become precious to her was about to be taken away.

Richard was watching her expressive face and now he put up a hand and touched her cheek. 'What is it, Deborah?'

'Nothing,' Deb said quickly. 'Nothing but the blue devils.'

She saw the lazy, masculine smile that touched the corner of his mouth. 'May I help banish them?'

Deb's eyes widened as she took his meaning. They were on her doorstep, in full view of anyone who chose to pass by. Yet Richard had never been particularly governed by convention and it did not appear that he was going to behave with propriety now…

He put out a negligent hand and drew her close to him. As soon as his lips touched hers, Deb felt her knees start to buckle. Richard kissed her deftly, expertly, with skill and assurance. There was something so seductive about such single-minded passion that Deb was afraid she might crumple to the ground on the spot, pulling him down so that he could make love to her there and then.

Richard drew her deeper into the shelter of the porch. It felt hot and still within the walls and the air was heavy with the burgeoning storm. Richard's hands were on her waist, where the material of her gown and chemise clung stickily to her skin. As he started to kiss her throat, Deb felt hotter still, as though she were dissolving. She tilted her head back against the wall and felt Richard's lips on the pulse at the base of her neck and his hand move to caress her breast with the gentlest of touches. Deb made a little sound of despair and longing.

Richard let her go and they stood staring at one another, the desire between them as elemental as sheet lightning.

'When—?' Deb whispered.

He did not pretend to misunderstand her. 'Tomorrow,' he said. 'Tomorrow I will send for you and we may go off somewhere and be alone together. Go on in, now, Deborah. Before I forget myself completely.'

Deb did go in to the entrance hall, but there she paused, watching through the window as Richard walked away towards the stables. She felt heated and impatient and near to madness. The clouds were massing overhead and the hall was dark.

Deb went into the drawing room, where she found Mrs Aintree arranging some of the late, pale pink roses that Olivia grew in such profusion at Marney Hall.

'Lady Marney called earlier,' Mrs Aintree confirmed, standing back to view her handiwork and twitching one spray of blooms slightly to the left. 'She wished to speak with you, Deborah. Apparently she has had a letter from your papa this afternoon.' Mrs Aintree nodded towards the mantelpiece. 'There is a letter for you too…'

The miserable feeling that had plagued Deb before now hardened into something more fearful. She snatched up the letter and took it over to the window. She could see Richard in the stable yard, exchanging a few words with the groom, laughing now, raising a hand in farewell as he turned Merlin through the gates. The groom was watching his departure with good-humoured approval, as well he might…

Deb broke the seal on the letter. After the conventional greetings, Lord Walton moved straight to business.

*I am gratified to hear of your betrothal to Lord Richard Kestrel, although I should have been more appreciative had he sought my permission sooner…*

Deb smiled slightly. It was the closest thing to approval that her father was ever likely to express. So Richard had been right—marriage to a rake was by no means unacceptable to her family provided that he was rich and well connected. Her heart warmed slightly—until she remembered that the engagement was only temporary.

*It would please me if you would still come to visit us at Walton next month, despite the unfortunate circumstances surrounding the cancellation of your brother's marriage...*

The fearful feeling solidified into a block of sheer ice in Deb's stomach. The hand holding the letter fell slowly. 'Do you know what this is concerning Guy's wedding, Clarrie?' she said.

'Oh, yes,' Mrs Aintree said cheerfully, clipping a blighted rosebud from the stem. 'Lady Marney was telling me. The most shocking thing! Your brother's fiancée has eloped with your cousin Harry. Surely your father mentions the circumstances in his letter?'

The closewritten lines blurred before Deb's eyes. Her father might well have related the entire matter, but she could not seem to make sense of it. All she was able to see was Richard Kestrel riding out of the stable yard, magnificent on his raking black hunter, the epitome of everything that she desired. Richard Kestrel, the man to whom she was betrothed. Except...

Deb licked her dry lips. Except that the wedding was cancelled and with it all necessity of arriving at Walton Hall with her fleeting fiancé in tow. For cousin Harry had run off with the bride, thereby removing both reasons for the betrothal in one fell swoop. Deb reflected with irony that had she known Harry had a penchant for Guy's intended she could simply have encouraged him to do the deed sooner and save herself the trouble of advertising. If only she had known...

She scanned the letter again, trying to breathe properly.

*Living in such close proximity, one assumes that their acquaintanceship developed into a wholly unsuitable intimacy...* her father wrote disapprovingly.

Deb sighed. 'Oh, dear. Poor Papa! Losing an heiress

daughter-in-law *and* the chance to secure cousin Harry's acres as well.'

Mrs Aintree was shaking her head. 'The best-laid plans…'

'Yes, indeed,' Deb said slowly. She rubbed a hand across her aching brow. 'Well, I am justly served for my own pretence now, I suppose. I must break my betrothal to Lord Richard as soon as possible and acquaint my father of the fact.'

Mrs Aintree put down her scissors and stared. 'My dear Deborah, surely you will do no such thing? You have not been engaged above two minutes.'

Deb frowned. 'What is that to the purpose, Clarrie? I cannot continue to be betrothed to Lord Richard under false circumstances.'

'But you already are!' Mrs Aintree pointed out.

Deb struggled with her thoughts. 'Yes, they are false pretences in the sense that the world believes it to be a genuine betrothal—'

'And must continue to do so for the time being.' Clarissa Aintree came round to sit on the sofa and fix Deb with a severe gaze. 'If you break your engagement now, Deborah, everyone will believe you flighty. Worse, people will talk scandal.'

'But there is no scandal!' Deb ran a hand agitatedly through her hair, scattering some pins on the carpet.

'That has no bearing on the case,' Mrs Aintree said. 'People talk scandal regardless. It is a national pastime. Besides, if anyone had an inkling about your advertisement, I venture to suggest that *that* is scandalous enough to keep the whole of Woodbridge talking for months.'

Deb sighed. She could see the sense in Clarissa Aintree's argument, but she knew it was impossible to keep the truth from Richard. That would be deceitful and, in the end, pointless, for she would be obliged to tell him sooner or later that Guy's wedding was cancelled. A deep feeling of gloom possessed her. It was always better to tackle an unpleasant duty as quickly as possible.

She looked at the clock. 'I was not intending to attend the theatre with Liv and Ross this evening, but it seems that I must go,' she said. 'I know that Lord Richard will be there and I must acquaint him with the truth of the matter, and ask him what he wishes to do now.'

Mrs Aintree shook her head. 'Never ask a man what he wishes to do,' she said, 'or you may receive an answer that you do not care for.'

As she trailed up the stairs, Deb reflected miserably that, whatever Richard's response, she was unlikely to care for it. She could see only two alternatives. They could either break the betrothal immediately or wait a little and break it in a few weeks' time, and either thought left her with an unconscionably miserable feeling inside. She was the one who had instigated the false engagement, insisting that it be for a limited duration only. Yet now that it had run its short course, she was the one who did not wish it to end. She knew that she should examine the reasons why that was, and she knew that she did not want to do so. Her feelings were immaterial, for soon Richard would know the truth and their short but sweet time together would be at an end.

Tomorrow, he had said. But now tomorrow would not bring the ecstasy of physical pleasure. It would bring nothing but the end of the betrothal and the beginning of a new and more barren period to her existence. She was not sure that she could bear it.

Richard had only gone to the theatre that night on Justin's persuasion and then under protest. Justin was an admirer of Mr Oliver Goldsmith's plays. Richard was not. Yet when he saw Deb Stratton in the Marneys' box, the quality of his pleasure surprised him. He had only parted from her a few hours earlier and yet here he was, so delighted to see her again that he felt like a lovesick boy.

Richard had already come to accept, with resignation and humour, that he was hopelessly in love with Deborah Stratton and was falling ever deeper in love with her with each day that passed. He loved the artless candour that prompted her to say things and ask direct questions that other, more sophisticated women would prevaricate over. He loved the way that she watched him when she did not realise that he was already watching her. He was almost certain that she was falling in love with him, but he did not want to force the process, for he was afraid. He had seen the look on her face that day in the conservatory when he had almost told her that he loved her. She was not yet ready to accept a declaration. He faced the thought squarely. He was afraid that if anything upset the delicate balance between them now, he would lose her and never recapture the happiness that was so close within his grasp. Which was why he had not hurried the physical intimacy between them even when every fibre of his being was demanding satisfaction. He had schooled himself to wait, even though the suspense was killing him.

So when Richard studied Deborah's face that night and realised that something was troubling her, all his instincts immediately focussed upon her and what the difficulty might be.

She was sitting very tense and upright in her chair and for once there was no trace of good humour in her face. Indeed, she looked sunk in gloom. At one point she looked directly at him with a very speaking gaze, and Richard smiled at her. She did not smile back; instead her frown seemed to deepen and her blue eyes were cloudy with some emotion that he could not read as they rested on him.

The interval did not seem to come quickly enough.

They met in the theatre foyer.

'Mrs Stratton,' Richard said scrupulously, conscious of the press of the crowd and the curious eyes upon them.

Deb was not so reticent. It was clear that intense emotion was driving her, although Richard was not entirely sure what that emotion could be. She stepped close to him, one hand coming to rest on his lapel. 'I must speak with you.'

Richard could read the distress in her eyes. So could others. He glanced round. People were staring a little now. To hell with them. He covered her hand with his own.

'I will call on you in the morning—' he began.

'I cannot wait that long.' Deb spoke in an urgent undertone. She bit her lip. There was a deep frown on her brow. Richard drew her closer.

'Has something happened?'

'Something dreadful.' Her lips trembled. Her hand clenched on his jacket. 'Guy's wedding is cancelled.'

For a moment the words did not make sense to Richard. He was far more aware of the intimacy of her gesture and the appeal in her gaze. He felt a surge of pleasure that she had turned to him when she was distressed. Then the implication of her words hit him hard.

'Your brother's wedding is cancelled—'

'Yes, and there is worse—his bride has run off with cousin Harry!'

Despite himself, Richard's lips twitched. Rash elopements seemed to be a feature of the Walton family. He leaned closer still. His breath stirred her hair. She smelled distractingly of roses and honey. He was still holding her hand. 'That is unfortunate, but what in particular distresses you?'

He caught a flash of lavender blue as she looked at him and then quickly away. 'Our betrothal needs must be at an end.'

'You mean that as the reasons for our betrothal are removed, you wish to call it off?'

He felt her fingers tremble within his. She had lowered her head now so that Richard could not read her expression. All he could see was the complicated arrangement of curls held up by the diamond slide. He wanted to put a hand beneath her chin and tilt her face up to his, but that was a step too far for the Woodbridge Theatre.

'I think it would be for the best,' Deb said in a steady voice. 'Papa is insisting that we should still travel to Bath so that he may make your acquaintance. Unless you wish to be married off to me in earnest, I suggest that we tell him immediately that it was all a mistake.'

Richard thought quickly. To be married off to her in earnest was precisely what he desired, but he could see from Deb's panic that it was too soon for her. He cursed silently. Matters had been progressing so well. Too well. He had had a mere fortnight to woo her in form and now it was too soon to make a proposal of marriage. She would run from him and he would lose all the ground that he had so carefully gained.

She was running already. He could sense it. She withdrew her hand from his and it felt as though her presence was slipping away from him.

Richard turned them slightly so that Deb had her back to a pillar and his broad shoulders blocked out the inquisitive glances of the crowd.

'If you break the engagement, then your father may well insist you return to live at Walton Hall,' he reminded her gently. 'He will always be looking to find another suitor for you.'

He felt the shudder go through her. Was the thought of matrimony so dreadful to her that she trembled to even think of it? Richard feared it might be so. Her lashes flickered against her cheek.

'I shall contrive a way out of the situation,' she said obstinately. 'You should not be constrained by that, my lord.'

Richard felt the frustration rip through him. She did not want his help now. He had served his purpose and now he was dismissed. He found he was close to losing his coolness.

'You will contrive another scheme like this?' he asked drily. 'You have seen how well this one succeeded.'

That won him a quick glance. 'I thought,' Deb said coldly, 'that you would be pleased. Matrimony can scarcely be appealing to a man of your stamp.'

Richard stepped closer to her and Deb moved back, instinctively trying to put a little distance between them. She did not succeed. Richard followed her with deliberation until her back was hard against the pillar and he was blocking her escape.

'And what sort of a man is that?' he asked pleasantly.

Her blue gaze widened, both at his tone and because of his proximity, which made no concessions to the crowd of people about them. She tilted her chin and held his gaze defiantly. 'The rakish sort!'

Richard narrowed his gaze. Through his frustration and thwarted desire he was conscious that she was hiding something from him and was trying to distract him. She did not wish him to ask her how *she* felt about the broken engagement. She did not wish to be honest about her own emotions. It was the one area in which she had always held back from him.

Richard scanned her face, noting the stubborn set to her mouth and the determination in her eyes. He could think of only one way of breaking through that façade—to shock her.

He drew closer still, resting one hand against the pillar so that his arm brushed the curve of her breast. She tried to shift away from him, but was trapped by his body. He pressed his leg hard and most improperly against hers, through the slippery silk of her dress. Immediately he was aware of the heat emanating from her. She felt as though she was burning up with fever. Her face had flushed and he heard her swift, indrawn breath. He bent closer, speaking for her ears only.

'Since you consider me to be a rake, I have a question for you. You have a habit of changing our agreements after they are made, Mrs Stratton. What I would like to know is whether you intend to release me from my other commission as well.'

He saw her eyes widen to their fullest extent as she took his meaning. She cast a swift, instinctive look over her shoulder. 'We cannot talk about that here.'

'Yes, we can. Do you still wish us to be lovers?'

Her head came up with a jerk. There was a silence between them whilst their gazes met and locked. Around them the throng swelled and chattered. Someone bumped into them and apologised. Neither of them spared a flicker of attention.

Deb cleared her throat. Her voice was husky. 'If you must have an answer now, then I do not know.'

'Not good enough.' Richard bent closer and let his lips brush her ear. 'What is it to be, yes or no?'

He felt the tremor that ran through her. Her eyes did not leave his.

'I cannot—'

He took his hand from the pillar and caught her wrist tightly. 'Yes, you can. Tell me.'

Her breasts rose and fell rapidly with the agitation of her breathing. 'Very well. The answer is yes.'

'Yes, you wish me to be your lover?'

'Yes.' It was a whisper.

'You do not wish us to be betrothed, but you still wish to take me to your bed?'

'Yes!'

Several heads turned. Deb, face scarlet, moderated her tone. 'We should return to the auditorium. I do believe the second act is about to begin, my lord.'

Richard stood back, releasing her wrist. 'I do believe it is,' he murmured.

He watched her as she scurried away and up the stairs to the Marneys' box. He realised that his fists were clenched and he relaxed them very slowly. Damnation. He had not intended to push her so far or so hard. Yet he had had the answer he wanted and he knew there was not a hope in hell of going back now. He would be Deborah Stratton's lover, betrothal or no betrothal. The time had come.

# Chapter Fourteen

*Please meet me at Kestrel Beach this afternoon at two of the clock. There are matters we need to discuss in private.*

Deb's fingers shook a little as she pushed away her plate of toast. Richard's note had arrived with breakfast and it was sufficient to reduce her appetite to zero. Regardless of the word 'please' at the beginning of the sentence, she recognised it for what it was—an order rather than a request. She had every conviction that if she did not comply he would come and fetch her.

So the moment had come, just as Richard had promised. Last night she had broken her engagement because she had not seen what else she could do. Last night she had also stated unequivocally that she still wanted Richard Kestrel to be her lover. It appeared that Richard was about to take her at her word.

Deb shivered and Mrs Aintree gave her a look of concern. 'Do you think that it is time to light a fire in the mornings, my love? These autumn nights are drawing in now and we do not want the house to become damp.'

'Yes…no…I do not know,' Deb said, her mind still pre-occupied with images of herself and Richard locked in ardent embrace. 'That is, yes, we could do so.'

Mrs Aintree looked even more worried. 'Have you taken a chill, Deborah? You do not seem quite yourself this morning and look a little flushed.'

'I am quite well,' Deb said hastily. 'I beg your pardon, Clarrie, I was not attending. I believe I am a little tired. The play did run on last night.'

'Perhaps you should rest this morning,' Mrs Aintree suggested. 'Recover your strength.'

'Yes,' Deb said, trying not to think too much about what it was that she was mustering her strength *for*.

The morning dragged. Deb went into the drawing room and tried to read *La Belle Assemblée* but could not concentrate. Then she fidgeted around with Clarissa Aintree's flower arrangement and quite spoilt the elegant display of roses. She considered going to visit Olivia, but was afraid that she would blurt out the whole of the scene that had taken place with Richard the previous night and the scandalous and shocking afternoon that she was planning. Then she realised that she had not thought of a suitable excuse to explain her absence to Mrs Aintree and spent a fruitless ten minutes racking her brains to come up with something. The clock crept around towards eleven thirty and she ordered an early luncheon, then thought that she should not go to the beach too early for fear of appearing too eager and shameless. The absurdity of this then struck her, for had she not brazenly requested that Richard seduce her? It was a little too late to worry about appearing wanton.

She sat at the table, picking at her food and thinking about this. What she was planning to do was both brazen and abandoned, and yet now that the moment had come she could not seem to help herself. It was anticipation, not dread, that was tripping along her nerves now. She had thought she would never feel like this again, would never forsake the principles that had guided her since Neil's desertion, but she ached for Richard with a desire that was as strong as it was sweet. She shivered and pushed her plate away. She simply was not hungry, at least not for the food.

Finally it was a quarter before two. Deb changed into her red riding habit and went down to the stables.

'Please tell Mrs Aintree that I have gone riding and may well visit my sister after at Midwinter Marney,' she instructed the groom as she dismissed him. 'I am not certain when I shall return, though it may be well into the evening.'

The sandy track through the forest was cool and green, but it did little to soothe the anxiety gnawing at Deb's stomach. In the end she gave an exasperated exclamation and kicked Beauty to a gallop. It was almost as though she was trying to outrun her demons. They hurtled down the sandy path and broke through the trees and out onto the beach. The curve of sand spread out before her, a perfect semicircle of white with the dunes glistening golden at the end where the low cliffs met the sea. The breeze stirred the marram grass.

There was a thunder of hooves and Deb swung around in the saddle. Richard was galloping towards her across the sand and without hesitation Deb dug her heels into Beauty's sides and galloped across the wide expanse, the sand flying from the hooves, the water spraying out in an arc as they caught the edge of the incoming tide.

This time it was Deb who won the contest. She reined in Beauty, the colour high in her cheeks, eyes bright and her hat askew. 'Oh, that was wonderful!' she burst out.

Richard was smiling at her enthusiasm and suddenly some of her nagging anxiety eased. His gaze was warm and he held out his arms to her to help her from the saddle. After a moment she allowed him to help her down—and felt a little *frisson* of disappointment when he let her go promptly.

'Are you hungry?' he asked, and Deb found herself blushing to the roots of her hair. She met his eyes, then burst out laughing.

'It is not very romantic but I confess that I am. I could not eat any luncheon.'

It was odd how the ride across the beach had broken the tension between them. Richard led her across to a knot of pines, where Deb was astonished to see that he had set up a picnic beneath the trees. There was ice-cold white wine and there were tiny chicken pies, smoked ham, strong cheese and fresh bread.

'Was this what you intended us to do this afternoon?' she said, eyes widening.

She saw his wicked grin. 'What did you imagine that I intended?'

Deb held his eyes. 'I thought…oh, you know what I thought! Do not make me spell it out…'

Richard laughed. 'That comes later…' he said, and Deb felt hot and cold at the same time, for she could not tell if he was in earnest.

They sat beneath the pine trees and ate the food that Richard had brought; under his prompting, Deborah talked about her childhood near Bath and her family and her life since she had moved to Midwinter. They had talked before during the short weeks of their betrothal, but strangely, given what was to follow, this was the first time that she felt entirely at ease with him.

After a while she stopped talking. She felt a little embarrassed. 'I have told you a great deal about myself, my lord, and in return I know almost nothing about you,' she said.

Richard looked at her. He was propped on one arm beside her. The sunlight was in his thick dark hair, turning it a rich conker brown. There was a smile in his eyes that made Deb feel very warm.

'You have known me for over a twelvemonth,' he pointed out.

Deb frowned a little. 'I know that you dance well and can charm the dowagers,' she said. 'I even know that you were in the Navy and now you have turned spy catcher. But I do not really know *you*.'

'Do you need to know me?' Richard asked.

'You mean because we no longer need to pretend that we are betrothed?'

'No, I mean do you need to know me in order for me to become your lover?'

Deb almost choked on her wine. He was watching her but there was no amusement in his gaze.

'I thought not,' she said slowly. 'But I think that I was mistaken.'

Richard nodded. The wicked smile that she had missed lit his face then and he tumbled her down into the grass beside him. Deb gasped as her bonnet rolled away into the sand and she found herself staring up at the bright blue of the sky through the interlacing of the pine branches. Richard's arm was still about her waist and she could feel the press of his body against hers as they lay close, but he made no attempt to kiss her.

'This is nice,' Deb said, wriggling a little to get more comfortable on the soft sand. 'I seldom look at the world this way. It is not considered ladylike to lie flat on one's back and look at the sky.'

'It is even better at night,' Richard said. 'One can lie back and look at the stars and feel very small.'

Deb turned her head and looked at Richard instead of the sky. He was very near and it seemed strange to be studying him at such close quarters. Strange but exceedingly pleasant. He was looking at her too. She could see the tiny lines around his eyes and mouth that deepened when he smiled, and the deep, soulful blackness of his eyes. Knowledgeable eyes that Deb fancifully imagined could read her every thought. She shivered lightly.

'Could we do that?' she asked. 'Lie here and look at the stars?'

'We can do whatever we like,' Richard said.

Deb's shivers deepened. 'Has that always been your guiding principle?' she questioned lightly.

Richard released her and turned over to lie on his back, hands behind his head. 'It was for many years,' he said.

'And now?'

'Now I hope that I am not so careless for the feelings of others that I take what I want without consideration.'

His gaze challenged her and Deb felt the trembling intensify within. He would not be going against her wishes when he took her. There was nothing that she wanted more.

She rolled on to her stomach the better to study him. She looked down at his face and felt her lips curve in a smile.

'What makes a man become a rake and a gambler?' she asked.

'Boredom, lack of employment, too much time and too much money,' Richard said lazily. He turned his head and their eyes met. 'There can be no excuse for it.'

Deb frowned. She had not expected him to be so condemnatory. 'You are very hard on yourself, Richard.'

Richard's expression was shuttered. 'I was a spoilt young man. I confess it. I was meant for the church, you know.' His smile was self-mocking. 'How inappropriate would that have been?'

Deb stifled a laugh. 'The church? Was that your father's idea?'

'It was. He did not know me very well.' Richard sighed. 'I do not believe he knew any of us very well, to tell the truth. He had an image to which he wished his sons would conform, and none of us did.' He sighed. 'Papa thought that inherited wealth should not excuse a man from the necessity of doing something useful with his life and I agree with him on that. However, he also thought it his right to dictate what I should do. Naturally I rebelled against his views. I set forward to cut a swathe through the bored ladies of London society and prove emphatically that I would make a shockingly poor parson.'

Deb saw the hard lines settle deeper on his face. She could not help herself. She reached across and brushed the hair back gently from his forehead. He did not move to repulse her and yet as soon as she had done it she felt a little shy, and withdrew her hand at once.

'Do you regret your behaviour?' she asked.

'In part.' Richard turned his head slightly and looked at her. 'I regret the selfishness and the hurt I inflicted so thoughtlessly—' His gaze slid away from hers as though he could not quite bear the candour of her gaze.

'Lady Diana Elliot?' Deb asked.

She heard him sigh. 'That was probably the worst of my excesses. I treated her with absolute disrespect because I simply did not care. I am not proud of that.'

There was a little silence. The late summer breeze sighed through the marram grass and caught up a handful of sand, spinning it around in a miniature whirlwind. Deb let the grains run through her fingers.

'Was it boredom that prompted you to join the navy?' she asked.

Richard's eyes were narrowed against the sun, where it slanted through the pines and fell in dazzling bars on the white sand.

'It was. It seemed rather amusing at first and it annoyed my father almost as much as my refusal to become a priest.

His idea of gainful employment did not involve risking one's life for one's country.'

'And yet you seem to have been rather good at it.'

Richard shifted and Deb sensed that he was a little uncomfortable. 'I did well enough.'

'Ross said that you were courageous to within a point of rashness,' Deb said.

Their eyes met in a split second of tension, then Richard smiled. 'So you have been asking Ross about me, Deborah? I rather like that.'

Deb blushed. 'I was curious.'

'It seems to be one of your besetting sins,' Richard said, a little drily.

Deb blushed harder. 'I confess that I do not calculate matters as you do. I act on impulse, I ask questions if I am curious, I always speak before I think it through.'

Richard laughed. 'And I like you for it.'

Deb drew a circle in the sand with her finger. 'It gets me into trouble.'

'Yes,' Richard said. 'I imagine it does.'

'I released mice into the ballroom at Olivia's come out and terrified Mrs Aintree when I was twelve by setting the conservatory on fire.'

'Why did you do that?' Richard asked.

'I was trying to ripen the fruit,' Deb said gloomily. 'Mama had some ornamental pineapple trees and I had not realised that growing fruit was a slow and delicate process.'

She drew a few wavy lines around through the sand circle. 'And then I eloped with Neil. That was the most impulsive and foolish thing that I ever did.'

Richard was watching her, an intent expression in his dark eyes. 'And why did you do that?' he enquired.

Deb did not meet his gaze. She sat up and drew her knees up to her chin.

'Mama was forever throwing eligible men in my way,' she said, 'but they were all old and gouty and dull as sticks. Then Papa suggested that as I could not find a man to suit me I could marry cousin Harry. His land marched with Papa's and it seemed a good match, but I found Harry's fat white hands and his bad breath to be quite unappealing.'

'Understandably.'

'Well, I am glad that you *do* understand,' Deb said, 'for Papa was not so sanguine. Then Neil came to Bath on furlough and he looked so dashing in his red uniform that I fell in love with him at once. He courted me in secret.' She sighed. 'I suppose that I should have realised that he had no integrity, but it all seemed so exciting. I was bored and did not care about Neil's family or where he had come from. I thought that he truly cared for me too. We eloped to Gretna and then...' She frowned. Without realising it, she had strayed very close indeed to dangerous territory. It seemed that Lord Richard Kestrel had a way of making her confide without even realising. She shifted uncomfortably.

'And then?' Richard prompted.

Deb averted her face, wishing that she were still wearing her bonnet and could profit from the shelter it afforded her. 'And then I found myself living in a poky boarding house in Brighton,' she said. 'Papa refused my dowry because we had eloped and Neil blamed me, of course. He would shout and swear at me, then go out carousing with his friends and return drunk, or not at all...' Deb rubbed her forearms vigorously with her hands to dispel the goose pimples on her arms, but the chill inside was more difficult to banish. 'I was young and inexperienced and it made the disillusion more difficult to bear. Then Neil's regiment was ordered to India when we had been married but three weeks and he could not wait to go. That made me realise once and for all what a fool I had been. He died a mere six weeks later, although I did not know it for some time. I...' She made a sudden gesture, obliterating the sand circle with her hand. 'But that is quite enough on that...'

She knew that Richard would conclude that her memories were too painful. Everyone always made that assumption. It was true, but not for the reasons that they supposed. People imagined Neil Stratton to have been a cruel husband, a lout and a womaniser. That was also true. Fortunately no one ever guessed that he had also been a fortune-hunting bigamist.

Deb looked up suddenly and met the warmth of Richard's regard. She was struck by his expression. He did not look as though he was speculating about the truth. He looked as though he had merely accepted what she had said...and still liked her, despite the impetuous foolishness that had got her into such trouble. For a second she trembled on the verge of telling him the entire truth. Then she blushed and looked down.

'I believe that you have skated over your own experiences in order to question me about mine,' she observed, turning the subject. 'You did not mention what happened when you were invalided out of the Navy...'

She saw Richard's face harden. 'There is little enough to tell. I took a bullet in the shoulder and then caught a fever; by the time I had recovered my strength and my own mind again, my father had arranged for my commission to be withdrawn.'

Deb stared at him, her attention arrested. 'You mean that whilst you were ill he...he destroyed your livelihood? How disgraceful!' She had seldom felt so indignant in her life.

She saw Richard smile at her vehemence. 'No doubt he thought that he had the right. He had never wanted me to be a sailor. He thought it too dangerous, though he had sons to spare. He argued that I had had my chance when he had offered me a good living and the opportunity to pursue a career in the church.'

Deb shook her head stubbornly. 'That does not excuse him! To make such an arrangement whilst you were sick and unable to reason with him—' She broke off. 'I do not suppose that that would have made any difference.'

'Very likely not. He was not open to reason. And he had powerful friends.' Richard sat up. 'He did not require my permission to change my life.'

'No, but...' Deb frowned deeply. 'That is not the point. He did not respect what you wished to do.'

'Just as your father did not respect the fact that you had no wish to marry your cousin,' Richard pointed out. 'We were both subject to parents who thought that they knew what was best for us.'

'You sound very calm,' Deb said, still feeling indignant, 'but it cannot have been easy nevertheless.'

Richard shifted slightly. 'It was not. I hated him for what he had done. So I went back to the other life I knew irritated him—that of drinking and gambling and flirting and wasting my time...'

'How did you get your commission back?' Deb asked.

Richard grinned. 'When Justin inherited the title he called me in and told me that I could go to hell if I pleased, but not with his blessing. He threatened to cut me off if I did not go back to doing something useful!'

Deb gasped. 'What happened?'

'We had an almighty argument. I was so angry that I would have called him out if I could have done,' Richard said ruefully, 'but I soon saw the hard truth in what he said. He gave me back my sense of purpose.'

Deb stared up at the fluffy white cloud that had, for a brief moment, obscured the sun.

'A sense of purpose…' she murmured. 'I have never felt the need for one of those.'

'No?' Richard's voice was soft.

'No.' Deb stretched in the warmth as the sun came out again. 'I live from day to day. It is enough for me to enjoy the peace of Midwinter and a quiet existence.'

'You do not find it *too* quiet?'

Deb smiled a little. Nowhere could be too quiet to keep her secret. 'It used to be a very slow place, but then you came…'

'And are you sorry?' Richard's breath drifted across the soft skin of her throat, making her shiver a little.

'No…' Deb turned her head and looked at him. There was an expression in his eyes that made her a little breathless. 'We grow melancholy with all this confession,' she said, moving a little away from him and attempting to shake the sand out of her skirts. When she tried to dust it off, it clung stickily to the folds of her riding habit. 'So that is why ladies are not encouraged to lie in the sand,' she said with a sigh. 'I knew that there would be a practical reason.'

Richard laughed. 'I think it is more to do with the fact that lying down is in itself a rather dangerous occupation,' he said, 'particularly when there is a gentleman present as well.'

Deb eyed him cautiously. 'That also makes a deal of sense, especially if the gentleman in question is a rake.'

Richard was laughing at her. 'Do you not trust me, then?'

'Can I?'

'Of course. I promised that I would never do anything that you did not wish me to.'

'So you did.' Deb's lips curved in a little smile. 'I do not believe that that sets much of a limit on your actions.'

Richard laughed. 'You are very honest, Deb.'

'I cannot see any point in being otherwise,' Deb admitted, 'when I was the one who shamelessly propositioned you.'

'You did not seem so sure last night.'

Deb gave a sigh. 'Oh, I was sure. I merely had difficulty in admitting it in public.'

The heat of Richard's gaze scorched her. 'And now that we are in private?'

Deb's pulse raced. 'I am frightened.'

'So you should be,' Richard said.

He reached for her; before she had time to react, he had tumbled her into his arms. His lean features had hardened with purpose. This time he did not merely hold her close, but brushed his lips tantalisingly over hers. Deb arched against him and instantly his mouth firmed over hers, exerting pressure against her lips, which parted involuntarily to admit the thrust of his tongue.

Deb was lost. She felt hot and dizzy and adrift. Her breath caught and she instinctively tried to retreat as Richard's masculinity threatened to overwhelm her. He showed no gentleness now and would not allow her to withdraw. His grip tightened, holding her fast as his mouth ravished hers with slow seduction.

'I want you to know exactly what it is you have asked for…' he murmured, when his lips left hers.

Deb made an incoherent little sound as his fingers skimmed her cheek and slid down her neck, gossamer light. Richard bent his head to tease the pulse that beat in the hollow of her throat and Deb's entire body jerked with response. She felt heavy and languid, every inch of her skin vividly alive to his touch. His hand moved to the high neck of her riding habit, slipping the mother-of-pearl buttons from their loops one by one. His palm brushed the curve of her breast through the material of her gown, and then Deb felt his fingertips within the bodice, stroking lightly over the cotton of her chemise.

She had already been trembling at the unexpected contact but now intense shivers racked her whole body. Richard cupped her breast, taking the soft weight into his palm before continuing the caresses that were driving her to the edge of madness. She had never experienced anything like it. When Neil had touched her, clumsy and selfish in his pursuit of pleasure, she had frozen and felt nothing but revulsion. Under Richard's gently stroking hands she felt as though she was melting with excitement and desire. And when he brought his lips back to hers, kissing her again with an imperious demand that drew a heated response from her, she forgot everything except the need to satisfy the glorious, painful claims of her own body.

Richard eased away. With his lips a bare inch away from hers he said, 'As I said once before, anticipation provokes the greatest excitement of all...'

Deb groaned with frustration. She opened her eyes and slowly the blue sky and the puffy white clouds and the shifting leaves came back into focus.

'Damnation, Richard,' she said, her temper catching alight, 'I would like to make you suffer the way that you do me.'

Richard's smile was wry. 'I think you will do exactly that, Deborah,' he said. 'In fact, you already do. Wanting you and yet not taking you plagues me like nothing I have ever experienced before.'

There was a heated silence.

Deb scrambled to her feet. 'I can hear the servants coming back to tidy our picnic away,' she said, her fingers slipping on her buttons in her haste to make her bodice respectable again. 'I think that I shall walk down to the sea before...'

'Before?' Richard asked mockingly.

Deb did not reply. She could not.

The sun was starting to edge lower in the sky although the sand was still hot and threw back a warmth that scorched Deb's face. She felt shaken and restless and unsatisfied, but beneath that was a still more disturbing and complex emotion. The day, with its confidences and its intimacy, had made her long for much more. She did not want this time together to end.

She was aware of Richard getting to his feet and following her and by the time she reached the water's edge he was by her side. He took her hand and interlaced his fingers with hers and she could not prevent the little sigh that went through her. Richard felt it and stopped walking. He pulled her around to face him.

'Deborah? What is the matter?'

Deb looked into his eyes. The sunlight off the sea was blinding and she could not read his expression.

'I was thinking about you,' she said honestly. 'Worrying about you, truth to tell. You said that you joined the Navy because you were bored and it made me think that you must have taken up this spy catching for the same reason. And Ross says that you can be reckless.'

Richard laughed. Carefully, aware of the servants who scurried about tidying up the remnants of their picnic, he drew her into his arms for a brief embrace. This time his touch was gentle and tender, offering comfort, not passion.

'Do not worry about me, sweetheart. I am always careful.'

Deb shook him slightly. Pressed close to his chest, she could smell the scent of his cologne mingled with the woodsy smell of the pines and the fresh salt air.

'Must you always be like this?' she demanded.

Richard's lips brushed her hair. 'Like what?'

Deb looked up, her eyes stormy. 'So careless and nonchalant and… Oh, you know what I mean! You pretend that nothing is of importance to you.'

'Some things matter to me a great deal,' Richard said, and again Deb heard the deeper feeling in his voice. He released her and his tone was cool and his own once more.

'Did you intend to go paddling in the sea or merely to get your riding boots wet?'

Deb looked down. The incoming tide was swirling about her ankles and had already splashed her boots and darkened the hem of her dress with patches of water. She gave an exclamation. 'Oh! I would love to take my boots off and run through the surf, but—'

'But?' Richard queried, his brows quizzically raised.

'But it is like lying in the sand—quite inappropriate for a lady!'

So saying, Deb bent and unbuttoned the boots, throwing them carelessly up the beach and, with a whoop of sheer excitement, ran into the waves.

The chill shock of the water brought her up short as it swirled about her knees and she gasped aloud. 'It is so cold!'

Richard was almost doubled up with laughter. 'Of course it is. Why do you think I did not venture in?'

In reply, Deb scooped up a handful of water and threw it at him. It missed him, but he set off down the beach towards her threateningly and with a squeal Deb ran, splashing through the water, her hair tumbling down her back. The sun was warm on her face, but the water was numbingly cold and her stockinged feet sank into the sand, slowing her progress. In the end she collapsed on a sand dune, out of breath, her skirts soaking and her face flushed.

Richard was still laughing as he joined her. 'You, Mrs Stratton, are the most complete hoyden!'

'I was never like this until I met you,' Deb said pertly,

squinting against the sun. 'You are a bad influence, Lord Richard.'

Richard put a hand down and pulled her negligently to her feet and into his arms. Deb could feel the sea water soaking through her dress and into the crisp linen of his shirt. Her body warmed as it took heat from his and their blood beat together.

'You were always like this underneath the surface,' Richard said softly. 'I knew it as soon as I met you.'

Deb's breath caught. 'I was trying to be as cool and composed as Olivia—'

Richard's voice held a betraying tenderness. 'Please do not. You have too much life and vitality to repress it beneath convention.'

The sun dipped behind the trees and Deb shivered a little. Her dress was sticking to her damp legs and her toes were cold. Richard tried to release her hands.

'We should go back,' he said.

Deb hesitated, holding on to him when he would have turned away. 'Must we?'

The breeze blew chill against her skin. Now that the sun was going down the air seemed much cooler. In an hour, it would be dark.

Richard looked at her. 'You should change out of those damp clothes.' His tone was completely neutral.

Deb knew what he was doing. He was giving her one last chance to change her mind and run away. After this, the die would be cast.

She tugged on his hand. 'I do not wish to go back. We could send a message with the servants to tell Clarrie that I will return later this evening. I want to listen to the sea at sunset and watch the stars come out.'

Richard gave her a long, hard look and Deb trembled inside. All day there had been an edge of dangerous attraction between them. It had lain buried when they had been speaking of their past and when they had sat together in the bright sunlight. It had mingled with the pleasures of riding together and eating and drinking, and playing in the sea. It had deepened with the intimacy that had sprung up between them as they shared some of their secrets. It had flared into life when Richard had kissed her. But when the darkness came and she was out here with him in this wild and empty place, then…then that dangerous attraction would come to the fore and she would have no will to resist it, no desire but to have one night in heaven to end this perfect day.

# Chapter Fifteen

The servants had packed the remains of the picnic away and had received, blank-faced, Richard's instructions to return to Mallow House and inform Clarissa Aintree that he would be escorting Mrs Stratton home later that evening. Richard had brought the horses across to where Deb was sitting by the sandy track that led away from the beach towards Kestrel Forest. He looked at her as he approached. She was watching the sun, bright red and round as a dinner plate, sink behind the pine trees and cast the last of its light across the rippling sea. Her hair was loose about her shoulders in a golden cascade. As Richard came up she turned to look at him.

'I thought that we were to stay here for a while and watch the moon come up?'

Richard bent to adjust the Merlin's girth, then straightened up.

'I had a better idea,' he said slowly, watching her face. He wanted to see her reaction to his words. 'As you know, Justin has an old hunting lodge in the forest, barely more than a cottage. None of us has been there for an age and it is very probably damp, but there is a splendid view across the terrace to the sea.'

Deb's face lit up and the tense feeling inside Richard eased slightly. He wanted her to be very certain of what she was doing. In the past, the women he had trysted with had been skilled seducers in their own right, bored wives looking for a little entertainment, professional courtesans whose amatory expertise was at least the equal of his own.

Deborah Stratton was different. Vivid, passionate, spontaneous, she was nevertheless an untried innocent in the ways of love and her vulnerability called up every protective instinct he had ever possessed.

It also sharpened his desire to a very fine edge and his possessive instincts to an almost intolerable level. He wanted to make her forget Neil Stratton forever. He wanted her experience of love to be with him and him only, he wanted to imprint himself on her in the most deep and masculine and primitive way possible.

He knew he had to keep a grip on his self-control or he would be completely lost.

He helped Deb up into the saddle, then swung up on to Merlin's back and drew ahead along the track. The pine trees mingled with old oak and beech here and grew close to the sandy path. The forest was shadowed and still in the twilight. There was no sound now except for the soft clop of the horses' hooves and the cawing of the rooks as they returned to roost.

The path wound slowly around the headland and the trees drew closer and the darkness deeper. There was a silence between them now, but it was not easy. Richard wondered if Deborah was about to turn tail and flee. He held Merlin back to fall in with her, dropping a hand over hers on the reins.

'The house is up ahead, around this bend.' He felt the tremor that went through her and stilled, holding his breath against the thought that she might take flight. He reminded himself that if she did so, that would be perfectly acceptable. The hunger within him would have to remain unslaked. It was imperative that he did nothing to frighten Deb away now or she would never trust him again.

'Do you wish to continue?' He kept his voice light and felt in response a very slight nod from her. Releasing her hand, he kept the horses close together, reassuring her with his presence beside her as they rounded the corner and came out from under the trees into a clearing on the edge of the forest.

He heard Deb catch her breath. Whilst they had been riding the sun had sunk below the horizon and the sky overhead had deepened to a sapphire blue, paling to turquoise where it met the sea. The first white pinpricks of the stars pierced the dark and down on the beach the sand gleamed and the drag of the surf was a muted roar, soothing in its repetition.

Deb rode forward slowly to the edge of the terrace. The house was behind them, closed and silent, waiting. It was tiny—one room and a scullery and closet below, and a tower room upstairs with huge windows facing east across the sea.

'It is very beautiful.' Deb's voice was soft. She half-turned in the saddle to look at him. 'Thank you for bringing me here, Richard.'

Richard dismounted and helped her down, holding her body close to his. Apart from one tiny tremor that he felt go through her, she made no move either towards him or away, but held herself steady as though barely breathing. He knew that she was trembling inside and it lit a passionate flame in him even as he felt a new wash of gentleness go through him. In the gathering darkness he could no longer see her features clearly, but her hair brushed his cheek and he caught the faint scent of honey and roses, the perfume that he always associated with Deborah. It was enough to turn his bones to water. He almost kissed her there and then, forgetting his vow to treat her gently and make love to her sweetly and slowly. He cleared his throat.

'Sometimes the moon rises directly above the sea and lays a trail clear across the waters,' he said. 'On summer nights when we were boys we would sit here on the terrace, telling tales of pirate ships and sea monsters. I did not know then that I would come to love the sea so well—'

He broke off as he saw her smile. 'You speak like a poet,' she teased. Her voice sank to a whisper. 'Love by the light of the moon…'

Richard caught a sharp breath, took her hand, and drew her across the terrace to the door of the house. The sand crunched beneath their feet. The door swung open beneath Richard's touch and then they were across the threshold with not a word spoken between them.

There were practical matters that needed attention. Richard remembered where to find candles and there were the makings of a fire in the grate, but once he had seen to Deborah's immediate comfort he had to go out to attend to the horses and stable them at the back. He hesitated in the doorway, looking back at her. In the candlelight she looked so pale he thought that she might faint. Her face was all eyes and she watched him with the apprehensive intensity of a mouse watching the cat. Richard's heart smote him. All the casual confidence with which he normally approached his conquests died away and he felt as untried as a green boy.

'I will fetch some water from the well,' he said. 'Are you hungry or thirsty? I do not suppose that there is any food, but there may be a bottle of brandy hidden away somewhere. Are you cold? There are blankets upstairs and the closet is by the scullery.'

The paucity of what he was offering her suddenly struck him. Oh, hell, what a stupid idea this had been! A mouldering house hidden away in the forest with no fine sheets nor champagne, no food, nor the soft scent of flowers, or warmth, nor comfort… He clenched his fists in an agony of self-reproach, within an inch of taking her hand and dragging her back to civilisation and handing her over to Mrs Aintree, never to touch her again.

And then she smiled at him, very sweetly. 'Richard,' she said, 'go and stable the horses.'

He was as quick as he could be, to the general disgust of Beauty and Merlin who objected to the cavalier manner in which he thrust them into the stalls and removed their tack without rubbing them down. Fortunately Justin had kept a small supply of hay at the lodge for those occasions on which he and his brothers chose to ride into the forest. Richard left the horses munching crossly and hastened back to the house, closing the door and, after a moment's hesitation, shooting the bolt home.

The room was empty and Deborah was nowhere to be seen. The door to the scullery was closed. Panic clutched at him. Surely she could not have run away when his back was turned? Had she locked herself in the latrine? What a damnable thought. Was she so nervous that she could not face him, let alone go through with this one night of passion, the idea of which was even now turning to ashes in his mouth? Had she run away into the forest alone and in the dark? It was the sort of impulsive act that he could quite easily imagine Deborah doing, only to regret her actions later. His hand hovered over the latch and then he heard a sound from above. He let his breath out on a huge, shaky sigh of relief Thank God she was safe. Much more of this and he would be incapable of blowing out a candle, never mind making love to Deborah. He felt exhausted.

'Richard, come and see!' Deb's voice floated down the stairs, an edge of pleasure and excitement clearly audible in her voice.

The tight anxiety in Richard's chest eased and he took the stairs two at a time, reaching the door of the tower room and stopping dead on the threshold.

In the time that he had been away, Deb had managed to light a fire in the grate and it glowed with a heart of warmth. Two candles burned on the wooden table by the door, casting their flickering shadow over a bed piled high with cushions and blankets. There was a faint fragrance of lavender in the air.

'I found the linen in the Armada chest,' Deb said, gesturing towards the bed. 'Everything has been stored properly and is quite dry…' Her voice faltered and Richard saw the flash of anxiety in her eyes and smiled at her. Even now she could not be coy about why they were there. She would not hide behind pretence or bashful words. He loved her for it. In fact, he could not imagine ever loving her more…

She was standing by one of the long windows and he reached her side in two strides, wrapping his arms about her and pulling her back against him. His chin rested on the top of her head. He could feel the tension in her now, the tiny trembles that racked her body. She turned slightly so that they were looking out to sea, where the moon, three-quarters full and hard as silver, was climbing from beyond the long line of the horizon. For a moment there was no sound but the wash of the waves and the humming of the breeze about the eaves. A ship slipped across the edge of the bay, the moonlight reflecting briefly on its sails.

'A privateer?' Deb said. She turned her head and slanted a look up at him. 'Should you not go and raise the alarm?'

Richard smiled. 'I should, but I shall not.'

There was a pause. 'I found the brandy,' Deb said. She turned in his arms so that she was facing him. Her cheeks were a little flushed. 'I thought perhaps that it might be a good idea.'

'We won't need it,' Richard said. He looked down at her, scanning her face as though trying to memorise her, feature by feature. There was a silence. After a moment, a tiny hint of frown touched her brow.

'Richard? Are we going to make love or not?'

He stared down into her face for one long moment more whilst the fierce desire returned like the cut of a whip to rage through his body. Then he smiled at her, his slow, wicked smile. 'Yes, Deborah,' he said, 'we are.'

Deb was terrified. She wished that she had taken several large swigs from the brandy bottle before Richard had come back. She wished that she had ridden away when he had given her the chance. She wished that she had never advertised for a fiancé in the first place, let alone entertained the ridiculous idea of asking Richard Kestrel to teach her about love.

Except that it was too late now. Except that she ached for his touch and wanted him with a desperation that knew no bounds. She always had, ever since she had first met him. The knowledge shocked and excited her in equal measure. There seemed no room for shame, no matter that she knew it was morally wrong. And now she was about to get what she wanted.

*Be careful what you wish for…*

The words of warning that Mrs Aintree had imparted to her as a child echoed in her head and almost raised a feverish laugh within her, except that Richard was kissing her now and all other sensations died swiftly under the devastating power of his touch. His mouth was warm and strong against her lips, caressing her, tantalising her. His hands slid down to clasp her waist and draw her closer against his body, so close that she could feel his hardness pressed against her. Again the shock and the helpless arousal flooded through her, turning her limbs weak with longing. She clutched at his shoulders, pulling him tight against her. Her nipples stiffened and peaked against the relentless pressure of his body and a tingling sensation of delight filled her abdomen.

His tongue curled lazily, sensuously against hers, and Deborah felt as though she was melting in the heat, slivers of white-hot desire licking through her blood.

Richard pressed her back against the wall, using his hips to hold her body still. She could feel how aroused he was and the shock roared through her again, her senses swimming. She felt his fingers once more at the buttons of her riding habit. He was shaking almost as much as she; the buttons slipped between his fingers. The knowledge that she could do this to him sent a heady feminine satisfaction through her and she slid her hand inside his shirt, revelling in the gasp he gave as her hand touched his naked chest.

The fastenings on her gown eased and Deb arched against his hands, obeying an instinct as deep as time. His fingers skimmed her nipple, cupped her breast, and then the bodice of the riding habit fell away, leaving her in her chemise and skirts.

'You wear no stays…'

Deb opened her eyes. For a moment the candlelight seemed very bright, hurting her eyes. Richard was staring at her as though she was the most exquisite thing that he had ever seen and it was oddly humbling. His hands were resting gently on her bare shoulders amidst the tangle of her blonde hair, and his eyes were devouring the curves of her breasts where they rose above the edge of her shift.

Deb cleared her throat. 'I seldom do, and never with a riding habit. I find tight underwear too constricting.'

Richard gave a muffled groan, as though the thought was too much for him. 'Oh, Deborah—'

His agony shot her though with all the stunning power of a lightning bolt. Suddenly, feverishly, she reached for him, undoing the buttons of his shirt in haphazard fashion, running her hands with glorious triumph over his bare shoulders, pressing her lips to the warm skin of his chest.

Richard's response was instantaneous. He picked her up and tossed her on the bed, where she lay amidst the tumble of lavender-scented blankets and cushions, slightly winded and wholly aroused. The bed was soft against her back and she sank into its depths, borne down a second later by the weight of Richard's body against hers. Deb struggled to right herself but was held still; Richard was deliberately kneeling on her skirts, keeping her flat on her back whilst he caressed her breasts through the thin cotton of her bodice, then eased it aside so that she was naked to the waist.

Deb wriggled desperately. His mouth swooped down and took one of her nipples, and she shuddered beneath the hot stroke of his tongue. The air was cool on her exposed skin and his hands and lips roamed at will, tasting and touching. He tangled one hand in her hair and drew her face up so that he could kiss her again, a burning kiss that branded itself on her soul. The friction of his bare chest against her breasts was intolerable pleasure. Deb writhed beneath him, clutching him to her.

Her skirts and petticoats were becoming a problem, tangled as they were about her legs. She thought that Richard would remove them, but when he drew away from her for a moment it was to rip off his own clothing, not hers. His boots crashed against the leg of the table as he discarded them. The candlelight trembled. Deb half-sat on the bed, her hair sliding over her bare shoulders and down her back, her eyes wide as she took in his nakedness.

'My goodness…' The breath trembled in her throat as her gaze travelled over the width of his shoulders, the long line of his back, the narrow waist, the firm curve of his buttocks. In the golden light he looked beautiful. Deb swallowed hard.

'Richard…' she said beseechingly.

He gave her no time to be afraid. One moment he was standing before her and the next he was kneeling beside her on the bed again, holding her upper arms as he kissed her with a searing intensity. Deb collapsed back on the cushions, her eyes closing. A moment later they opened wide as she felt Richard's hand steal up her thigh, pushing her skirts up as he went, parting her legs.

'Do you not mean to take it off?' she whispered and felt all the breath knocked from her body as he replied, 'Not this time.'

Understanding and desire hit her in a headlong wave. He did not intend to remove the rest of her clothing. She was naked to the waist, but below that was the heavy velvet skirt of her habit, the froth of her petticoats, her stockings, her boots…

She dug the heels of her boots into the bed and arched upward as she felt him spread her legs wider. This was beyond anything that she had ever dreamed. The shattering intimacy of it held her spellbound. It was inevitable but natural; she was desperate for him and this was perfect… It was heaven. She wanted him. All of him.

A moment later she felt the hard warmth of him pressing inward, filling her slowly and with such gentleness that she almost cried out. She could feel him shaking and knew the control he was exercising not to allow his desire to override all else. A fierce hunger took her then and she lifted her hips to draw him in, wrapping her legs about him in a tangle of velvet and lace. The rub of the material was unbearably stimulating against her bare skin. She dug her fingernails into Richard's shoulders and felt the moment that his control gave way, his need for her overcoming all else. With a shout he held her hips still and drove into her, all control lost as his head came down and his lips ravaged her mouth as thoroughly as his body took hers. Deb's whole being exploded with a dazzling burst of pleasure. The fire raged through her, drawing her down, tumbling her over, until she lay panting and still amidst the scattered bedclothes, with her mind in splinters and her body still shaking with the glorious disbelief of discovery.

She must have slept briefly, for when she awoke the moon had risen higher and its silver light was spilling into the room and paling the light of the one candle that still burned.

She could feel Richard's hands moving over her and she shifted slightly, struggling against the drugging satiation that weighted her limbs.

'Do we have to go back now?' she murmured, a faint chill touching her heart at the thought.

Richard did not answer for a moment. Something gave— her skirts and petticoats, finally drawn away from her and tossed on the floor. He had already removed her boots and stockings. Now she was as naked as he. She turned towards him and saw that he was watching her with those dark, dark eyes.

'Do you want to go back?' he said, and Deb had the oddest feeling that he was asking about more than the journey home.

She looked at him. The chestnut hair tumbled across his

forehead and she raised her hand to caress his cheek where the stubble already darkened his jaw.

'No,' she said, a smile curving her lips. 'I wanted a whole night.'

He put out an arm and drew her into the curve of his shoulder. 'I hope that nothing I have done has made you change your mind…'

Deb smiled against his chest. 'No. You were everything that I had hoped for. It is almost a pity that you have given up a career as a rake, for I can see why you were so prodigiously successful.'

'Thank you,' Richard said.

'I was certainly not thinking of England, or of planning my weekly menus,' Deb confessed.

'Menu planning?' Richard's voice sounded lazy, faintly amused. 'I should hope not.'

'When Mama advised Olivia on the duties of a wife, she said that planning one's weekly menus was an excellent way to get one through the ordeal of a gentleman's ardour,' Deb said. 'It distracts the mind and at the end of it one also has a useful list.'

'That must be where Olivia and Ross have gone wrong, then,' Richard said easily. 'I knew there must be a simple explanation.' He pressed a kiss against her hair. 'Alas that your menus for the week must go unplanned, my sweet.'

Deb snuggled closer. It was warm in the nest of blankets and she felt cosy and cherished and very happy. When Richard started to stroke her breast very gently she also felt surprised. She had thought her body completely satisfied, and yet now the blood was singing softly through her veins again and she felt as though she was opening like a flower in the sunshine.

'Richard…' she whispered.

In reply, he shifted slightly so that her body was more

exposed to the touch of his lips and hands, alternately stroking and soothing, arousing and calming. She burned wher-
ever he touched her and tingled beneath him, knowing that
he watched her every reaction. She was melting again,
yearning for him and the sweetest, sharpest pleasure that he
could give her.

'You wanted a whole night,' he whispered in reply. 'Be
careful what you wish for…'

His hands stroked the soft skin inside her thighs and then
he slid down her body and his tongue touched the secret
hidden spot at the centre of her being. Heat lanced through
Deb and she jolted with the shock of it. Such devastating
pleasure… She had had no idea…

'Would you like me to do that again?' They might have
been at a garden party were it not for the hard, hot undertone
of desire in his voice.

Deb twisted on the blankets, her hands bunching tightly
in the material. 'Please…'

She had never known such intensity of feeling, never
even guessed at such sensations. Once again her body was
convulsed with the purest bliss and she lay shaking and
devastated in his arms.

He did not let her rest. His fingers drifted back between
her thighs and resumed a slow and tortuous stroking. Her
body was tight and she wriggled in protest against the renewed touch but he persisted, giving her no choice but to
accept his caress. To Deb's amazement, her body quickened
again, her blood beating feverishly as the heat pooled within
her. She gave a little gasp of need and Richard's mouth
covered hers, drinking deep. He was above her and inside
her again, and Deb reached for him and ran her hands over
the hard muscles of his back and down over his buttocks.
She felt the shudder that went through him whenever she
touched him and it made her feel triumphant. This time was

slow and the sensation of possessing and being possessed filled her senses and overwhelmed her beyond thought. Richard dipped his head to her breasts and the hot pleasure stirred through her once again and she tangled her fingers in his hair to hold his head there, feeling a spasm jerk through her each time he used his teeth against her skin.

She was drowning. The faint ebb and flow of the tide outside mingled in her head with the flow of her body until she could bear it no longer. She felt Richard bite down gently on her breast and she cried aloud as she tumbled over the edge of mindless delight, feeling him fall with her into the darkness where sheer ecstasy and sheer exhaustion held her captive and dropped her into the deepest sleep.

Richard eased himself quietly down the stairs and opened the door of the house. The night air flooded in, cold and crisp, laced with sea salt and something else that caught his attention. Smoke. Somewhere, nearby, there was a fire.

He was not certain what impulse had made him drag himself from the warm haven of the bed to check that all was secure outside. He had not wanted to leave Deb, not then, not ever.

He trod silently across the yard to the stables. The horses had smelled the smoke too and were bumping nervously in their stalls, but nothing else seemed amiss. Richard walked to the edge of the terrace. The smell of smoke was stronger here, but it was the wood smoke of a bonfire rather than anything else.

Richard paused. Although the idea seemed preposterous, he was almost certain that the privateer they had seen earlier was moored in Kestrel Creek, a quarter-mile to the east, and the smoke was from a bonfire on the beach. It would be unconscionably dangerous for a pirate to drop anchor anywhere near the coast, particularly if he was French. Yet it was not as unlikely as it seemed. Someone had been to the house since he and Justin had last used it back in July. The bottle of brandy that Deb had found earlier was not the half-drunk version that they had left three months ago, but a new bottle and a very fine one at that. Then there had been the tiny, perfectly made wooden ship that he had found on the windowsill scratched with the initials DDL…

Richard went across to the water butt and doused his face, enjoying the cold shock of the water. He shook his head vigorously, sending the water droplets flying. That was better. He could think clearly now.

He should wake Deb now and escort her home, though he had the deepest of misgivings. Without a pistol it was dangerous to travel through the forest at night, particularly if the smugglers and the revenue might be out, let alone any other nefarious characters. The last thing that he wanted to do was put Deb in danger. He had already created sufficient difficulties for one night. He leaned both hands on the stone wall of the terrace and took a deep breath. Whatever he had been thinking with earlier, it had not been his brain. He had compromised Deb thoroughly with this episode and now he would ruin her if he did not return her to Mrs Aintree's care immediately. It must be close on midnight.

Richard stretched and tilted his head to look up at the darkened window. Before that night he had thought that he could not possibly love Deb more, and yet now he was fathoms deep in an emotion he had never dreamed possible. He wanted to hold her close and never let her go ever again; he wanted to cherish and protect her, to make love to her again until her quiescent body quivered beneath his touch with all the passion of which she was capable.

He wanted to tell her that he loved her.

Tomorrow. Tomorrow he would tell her and he would propose marriage to her properly, not as some sort of fleeting arrangement to outwit the demands of her father. If she did not like it, then it was too bad. At least he would have been honest with her and told her of his feelings. If he did not, he thought that he might explode.

He went back into the house and felt his way up the stairs gingerly, guided by the moonlight. Deb had not stirred. She was nestled deep into the blankets and he paused to look down at her sleeping face whilst a huge wave of love and longing swept through him and stole his breath. He put out a hand to shake her awake and tell her to dress, but before he touched her she opened her eyes. In the moonlight her face was beautiful and bemused and her eyes deep pools of blue.

'I love you,' she said dreamily, and she reached for him, pulling him close. He knew that she was almost asleep and possibly did not even know what she said, but the impulse to wake her properly and take her home died in that moment.

For a second time that night Richard discarded his clothes and slid under the covers beside her. She turned towards him in her sleep, snuggling close with the trusting confidence of a child. Richard obligingly angled his body to accommodate hers. He fell asleep with her head resting over his heart.

## Chapter Sixteen

Deb had no idea of the time when she awoke. The moon was pouring its light into the tower room and the soft hush of the waves was as sweet and soothing as a caress. Deb lay with her eyes open, watching the shadows shift on the ceiling and breathing in the scent of lavender and spent candles. She felt warm and languorous and, for some reason, wide awake.

She sat up, drawing the covers close about her. Beside her, Richard shifted slightly in his sleep and turned towards her, but he did not wake. A small smile curved Deb's mouth as she looked down at him.

She examined her feelings. One of the things that she had been afraid of was that the feeling of wanton happiness would burst like a bubble, leaving her as disillusioned with herself as she had after Neil's betrayal. This time, after all, she had knowingly given herself to a man. She had sought his embrace with a brazen disregard for propriety and practically demanded that he make love to her. She smiled a little to herself at the memory of it. She did not feel cheapened, or dishonoured, or immoral. With Richard she felt warm and happy and cherished. She was not sure what constituted the difference, but it was there and she was in no mood to question it. She slipped from the bed and stole across to the window. The view was so beautiful that it made her catch her breath. The bright light of the moon spilled across the sea, turning the beach to silver and painting the trees in shades of black and white.

'Deb?'

Richard was behind her. She felt the warmth of his naked body against her, a counterpoint to the chill of the cool night air from the window. He slid his arms about her and drew her head back against his chest.

'I woke,' Deborah said. 'It was so beautiful that I wanted to see…'

Richard's lips touched her collarbone and drifted along the line of her shoulder. Deb shivered, but not from the cool draught. His hands spread across her bare stomach and she felt her muscles contract beneath his caress. When his hands moved up to her breasts she was already waiting for their touch and arched back against him, helpless in her desire. His cheek brushed hers, hard against her softness.

'The night is not over yet…' he reminded her, and her heart leaped at his words and the heated images they provoked.

He turned her into the window alcove, so that her back was against the hard stone of the wall, and kissed her until she was mindlessly adrift and lost in sheer bliss. He lifted her up and held her trapped between his body and the wall. She obeyed without hesitation his instruction to wrap her legs about him, sliding down to find herself impaled, senses utterly ravished at his deep invasion of her body. The stone was cold behind her, but the heat of his body scorched her. His hands steadied her, holding her still to meet his thrust. The shocking delight of what she was experiencing, combined with the insistent tug of his mouth at her breast, was enough to send her mind spinning away into silken darkness and she screamed aloud, wilting in his arms, shattered and pierced by the devastating bliss.

Then he took her back to the bed and kept her there until she had no notion of what was moonlight and what was breaking daylight, and was so lost in blind ecstasy that she did not care either way.

Olivia Marney was in her bedroom, sitting before the mirror whilst Jenny carefully unpinned the emerald-encrusted bandeau that nestled amongst her curls. It was very late and she felt tired. The evening, a dinner at Saltires, could not be accounted a complete success. Lily Benedict had been in a scratchy mood and had made several sharp remarks about Deb's absence that evening and the coincidental disappearance of Lord Richard Kestrel. Fending off her barbs had given Olivia a headache, and her spirits had not improved to see that Ross seemed sunk deep in thought and barely made any attempt to join in the conversation. Occasionally he would look at her across the table, a deep impenetrable look that Olivia could not read. Until that evening she had thought that they had been achieving a better understanding. They had talked on a number of topics recently, including Deb's supposed false betrothal and Richard Kestrel's honourable intentions. On more than one occasion, Olivia had thought that Ross might even be intending to kiss her, for there was a certain look in his eye. He had not done so, however, and now he was not speaking to her again. She felt utterly cast down.

When they had returned to Midwinter Marney Hall that evening it was to find the servants in a panic for the second time in as many days. A message had come from Owen Chance that the smugglers and the revenue men were out, and they should stay within doors and make sure that all was secure. Ross had muttered something about going down

to the farm to check that the livestock was safe and Olivia
had watched him go in bafflement and not a little irritation.
She had trailed her way upstairs to her bedroom and rung
for the maid.

Now it was twenty minutes later and Olivia was in her
petticoats, with a dressing robe over, waiting with ill-
concealed impatience for Jenny to finish her ministrations.
Whilst the maid fussed about her, Olivia's ill temper grew
until it reached epic proportions. All the exasperation she
had felt with Ross over the past few weeks was growing
into a tidal wave of frustration. What was the point of pre-
senting an exquisitely prepared face to the world when her
husband appeared to prefer the company of his pigs? Olivia
picked up the pot of rose-scented skin cream from her dressing table and just managed to repress the impulse to throw
it into the fireplace. So much for Deb's aphrodisiac! It may
have made her skin softer, but it had had absolutely no
positive effect on Ross and what was more, it did not smell
of roses at all but of a rather unpleasant hint of goose fat.

There was a discreet knock at the bedroom door. Jenny
went across and, after a low-voiced colloquy, brought Olivia
a note.

'Excuse me, madam. Mr Ford says that this has just arrived from Mallow. He did not wish to disturb you, ma'am,
but the boy said that it was urgent. He is waiting for a reply.'

Olivia felt a clutch of fear. The combination of Deb's
absence from dinner and the scare about the smugglers suddenly came together as an unspecified dread. She unfolded
the note slowly and read it. Then she read it again, biting
her lip as she did so.

Mrs Aintree's words were both discreet and carefully chosen, but there was no denying their underlying message.

Mrs Stratton, she wrote, had sent a message earlier in the
evening to say that she had decided to prolong her outing

with Lord Richard Kestrel and that he would escort her back home later that night. She had not returned in time for dinner, nor by eleven, when Mrs Aintree had decided to retire. An hour later they had received the warning about the smugglers, and shortly after that Mr Chance had arrived at Mallow to tell them that there had been a chase and that the villains had opened the sluices on the Winter Race to flood the roads about Mallow and create a diversion. Given both the danger of flooding to Mallow House itself and the fact that Mr Chance wanted to check that none of the Mallow servants was involved in criminal activity, he had demanded—politely, but demanded nevertheless—that the household be mustered. Mrs Aintree had been obliged to comply with his request and summon everyone within the house.

And Deb had not been there.

Mrs Aintree wrote that she had passed the matter off as best she could by claiming that Deb was staying at Midwinter Marney with her sister. Mr Chance had accepted her excuses on Deb's behalf very smoothly. But the truth was out.

Olivia put the note down slowly. She did not think that Owen Chance would be unchivalrous enough to challenge Mrs Aintree's claim of Deb's whereabouts even though he might believe it was not true. But the servants at Mallow knew that Deb was not there, and the servants at Marney knew she was not staying there… And servants talked. Olivia remembered Lady Benedict's malice with a shiver. The scandal was out and it would ripple through the neighbourhood like a breeze across the river. It would not be long before the whole of Woodbridge would know that Mrs Deborah Stratton had been missing when a muster was called at Mallow in the middle of the night. Soon after that, someone—Lady Benedict, no doubt—would observe that had not both Lord Richard Kestrel and Mrs Stratton been missing from the dinner at Saltires, and how piquant it would be if they had been together… Engagement or no engagement, Deb's reputation would be in tatters.

Olivia glanced at the clock. It was almost two in the morning and Ross had been gone a half-hour.

'Where is Lord Marney?' Olivia demanded, suddenly furious that Ross was not there to help her decide what to do at a time like this.

Jenny looked startled. 'I believe that he is still down in the farmyard, milady. Should I ask Ford to send for him?'

Olivia made an exasperated sound. 'I shall find him myself! Jenny, a pen and paper…' She scribbled a note and thrust it at the maid. 'Give this to the boy from Mallow.' She pulled the remaining pins from her hair with impatient fingers, shook out her curls and thrust her feet into her slippers. Grabbing Mrs Aintree's note, she made for the door.

'I am off to find Lord Marney,' she said, over her shoulder.

The maid looked astonished. 'But, madam, your hair!' she wailed. 'Your slippers! The farmyard!'

But Olivia was gone.

It took Olivia ten minutes to walk from the main house to the home farm, which was close by. During that time she barely thought about what she was doing. She was fuelled by her anger with Ross and her concern over Deb's situation, and for once she had thoroughly lost her composure. She arrived in the farmyard, panting slightly, and looked around for her husband.

He was not difficult to find. The door of the second pig pen was open and Olivia could see Ross leaning on the wooden rail of the stall. One lantern burned on the windowsill. Olivia did not normally enter the farmyard, for it was not only dirty but prodigiously smelly as well and the pigs were the worst offenders. Tonight, however, she had no thought for either the dirt or the smell. She erupted through the door, waving Clarissa Aintree's letter agitatedly.

'Ross, the most dreadful thing has happened—'

She stopped dead. The air was full of the scent of roses and two of Ross's prize Gloucester Great Spot pigs were enthusiastically mating in the pen in front of her. Olivia gave a little squeak and covered her eyes with the letter.

'Ross! Are you so depraved that you come down here deliberately to watch your pigs at sport—?' she began wrathfully, only to break off as she heard her husband give a guffaw of derision.

'Of course I do not, Olivia. What a ridiculous notion!' Ross ran his hand through his hair. He was frowning. 'To tell the truth, I have been worried about their recent enthusiasm for procreation.' He nodded towards the jar that Olivia could dimly see on the windowsill. 'Ever since you gave me Rachel Newlyn's potion to help them with their skin complaint they have not been able to keep away from each other. I fear that they will be quite exhausted.'

Olivia stared at the frolicking pigs and then at the pot of ointment. She sniffed the air delicately.

'The liniment does seem to have a very sweet aroma,' she said faintly. 'Has it worked to cure their skin ailment?'

'I have not been able to keep them still for long enough to check properly,' Ross said ruefully. 'When they are not mating they are skipping around full of vigour. Betty used to be the most slothful of animals. I cannot explain it at all.'

Olivia rather thought that she could. She stared at the pot again whilst the heat came into her cheeks and the smell of goose fat on her own face seemed to overwhelm the sweet scent of the roses. There was no denying that Rachel's potion was exceptionally good for the complexion. Her skin felt as smooth as silk.

'Oh, no…' she said faintly.

Ross had come across to her and taken her gently by the arm, steering her away from the pen and its happily cavorting animals.

'I am sorry,' he said. 'Is there something the matter, Olivia?' His gaze travelled over her, from the dishevelled tumble of her fair hair to the slippers that were now somewhat the worse for wear. His eyes lingered thoughtfully on the diaphanous dressing robe and the petticoats beneath, before he seemed to drag his thoughts away and focus abruptly on her face.

'Olivia?' he said again. He was holding her gently by the elbow. 'There must be some reason that brought you down here in your slippers. Is something wrong?'

Olivia dragged her thoughts away from aphrodisiacs for pigs and goose-grease face cream.

'Oh, yes, the most dreadful news!' She waved the letter again. 'Deb has been missing all night and I dare swear that she is with Lord Richard Kestrel!'

Ross grinned. 'So that is how he thought to persuade her into marriage!'

Olivia slapped his arm. 'It is not funny, Ross! There has been a muster at Mallow House to try and catch the smugglers and everyone was hauled from their beds and Deb was not there! Now everyone will know where she has been and who she was with!'

Ross's face stilled. 'That is unfortunate,' he said, 'but it is Deborah's choice to behave in this manner and therefore her difficulty, not yours, my love.'

In her distress Olivia missed the endearment. She was almost in tears.

'But Deb is ruined! Do you not understand? She is spending the night with Lord Richard and now everyone will know and her reputation will be in tatters.'

'Deb will be quite safe,' Ross said soothingly. 'Come back inside or you will be frozen.'

Olivia abruptly became aware of her flimsy robe and chilled feet. She waited whilst Ross blew out the lantern and bolted the door on the still-snuffling pigs. Then, to her great surprise, Ross swept her up off her feet.

'Keep still,' he instructed softly, as she made a faint protest. 'If you struggle, you may fall in the slurry.'

It was enough of a threat to keep Olivia still as a mouse all the way back to the Hall. It was also inevitable that during the course of the journey she should become aware of the warmth and strength of her husband's hands through the slippery silk of the dressing robe. Sliding her arms around Ross's neck purely in order to hold on, Olivia felt a traitorous and unexpected little shiver of desire run through her.

'I told you that you would catch cold.' Ross sounded briskly practical.

'Yes,' Olivia said faintly. 'I think you might need to take me to my bedroom...'

She felt rather than saw the look that Ross slanted down to her. Her heart was suddenly beating very swiftly as Ross carried her into the house and up to her room. But when he placed her very gently on her bed and straightened up, he said stiffly, 'I will send your maid to you.'

His obtuseness was the last straw for Olivia. Would they never, ever be able to reach some sort of understanding? She felt quite hopeless and furiously angry. She moved quickly, dashing over to the dressing table and grabbing the pot of ointment that had been sitting there.

'Ross, take this! Take it and go! You may be sure that your pigs will be the better for it.'

Ross was looking understandably confused. He looked from her stormy face to the pot in his hand.

'I beg your pardon, Olivia?'

Olivia could feel a curious sensation building up inside her like a volcano about to blow its top. She kicked her dirty slippers off and sent them sailing across the room with a violence that made Ross flinch.

'This is the pig ointment, Ross! Lady Newlyn sent two pots. I have been using the pigs' unguent on my face and you have been using my—' Olivia caught herself up quickly before she could utter the word aphrodisiac. 'You have been using my rose-scented cream to try and cure their skin condition.'

Ross took the pot and looked at it, then back at her. Not a muscle moved in his face.

'I hope,' he said politely, 'that this has been beneficial for you, Olivia?'

'Perfectly, thank you,' Olivia snapped. 'My skin smells a little of goose grease, but it is very soft.'

She thought that she saw Ross's lips twitch, but could not be certain. 'So the pigs' skin cream was meant for you...' he began.

Olivia was beginning to wish she had not said anything at all. She felt hot and shaky and quite uncertain of how the conversation might progress now that it had begun.

'Yes,' she said, 'but I shall not press for it to be returned, having seen what it has done to your pigs.'

Ross was still watching her, an unfathomable expression in his very blue eyes. 'Did you know about it's...ah... invigorating...capacities?'

Olivia evaded his gaze. Her shakiness seemed to be getting worse as they approached the crux of the matter.

'I had been told to use it sparingly,' she admitted, 'but I never imagined what the effect might be. I expect that you

have been plastering it all over the Gloucester Great Spots
in order to cure them—'

'And instead I have made them quite astonishingly ram-
pant,' Ross finished drily.

'Ross!' Olivia blushed crimson with shock and mortification. Ross took a step closer to her.

'What on earth would have happened had you used it
yourself?' he mused.

Olivia toyed with the tie of her dressing robe. 'I cannot
bear to think,' she said crossly.

'Really?' Ross drawled. 'So whatever possessed you to
try the potion in the first place?' He was lounging at the
foot of the bed now and Olivia was annoyed to see that he
looked rather amused. The torment inside her tightened as
she looked at him laughing at her. She made a last, desperate
attempt to hold on to her temper. Ladies did not show anger,
she reminded herself. It was not the done thing.

'Deborah passed it to me,' she said tightly, and closed
her lips to forcibly prevent any other words from spilling
out.

Ross raised his brows. 'That may account for many
things, my dear Olivia, but it does not answer my question.
Why on earth would *you* want to use it?'

The mockery in his tone was too much for Olivia's over-
stretched nerves. Her anger erupted with the force of a tidal
wave. So long repressed, there was no stopping it. With a
gesture that would not have been out of place on the stage
at Drury Lane, she turned and swept her hairbrush and a
selection of bottles off the top of her dressing table on to
the carpet with a resounding crash. She swung round on her
startled husband.

'Why would *I* want to use such a thing? Perhaps it is
because I cannot seem to attract my own husband! The last
time that you came to my bed you swore not to trouble me

again! Perhaps I could not bear to imagine you taking solace in the arms of someone like Lily Benedict. Perhaps I was *jealous* of the thought of you even considering consoling yourself with another woman!' She paused for breath. Ross was looking absolutely riveted and Olivia was astounded to discover that she felt wonderful, vibrant and alive, and, for once, totally unguarded. That being the case, she carried on.

'Would it astound you to know, Ross, that I wanted you from the first moment that Papa introduced us? Oh, yes—' she saw his look of shock '—I wanted to marry you! I wanted you to sweep me off my feet!' She turned away. 'But you courted me with such decorum. It was very sweet but utterly unfulfilling. Yet it fitted with everything that Mama had ever told me about gentlemen requiring their wives to show no passion and conduct themselves with absolute propriety.' She gave a bitter shrug. 'So I thought that there was some fault in me for feeling the desire I did. I thought I would give you a disgust of me. So I subdued it and conducted myself in the manner a wife was meant to behave.'

Her gaze swept over him from head to foot. 'After a little while I forgot all about my girlish desires. I realised that you did not wish to be close to me. I would have given anything then just to be able to *talk* to you, Ross, but I could never reach you. You shut yourself away from me. So in the end I lost the habit of trying to please you.'

Ross had turned pale now. 'I thought that you wanted me to preserve some distance,' he said. 'I thought that you had ice in your veins. I did not want to trouble you with the memories of all things that had happened to me before I met you, or talk to you about matters I assumed would not interest you—'

Olivia laughed. The blood running through her veins felt so hot now she thought she might be in danger of taking a fever. 'So we are both as foolish as each other,' she said bitterly. 'There is a certain justice in that.' She shot him a look. 'Have I said enough yet?'

'Nowhere near enough,' Ross said. He was white, but there was a spark of something in his eyes and it lit an answering flame within Olivia. She spun away from him and picked up the thread of her thoughts.

'You asked why I wanted the rose-petal potion. Why not? I had nothing to lose and I thought that perhaps I might even kindle some degree of interest in my husband before it was too late. So I took the pot and I have been lathering myself in pig ointment this month past whilst your pigs have been frolicking in rose-petal aphrodisiac—' She broke off. 'Damn you, you are laughing! It is *not* funny, Ross!'

She realised all of a sudden how thin the line was between anger and despair and stopped before the tears could break. She could see her reflection in the inset mirrors, her hair tumbled, her breasts heaving with outraged fury. And she could see Ross, who definitely *was* laughing, coming towards her with a very purposeful look in his eyes. Panic seized her throat.

'And if you think for one second that I love you—' she gasped.

'Well,' Ross drawled, grinning openly now, 'I think it is a little too late for disavowals now, my love.'

'Arrogant beast!' Olivia glared at him, beating her clenched fist helplessly and with very little force against his chest.

'Sweetheart,' Ross said, trapping her hand and pulling her close. 'I love you too.'

Olivia opened and closed her mouth silently, like a landed fish.

'Perhaps we could talk now,' Ross said, with scrupulous politeness, 'unless it is too late.'

Olivia stared at him, knowing he was not speaking of the hour. 'I do not believe that it is too late,' she said huskily.

She licked her dry lips and watched, fascinated, as Ross's eyes fixed on her mouth and darkened almost to black with desire. He was still holding her hand and her skin burned beneath his touch.

'If you prefer to retire and would like me to send for your maid then I shall, of course, comply,' he said, but his eyes gave her a different message.

Olivia freed herself from his grip and reached out with both hands to grab him by the lapels of his jacket. 'Don't you dare,' she said, a second before his lips met hers.

When Deb awoke, the early morning light was pouring through the window and spilling across the bed. She was alone. She had already stretched out a hand instinctively and found empty space when memory returned to her and her spirits sank lower than a stone.

The night was over. It was time to go home.

She stretched and winced at the stiffness in her body and the unaccustomed soreness, the deep, tender ache inside her. It seemed to echo the ache in her soul. There was always a price to be paid.

The chinking sound of the harnesses came from below. Richard must be getting the horses ready to leave. She hurried from the bed and threw her clothes on haphazardly. She did not want to be naked when Richard came back. She did not want him to see her vulnerability now, in the bright light of day. Her mind could not encompass all the things that they had done. She did not want to have to think about it.

Nevertheless, she could not seem to help herself.

Deb sat down abruptly on the edge of the bed. A cold prickle ran down her spine and settled like a leaden weight in her stomach. Something was wrong and it was nothing to do with the night she had spent with Richard, nor the shockingly intimate and entirely pleasurable nature of their activities. Awareness had come to her during the night. She understood now the difference between how she had felt when she had found herself betrayed by Neil Stratton, and how she felt now. Both experiences, were they known, would bring her disgrace in the eyes of the world. Yet now she felt none of the shame that had dogged her for so long after her sham marriage was exposed. This time she had made her own choice freely and from something she had thought was physical desire. Now she knew how mistaken she was. Now she knew that she had fallen in love.

She let her hands fall into her lap and stared blindly out of the window. What an absolute fool she had been, thinking that she could dictate to Richard that she wished for a night of passion and then expect nothing to be different afterwards. The night had been all that she had wanted and more, glorious, blissfully fulfilling, but Richard had taken her soul as well as her body, and bound her to him with a love that could never be broken. She knew now that this was the man with whom she wanted to spend the rest of her life.

Looking back with the clear vision of hindsight, Deb could see that she had been falling in love with Richard for weeks. She had discovered so many different facets to a man she had once dismissed as nothing more than a society rake. She had agonised over his loneliness and cherished his tenderness. Yesterday afternoon they had spent a perfect time together, building intimacy upon companionship, deepening the feelings for him that she already possessed. They were feelings that she had held for him almost from the first. The dazzling attraction, the heated tug of desire were all as nothing to the things that she valued in him, the strength and the protectiveness and the humour and the intellect that teased and matched her own... She even had some half-remembered dream of telling him that she loved him…

She gave a little moan of distress, for there was no reason to suppose that Richard felt the same way. She had never asked him for his love, only his passion.

She beat an impotent fist on the bed beside her. She was a fool. She had held on so long to her mistrust and disenchantment that she had not been able to see when love had crept up upon her.

Moving slowly, she went to the head of the stairs and started to descend to join Richard below. She did not spare a backward glance for the bedroom with its tumbled blankets or the bed where she had slept curled next to Richard and had experienced such ecstasy in his arms. She would never forget such pleasure, but they had made a bargain. She had wanted a false betrothal and for Richard to be her lover. He had given her both of those things. And now it was over.

## Chapter Seventeen

Richard left Deborah, at her request, at the gate of Mallow House. It was raining, the water running in rivulets from Deb's hat and soaking into the velvet riding dress until she was drenched and shivering.

They had not spoken much on the ride back from the hunting lodge. When Deb had gone out on to the terrace the horses were ready and she had greeted Richard with a stilt-edness that was completely out of character. She realised that Richard thought she was shy in his company now and her misery deepened when she saw the tenderness that this evoked in him. Everything felt wrong. She was being dis-honest with Richard, she was not telling him how she felt, and yet she knew no other way, for if she weakened for a moment she knew that she would throw herself into his arms and beg him never to let her go.

He touched her wet cheek with gloved fingers when they parted.

'I will call on you later, sweetheart,' he said, and she nodded numbly. Later seemed a long time away and she wanted to wash and to sleep and have time to think what she would say when next she saw him.

Mallow House was very quiet as Deb let herself in and

crept upstairs. It was a half past nine, but no one seemed to be stirring. Deb was too exhausted to question why. She shed her clothes and almost fell into her big bed. She had only awoken an hour before and yet now she felt exhausted again.

When she finally awoke the afternoon was advanced and there was a suppressed buzz about the house. Deb sent for hot water and luncheon in her bed, and heard without enthusiasm that Olivia and Ross had called and needed to see her urgently in the drawing room. She felt a little sick. It was inevitable that Clarissa Aintree was aware of her absence the previous night and if she had told Liv and Ross... Deb hoped fervently that they were not going to ring a peal over her, but she thought it very likely. She might be seen as a widow of previously unimpeachable reputation, but it still could not excuse such outrageous behaviour. They would be disappointed in her; even though no one else would know about her bad behaviour, Deb did not like the thought of incurring the disapproval of those closest to her. It added another weight to her heart at a time when she felt most vulnerable. She could not regret what she had done, for the night spent with Richard had been the most perfect, special and tender experience of her life, but now the night was over and the light of day was cold indeed.

She sat passively whilst Mary dressed her hair and then went down to the drawing room. Ross was pacing the rug before the mantelpiece, a deep frown on his forehead. Olivia was sitting upright on a straight-backed chair, her hands locked together, a look of deep distress on her normally serene countenance. Deb forgot her own preoccupations and hurried forward.

'Liv?' she said. 'Has something happened?'

Olivia looked at her with a familiar expression of rueful

affection and complete exasperation. 'Sit down, Deborah,' she said. 'I have something to tell you.'

'I did not know about the smugglers being out or about the muster,' Deb said, white-faced. 'I had not intended to worry anyone—' She broke off as Ross gave an irritable sigh. She knew what he wanted to say—that she never thought through the consequences of her actions and, if she had, they would not now be sitting here contemplating the ruin of her reputation.

'I cannot understand how you could be so indiscreet,' he said.

Deb felt miserable. Looking back, she could see exactly how she had been so indiscreet, for she had given no thought to anything except Richard and her feelings for him from the moment that they had gone into the hunting lodge until they had returned that morning.

'It is clear that you have never tried to arrange a romantic liaison, Ross,' she snapped, angry at his condemnation and her own miserable feelings. 'It amazes me that anyone ever manages to be indiscreet when they have a whole host of interfering relatives—'

'Well, despite our interference, you have succeeded finely!' Ross thrust his hand through his hair with all the pent-up impatience he could not express in words. 'Really, Deb—'

'Ross,' Olivia intervened gently. 'It is not so bad. Mrs Aintree has put out the tale that Deb was staying with us last night and if we back her up—'

'Deb did not attend Lady Sally's dinner with us and everyone knows it.' Ross said bluntly. He shook his head. 'My dear Olivia, that story will not hold water for two minutes.'

'Then there is the fact that Deb is betrothed to Lord Rich-

ard,' Olivia continued. 'Yes, she has been reckless, but it
could be a great deal worse—'

'I broke the engagement two nights ago,' Deb said.

Both Olivia and Ross swung round to look at her with
identical expressions of horror.

'You broke the engagement,' Ross said carefully, after a
moment, 'yet you spent the night with the man? Will I ever
understand you, Deborah?'

'Oh, Deb!' Olivia wailed. 'Please tell me that no one
knows you broke it off!'

'I have not told anyone,' Deb said, 'but I intend to. With
Guy's wedding cancelled there can be no reason for the
engagement to continue—'

'No reason!' Ross exploded. 'Never mind the betrothal,
there is every reason for a *marriage* to take place!'

Deb tried not to cry. 'I will *not* marry Richard Kestrel!'
she said. 'Why should he be compromised into marriage
with me when the whole matter was my idea? I was the one
who instigated this! I *asked* him to be my lover!'

'Deb!' Ross and Olivia's outraged cries mingled with the
sound of the door opening.

'Lord Richard Kestrel,' the maid announced.

Deb froze. She had wanted to finish her discussion with
Olivia and Ross before she faced the equally difficult task
of speaking to Richard, but, since she had given the maid
no instructions to refuse him—and since he would probably
have ignored them anyway—she was not going to have that
chance.

She knew that she had to dismiss him. Their betrothal
was at an end and that one perfect night of passion was
over. Yet now when she saw him all she wanted to do was
run to him and throw herself into his arms. She loved him
hopelessly.

'Richard!' she said, and heard her voice break on the word.

Richard heard it too. He came across and took her hand and Deb could feel the warmth and reassurance flowing from his body to hers.

'Sweetheart—' His lips pressed her hair. His arm went about her. Deb leaned against his strength and fought against the feeling of coming home. She could not permit herself to depend on him.

Olivia was looking almost as relieved as Deb felt. Ross was looking murderous.

'What the hell were you thinking of, Kestrel?' he said to Richard. He paced across to the window. 'No, don't answer that. On reflection it's easy to see exactly what you were thinking of! When you asked my permission to woo Deborah, I did not appreciate what it was that you had in mind! Why the devil you could not have waited until you were married—?'

'Ross,' Olivia said again, putting a hand on her husband's arm, 'since Deb and Richard *are* to be married, I think we could put aside our differences.'

But Deb was not listening. She was looking from Ross's face to Richard's as the coldness clutched at her heart and seeped from there to every corner of her being. She freed herself of Richard's protective arm and took two steps backward.

'You asked Ross's permission to court me?' she said to Richard, her voice a whisper. 'You discussed *marrying* me? You hatched some plan with him and never spoke of it to me?'

She saw Richard's gaze snap back to her, saw his eyes narrow on her face. 'Deborah,' he began carefully, 'it was not in the least like that.'

Deb had started to shake. 'No? How was it, then?'

Richard drove his hands into his pockets. 'Can we talk about this alone?' he asked, with restraint.

'No!' Deb's chin came up. 'Since you discussed my future with reference to everyone else before, it seems appropriate that they can be party to the discussions now! After all, they already know far more about it than I do. Apparently I am to be married off without my knowledge!'

'It was not like that,' Richard said again, quietly but inexorably. 'Deb, I love you! I have loved you for months! I *want* to marry you.'

Deb felt hot, humiliated and hurt. All the time that she had been making plans for her temporary betrothal, Richard had been talking to Ross of quite a different scheme. He had fallen in with her proposal whilst planning something else entirely. And he had not told her.

She felt foolish and manipulated. Richard had told her that he had explained the situation to Ross, and yet that had not been true. He must have told Ross everything—that she had advertised for a temporary fiancé, that he was playing along with her until he could persuade her into a real betrothal. She had confided in Richard that her marriage to Neil Stratton had been unhappy and that she had no desire to wed ever again, and yet he had paid her scant heed. And last night… She covered her face briefly with her hands. Last night she had given herself to him body and soul. She had finally realised that she loved him with all her heart and that, although to overcome her scruples about marriage would require a leap of faith, she might even have been able to have had the courage. Under other circumstances…

'And when were you going to tell me of your plans for me?' Deb asked, her voice shaking. 'After you had told Ross and Olivia and everyone else, and conspired to make me accept you?' Her voice rose. 'No doubt I should be grateful to be offered marriage, with my tarnished reputation!' She swung round on them all, the pain lodged in a hot ball in her chest. 'But do you know—I am not grateful in the least! You are just like my father—' she turned on Richard '—planning to marry me off regardless of my wishes. You, and Ross, and everyone else who has made arrangements for me of which I was totally unaware! You cannot allow me to make my own choices, nor give me the freedom to do as I choose! That was all I wanted! To be allowed the choice!'

Richard put out a hand to her. There was something that looked like pain in his eyes and Deb could not allow herself to look on it because it moved her unbearably. She turned away but still she could not block out his words.

'I love you, Deb. I did not tell you or propose to you before because I was afraid. I knew of your doubts about marriage and I was afraid of losing the one thing that was becoming more precious to me as every day passed—'

Deb put her hands over her ears. 'I *trusted* you,' she said, and as she spoke she realised that it was true. 'I never thought that I would trust anyone again, but I trusted you.'

She whirled around and made for the door, pausing when she reached it. 'Let me be quite clear,' she said, her voice shaking. 'I do not wish to marry you, Lord Richard. I do not wish to see you again.'

Olivia came up to the bedroom and found Deb in a tearful heap on the bed. Deb felt her sister touch her shoulder gently and after a moment the tension went out of her body and she allowed Olivia to draw her close and give her a hug. It was unusual for Olivia to be so demonstrative, but Deb found it enormously comforting. She hiccuped a little and reached for a pillowcase to dry her tears. 'We cannot be forever crying over each other.'

'No,' Olivia said, proffering her own scrap of cambric

handkerchief. 'I am sorry, Deb. Sorry that I deceived you, I mean.' She grimaced. 'I knew Richard wanted to marry you, and I was so pleased!' She looked at Deb's tear-swollen face and shook her head slightly. 'He loves you very much, you know, Deb, and you love him too…'

Deb bit her lip on a denial. What was the point? She had admitted to herself only that morning that she loved Richard with all her heart. If she had not, she would not be feeling so distressed now.

She twisted her hands together. 'He did not tell me he loved me,' she said.

Olivia raised her brows. 'Did you tell him that you loved him?'

'No, but that is different.' Deb blushed. 'I only real-ised…' her voice dropped '…this morning, after we…'

Olivia laughed. 'Oh, Deb!' She sobered up. 'It was wrong of Richard to mislead you, but his motives were sincere. He knew that you had no wish to wed again and all he wanted was the opportunity to court you. He was in the devil of a fix, you know, wishing to reassure Ross and myself that his intentions were honourable, but also needing to win your trust—' She broke off. 'But you must discuss this with Richard himself. It is not for me to say.'

'I trusted him,' Deb said in a tired voice. 'I trusted him and he betrayed me.'

'Did he?' Olivia said, and Deb jumped at the ring of steel in her gentle sister's voice. 'You think that you are the only one deceived? And what sort of trust is it that does not even tell Richard the truth of your own situation? I'll wager that you have not told him about your first marriage, have you?'

Deb froze. She felt simultaneously hot and cold, her heart ice, the prickling heat breaking out over her whole body. 'You did not tell Richard that I was never married to Neil? Tell me that he does not know!'

'I have not told him,' Olivia said, 'and nor has Ross.' Her expression was hard. 'It is your place to do that—if you truly love him. If you trust him, you could tell him anything.'

'No,' Deb whispered. 'I cannot.'

Olivia shrugged, but her hard expression had softened into something like pity. 'That is, of course, your choice, Deb, just as it is up to you whether or not you marry Richard.' She stood up. 'I hope that you will feel well enough to go out later. Do not forget that it is the private view for Lady Sally's watercolour book tonight.'

Deb caught her breath. 'I cannot attend—'

Olivia looked cross. 'You must. Show some spirit, Deb!'

'Tell everyone that I am ill!' Deb begged. 'I cannot bear to go into company.'

'Since everyone is talking scandal about you,' Olivia said, with asperity, 'you will attend to quash the rumours. I have had enough of this, Deb! Stop feeling sorry for yourself. We shall collect you at eight.'

After she had gone, Deb rolled over with a groan and buried her face in the pillow. Then she sat up. What could she do? She could refuse to attend Lady Sally's soirée but she suspected that Olivia and Ross would drag her there.

She could break her engagement publicly and face the consequences.

She could return to Bath and throw herself on her father's mercy.

Except that she could not. That was how she had got herself into this difficulty in the first place.

She could marry Richard Kestrel...

She had to marry Richard Kestrel unless she wanted to be ostracised.

She loved Richard and *wanted* to marry him, but not like this...

'Damn it!' Deb said furiously, punching her pillow. 'Why must I always get into such a scrape?'

She knew that she was going to have to talk to Richard and put matters right. She knew that she was going to have to tell him everything that she had previously held back. She had had the courage to love and trust this far, and now she must take the final step. Then, and only then, she might make the match of her heart—but only if Richard still wanted her. And of that she was painfully unsure.

# Chapter Eighteen

There was no opportunity for Deb to speak privately to Richard at Lady Sally Saltire's ball that evening. It seemed absurd, for they were in the same room, partook of the same dinner and mingled with the same guests. Yet they were never alone and Deb could feel her frustration mounting as each hour passed. She fidgeted with the saltcellar and sprinkled too much on her food, she toyed with the wine in her glass and spilled it on the table and she felt cross and anxious and utterly miserable.

Outwardly it felt as though nothing had changed. They had not formally broken their betrothal, and Richard behaved with the same impeccable good manners towards Deb that he had always shown her in company. Only she was aware of the distance between them; the chilly edge to Richard's politeness and the withdrawal in his eyes. She wanted to put a hand out to him then, to draw him back to her and see that coldness melt into the warmth and tenderness that she had come to value and rely upon. Only the previous night he had held her in his arms and made love to her with exquisite love and gentleness. Now he was becoming a stranger. Deb felt very lonely.

At some point during the seemingly interminable dinner,

Deb resolved that something must be done. She decided to slip away to Lady Sally's study to write Richard a note, begging him to speak with her the following day. It was the best idea that she could devise and, as soon as she had thought of it, Deb was itching to put it into action. Eventually the dinner ended and the gentlemen withdrew and Deb, without further ado, excused herself from her hostess with vague suggestions of seeking the ladies' withdrawing room.

She never reached the study. She had passed the ballroom, shuttered and in darkness until the unveiling of the watercolour book took place, and was standing outside the library, when a strange smell reached her and immediately tugged at her memory. She stood still, racking her brains to recall the occasion on which she had smelled it before and wondering why it seemed so important to remember. And then it hit her. It was the odd, musty scent that had permeated the pages of the poetry book. She had come across it when they had found the coded message and she had known then that she would recognise it if she smelled it again.

It was here, a faint perfume in the air, in the passageway of Lady Sally Saltire's house. Deb stood still, puzzling, whilst her heart started to race. She took a few steps forward and the scent was stronger, battling with the perfume of the tiger lilies that stood on a plinth in the corner. It smelled of old, damp buildings and illness and musty clothes. It seemed to be seeping from under the nearest door like a gas. Stealthily, without pause for thought, Deb opened the door and slipped into the room beyond. She could see nothing. It was all in darkness, the curtains drawn. She was not even sure which room she had entered, except that it was hot and the smell of camphor overrode all other scents and was oppressive now. It made her want to sneeze. She pressed a hand to her mouth. She needed fresh air…

There was a movement behind her and a swirl of clear cool air as the door opened, but she never had time to profit from it. Something hit her hard on the back of the head and she went out like a doused lantern.

Her whole body ached. Her legs were trembling, her arms felt stretched beyond endurance, and in her head was a buzzing sound that made her groan. She tried opening her eyes, but the red and green flashes that exploded in her skull made her close them again. Her head felt unnaturally heavy and her whole body felt weighted with lead. She groaned again.

'Deb! Deborah!'

The sharp voice spoke in her ear and made her head jerk up again just as she was welcoming the blissful darkness back again. She tried to move, felt herself restrained and caught her breath on another wave of pain.

'Deborah!' It was Richard's voice. 'Wake up!'

'Yes, all right,' Deb said crossly. 'There is no need to shout!'

'Thank God.' Richard's voice held a wealth of relief. 'I was beginning to think they had hit you too hard and you would never come round.'

'That sounds very pleasant at the moment,' Deb said. It was no good, though. The insistent note in his voice was dragging her back from the edge of unconsciousness and making her aware of all the things that she did not like about her current situation.

There was plenty to dislike. For a start she was standing up, which accounted for the weak trembling of her legs, which protested that the most urgent thing for her to do right now was to lie down. Then there was the fact that her arms were by her side and tied tightly to something hard. Then there was the darkness. She could see nothing at all. She could feel, though. She knew that something—or someone—was pressed close against her and that there was a soft weight like a blanket draped over her head, adding to the general ache and preventing her from breathing deeply through its smothering folds.

'Richard?' she said cautiously.

'Yes?' His voice came softly out of the darkness, right by her ear. Deb realised that he was standing directly in front of her, his body pressed against hers.

'Why do you not release us?' Deb asked. 'Are we to stand here in the dark all night?'

'Very probably.' There was a hint of rueful amusement in Richard's voice now. 'I cannot release us, Deb, because I am tied to this easel with you.'

'The *easel*?' Deb's voice rose as the truth hit her. 'You mean that someone has tied us up in the ballroom where the watercolour book was displayed? Of all the fiendish ideas—'

'I am afraid so,' Richard said. He sounded, Deb thought, remarkably calm. 'You are tied to the front of the easel, Deb, and I am tied up facing you. I apologise that you are obliged to be in such close proximity to me, but I cannot move away.'

Deb shifted slightly as she began to assimilate the truth of their situation. It was as Richard said. She was standing with her hands tied behind her back, fastened to the easel. It appeared that their captors had made Richard face her and then tied him up directly in front of her so that his arms were about her and his body was pressing against hers. Deb gave a small, exploratory wiggle and almost immediately felt Richard go tense.

'Please do not do that,' he said politely. 'It is not helping the situation.' Deb went still.

'Why have they done this to us?' She whispered.

She felt Richard move slightly. The easel creaked again. 'To make fools of us—humiliate us.' His voice hardened. 'The spies grow so arrogant that they want to show us they know we are after them. This is a statement—one that shows their mastery. They want to ridicule us and show us they are too clever for us.'

Deb let her breath out in a long sigh. 'Then they do not intend to kill us.'

'I doubt it. We are to be a laughing stock rather than a sacrifice. When Lady Sally's guests come into the ballroom for the private view, the view they will see will be of us, tied up in this position. I have no doubt it will create a sensation, albeit not the one that Lady Sally intends!'

'Lady Benedict,' Deb whispered. 'I am sure she must be behind this. I cannot believe it is Lady Sally, so Lily Benedict is the only other person it could be…'

'This has all the hallmarks of her malice,' Richard agreed.

'Yet she was in the dining room when I left, as was Lady Sally and Sir John Norton. How could any of them be responsible for this?' Deb rested her aching head back against the cool wooden upright. 'It does not make sense!'

'No, I agree. Once we are out of this damnable mess we must put an end to their games once and for all.' His voice changed. 'What were you up to, Deb, to be caught in this situation?'

Deb shifted irritably. 'I smelled the same scent that was in the poetry book,' she said, repressing a shiver of horror. 'Camphor and fusty old clothes and illness. It is hard to explain. The smell was coming from one of the rooms, so I went in to see who, or what, was behind it—'

'And promptly walked into a trap.'

Deb wriggled pettishly. 'If it comes to that, how did they

manage to trap *you*? You are supposed to be good at this sort of thing.'

She heard Richard give an equally irritable sigh. His breath stirred her hair. 'I had other matters on my mind,' he said, with commendable restraint. 'A servant brought a message to me, Deborah, purporting to be from you. He said that you wished to speak with me as a matter of urgency and I was to meet you in the library. Naturally I thought—' He broke off with a shrug and the easel creaked in protest.

'You came because you wanted to speak with me,' Deb repeated softly. Despite the extremity of the situation she suddenly felt a lot warmer.

'And got knocked on the head for my pains,' Richard confirmed bitterly. 'I cannot believe that I fell for the oldest trick in the book. I suppose this is the nadir of my career as a spy catcher. I had best resign.'

'If you do, you will have to find another purpose in life,' Deb said.

'Very true.' There was an odd note to Richard's voice now. His hand reached for hers again, caught it and held it. 'Could you give me that purpose?' he asked.

Deb had nothing to go on but his voice and the touch of his body against hers. The first was steady but the second conveyed something sweet. All thoughts of the Midwinter spies fled as more important matters caught her attention. Hope trapped her and held her silent, somewhere between apprehension and desire.

'Listen to me, Deb,' Richard said abruptly. 'We do not have much time before they come to unveil the private view. I know I have gone about this all the wrong way. I know I have misled you and that it appears I gave no significance to your wishes, and I can plead no excuse other than that I love you desperately and have wanted to marry you for a very long time—'

'From the first?' Deb said, in a small voice.

She heard the smile in his words then. 'No. From the first I wanted to make love to you. I was a rake then, as you know.'

'And now?'

'Now I realise that my past indiscretions are likely to lose me the one woman that I want to marry. I understand that you would find it difficult to trust me, both because of your own experiences and because of my past behaviour. It is the ultimate irony of a rake's life, I suppose. All I can tell you is that if you choose to marry me of your own free will I should be the happiest man alive and I would never betray you.'

His words fell into the silence. Deb swallowed hard. He had been open and honest with her and had offered her all that she wanted, but there was something she had to tell him…

She took a deep breath. 'Richard…' Her voice trembled, then strengthened. 'Thank you for what you have said. There is something that you should know, however. I have not been entirely honest with you.'

There was a different quality to the silence now. It felt alive, waiting, trembling on the edge. Deb's nerve almost deserted her. She knew she had to finish this quickly.

'I was never married to Neil Stratton,' she said, in a rush. 'I did not know that he was already married when I eloped with him. He never told me. It was only after he died that I discovered he already had a wife and child.' Her voice faltered. 'By then, of course, Neil had seduced me and I was already ruined.' She shook. She could not help herself. 'We contrived a pretence, Ross and Olivia and I. I was to live here quietly in Midwinter and pretend to be the respectable widow that I was not.' Her voice rose a little. 'No one knew. Ross has paid to support Neil's real wife and child ever since—poor girl, she never meant to cause trouble, but her very existence spelt my ruin. I am sorry. I was so very stupid. I should not have trusted Neil—God help me, I thought it was exciting to be courted in secret and to run away to Gretna! I was so foolish and so impetuous and rash—' She broke off as Richard's lips brushed her cheek very softly.

'Deb,' he said.

'I am sorry,' Deb said again, wretchedly. 'I have been so afraid all the time and I tried so hard not to do foolish things, but sometimes I cannot seem to suppress them.'

'Did you think that spending the night with me was a foolish thing and to be regretted?' Richard asked.

Deb shook her head and unconsciously strained a little closer to the comfort of his body. 'No. It was a wonderful thing! But I never meant to fall in love with you, Richard, and I certainly never intended to marry, for I was so afraid of trusting again and being hurt and losing my self-respect. And I was afraid that when you knew you would have no good opinion of me—'

'Deb,' Richard said again. His voice was hard with suppressed anger and Deb shuddered to hear it, though she could not be sure whether it was turned against her or against Neil Stratton. And when Richard spoke again he had moderated his tone, though she could still hear the violence underneath.

'Do you think,' he said, 'that I give a damn about whether or not you were truly married to Neil Stratton? If you love me and wish to be married to me, then that is all that matters.'

Deb was trembling fiercely now. 'But I am a fallen woman, Richard! Even now, if the truth came out, I would be utterly ruined! That was one of the reasons I struggled so hard against my attraction to you, and why Ross and Olivia were shocked that I could make the same mistake twice, only this time knowing what I did, with my eyes open…'

'Why did you do it?' Richard asked.

Deb hesitated. 'I thought it was because I was attracted to you too strongly to resist, but the truth was that I was falling in love with you, and I *wanted* to love you and desperately wanted you to love me too.'

'That is more than enough for me,' Richard said, and Deb could hear the smile in his voice now and her heart started to ease, though she still hesitated.

'I do not understand why what happened before does not matter to you, Richard.'

'It matters to me that someone hurt you so badly,' Richard said. His voice softened. 'The rest is not important. How could it be, when you chose of your own free will to give yourself to me? Deb, it is *you* I love, not Mrs Deborah Stratton, widow, or Miss Deborah Walton, spinster, or however you or society wishes to describe you. It is what you are—warm and impulsive and vibrant and so alive—that is important to me, and if you love and trust me too, then that is all that matters.'

Deb smiled shakily. 'It is true that I was not sure if I could trust a rake,' she said shyly, 'but I know that you are not like Neil. You are an honourable man.'

Richard angled his head and kissed her hard, pressing her head back against the wooden bars. She gave a little gasp of protest and he straightened.

'You *can* trust me.' His voice was not so steady now. 'I swear it. I love you. I would never hurt you. God knows, Deborah, it must surely be apparent to you that I would walk across burning coals for you if I had to. I would probably *eat* burning coals if you asked me.'

Deb tilted her head up towards him. 'Richard...'

'Yes?' The word was like a caress on her skin. Deb wriggled.

'The burning coals will not be necessary. But we have been away from the dining room for a considerable time. People will have noticed.'

'They will indeed.'

'Taken with the rumours about last night, I fear that your freedom is lost. You will have to marry me.'

There was a pause.

'Are you proposing to me, Mrs Stratton?' Richard said, after a moment. Once again Deb could hear the amusement in his voice and she felt warm.

'I believe that I must. In a moment they will find us, you see...' Even as she spoke, Deb heard the scrape of a door and the sound of voices at the other end of the ballroom.

'They will whip off this damnable sheet and find you and me tied up together beneath it in a wholly scandalous and utterly compromising fashion. There will be no alternative other than a quick marriage to silence the gossips.'

She felt Richard bend his neck so that his lips could brush her hair. 'How quick?'

'Oh, as quickly as we can make it? By special licence? So that we can return to the hunting lodge for our honeymoon?'

She felt the easel shake as he laughed. The voices and footsteps were coming closer. The ballroom was filling up with Lady Sally's visitors.

'The hunting lodge...' Richard said. 'I am so glad that you enjoyed it.'

Deb could feel herself blushing. Suddenly the warmth of the sheet was stifling, the press of Richard's body stirring all the feelings they had explored with intimate delight the previous night. 'I did,' she said. 'I am sorry—I never thanked you.'

'It was my pleasure,' Richard said. 'Truly.'

His mouth captured hers, warm and tantalising, making Deb's mind reel. Briefly she freed herself.

'Richard! Any moment now they will see us—'

'Let them.'

He kissed her again and Deb succumbed to the pure pleasure of his touch. She burned at every point their bodies were in contact. The easel strained as they pulled on their bonds, prompted by an instinctive desire to hold one another. Deb gasped in frustration as she could not break free and gasped again as Richard angled his head to kiss her more deeply, pressing his hard body against every yielding line of hers. His tongue curled lazily against hers and an infinitely sweet sensation flooded Deb's veins and made her melt with longing. She clenched her fingers about the wooden upright of the easel.

'I love you,' Richard murmured, as his lips left hers to trace the line of her throat and move down to tease the soft skin above the collar of her gown. 'Always.'

'This is the moment that we have all been waiting for! Light the candles, please.' Lady Sally's voice spoke suddenly from nearby, making Deb jump. She tried to pull away from Richard, but he was having none of it and she would not have been able to put much distance between them even had he co-operated with her. Instead he nibbled gently at the sensitive skin below Deb's ear, sending goose bumps along her skin. She could have sworn that he was smiling. It *felt* as though he was smiling.

'Ladies and gentlemen,' Lady Sally continued, 'may I present my watercolour calendar, which I am sure will be the greatest of sensations—'

'Richard,' Deb whispered desperately, 'we mustn't—'

Richard's only response was to kiss her with prolonged and deliberate intensity until she forgot everything else and was grateful for the support of the wooden easel, without which she would surely have tumbled to the floor.

There was a flare of light as someone whipped the sheet from about them. Deb made an incoherent sound against Richard's mouth but he did not relent, continuing to kiss her with a purposeful pleasure that drew a roar of shock and scandalised comment from their audience. Eventually he let her go, and Deb blinked in the light. The ballroom was packed with people and illuminated with a hundred candles. In the long mirrors at the end of the ballroom, Deb could see their reflection. They looked utterly indecent, she tied with her hands behind her back and Richard with his arms about her in the closest and most private of embraces. Deb rested her head against Richard's shoulder in appalled resignation.

For once, Lady Sally Saltire looked shocked and was entirely silenced. For once, Justin Kestrel also lost his customary aplomb.

'Good God, Richard—' he began.

'Thank goodness you are here, Justin,' Richard said coolly to his brother. 'Untie these bonds so that I can kiss my fiancée properly, there's a good fellow.'

With superb aplomb, Justin Kestrel loosened the ropes that bound his brother to the easel and shook him formally by the hand once he was freed.

'Congratulations on causing a sensation, Richard,' he said.

Richard grinned. 'Thank you, Justin.'

Lady Sally hastened to help Deb and the biting ropes fell away, leaving her rubbing her wrists. Before she had time to feel any of the mortification that the situation surely demanded, Richard had scooped her up in his arms and kissed her with pent-up passion and a dizzying love that made her head swim. Lady Sally's guests started to applaud.

'I imagine that you will wish to continue your celebrations in private,' Lady Sally said, looking as though she was trying not to laugh. 'I will send for your carriage.'

'And I will send for the Bishop of Ipswich,' Justin said, 'with a special licence!'

Richard kept his arm protectively about Deb as he ushered her through the crowd and eventually they found themselves out on the steps of Saltires with the carriage waiting.

'What a shocking night,' Deb said, sighing, as she collapsed on the seat. 'Should you not go back and tell your brother what has happened?'

'I told Justin that I would talk to him later,' Richard said, drawing her close into his arms. 'I am all for neglecting business in favour of pleasure tonight.'

Deb sighed, snuggling close. 'Do you think that we might manage one more night of scandal before the bishop arrives with the special licence and I am at last respectably married?' she asked, a little wistfully.

Richard smiled as he drew her closer still. 'I think we might,' he said, 'and though I cannot wait for us to marry, Deb, I assure you that we shall never, ever be respectable.'

# Epilogue

'What an extraordinary business that led up to your brother's marriage,' Lady Sally Saltire said, a fortnight later as she shared a late-night glass of brandy with Justin Kestrel in her study at Saltires. 'Although I had predicted that Richard and Deborah would marry, I had not imagined that it would come about in such a sensational manner. The whole of Woodbridge is still agog!' She cast him a thoughtful glance. 'Who could have played such a trick on them?'

'I am sure that I have no notion,' Justin Kestrel said, his dark gaze betraying nothing but blandness.

Lady Sally knew him too well to be deceived. 'Nonsense, my dear Justin. There is something havey-cavey going on in Midwinter and you know it!'

'Mayhap so.' Justin's tone was as unrevealing as his expression and Lady Sally sighed.

'I can see that you mean to tell me nothing.' She fidgeted a little with her glass. 'Just so long as you do not suspect *me*, Justin.'

There was a flash of feeling in Justin Kestrel's eyes that looked oddly like pain and Lady Sally found her heart beating a little faster. It was surely a very long time since she and Justin Kestrel had had the power to hurt each other and yet it seemed that she still had feelings for him. No, she knew that she did. Feelings too complicated to give a name, too late to act upon…

'Tell me something, Sally.' Justin spoke slowly.

There was a tension in the room. It caught at Lady Sally's nerves, making her tremble. She wanted to tell Justin not to ask her anything too difficult, yet she was obliged to admit that she owed him any explanation that he cared to request.

'Why did you choose Stephen Saltire over me?' Justin asked.

There it was, the one thing that she had dreaded. She looked up from the amber swirl of brandy in her glass to meet his steady regard.

'He asked nothing of me,' she said, as lightly as she could. 'I was young and not very brave, and you…' she swallowed the lump in her throat '…you were too much of a risk, my dear. I sensed an intensity in you I was uncertain I could match. Whereas Stephen—' she smiled with affectionate memory '—Stephen was easy, straightforward, accepting. He made life easy for me too.'

The silence lingered until Lady Sally broke it by fiddling restlessly with the seam of her gown.

'So Richard and Deborah are wed within three months and I win my wager,' she said brightly. 'You had not forgot that we made a bet at Lord and Lady Newlyn's wedding, Justin?'

'No, indeed,' Justin said. 'What do you demand in payment?'

Lady Sally put her head on one side thoughtfully. 'Oh, merely that you attend the ball to celebrate the launch of my watercolour calendar, I think,' she said. 'Having lost one of my greatest attractions in the person of your brother, I need the cachet a duke will bring to gain the attention of the *ton*!'

'Nonsense,' Justin said. He smiled. 'I shall be there, nevertheless. That was a very easy stake to agree, my dear. You could have asked a deal more of me.'

'I dare say,' Lady Sally said. 'I did not wish to tempt fate, however.'

Once again a ripple of tension seemed to spread through the room. Lady Sally found herself unable to meet the Duke's eyes and this time it was Justin who changed the subject.

'I seem to remember that your prediction was that Lucas would be next to fall in love,' he remarked. 'Do you stand by that, Sally?'

Lady Sally bent her sparkling smile on him. 'Of course! I assure you that I am never wrong on matters of matrimony!'

'Another wager, then?' Justin suggested, with the shadow of a smile.

For once Lady Sally seemed reluctant. 'I am not certain—'

'Then you do not really have faith in your own prophecy?'

'It is not that.' Lady Sally flashed him a look. 'Lucas is less predictable, for he has not yet met the lady of his heart. Nevertheless, I believe that when he does—and it will be soon—the matter will be arranged in the shortest time.'

Justin nodded sagely. 'So why not take the wager?'

'Because I may—just may—lose this one and...' Lady Sally hesitated '...I am not certain what payment you would demand, Justin.'

Justin gave her a flicker of the wicked smile that had turned her heart inside out when she had been a débutante of eighteen.

'Take the gamble,' he said softly.

After a moment, Lady Sally held out her hand and his

own closed about it to seal the deal. This time he did not
kiss the back of her hand as he had done at the Newlyns'
wedding, but turned it over and kissed the palm.

'Do you wish to win or lose?' he asked her.

Lady Sally stood up. She felt very strongly that it was
time he should be gone, or she could not foretell the outcome of the evening. She had no wish to do something that
she might later regret, and talk of the past was notoriously
dangerous.

'I always win, Justin,' she said sweetly. 'Surely you know
that, my dear.'

But when the Duke had left and Lady Sally was all alone
in her big four-poster bed, she admitted to herself alone that
this time a certain whim in her made the thought of losing
*almost* more attractive than that of winning.

'I rely on you, Lucas,' she said as she blew out her candle. 'Do not let me down, or I very much fear that your
brother will catch me at last, and I have outrun him for these
fifteen years. Well, we shall see…'

And she fell asleep, to dream of the past and the as yet
unpredictable future.

\*    \*    \*    \*    \*

# Harlequin® Historical
### Historical Romantic Adventure!